SARDINE

in outer space

6

4.5/1 pt

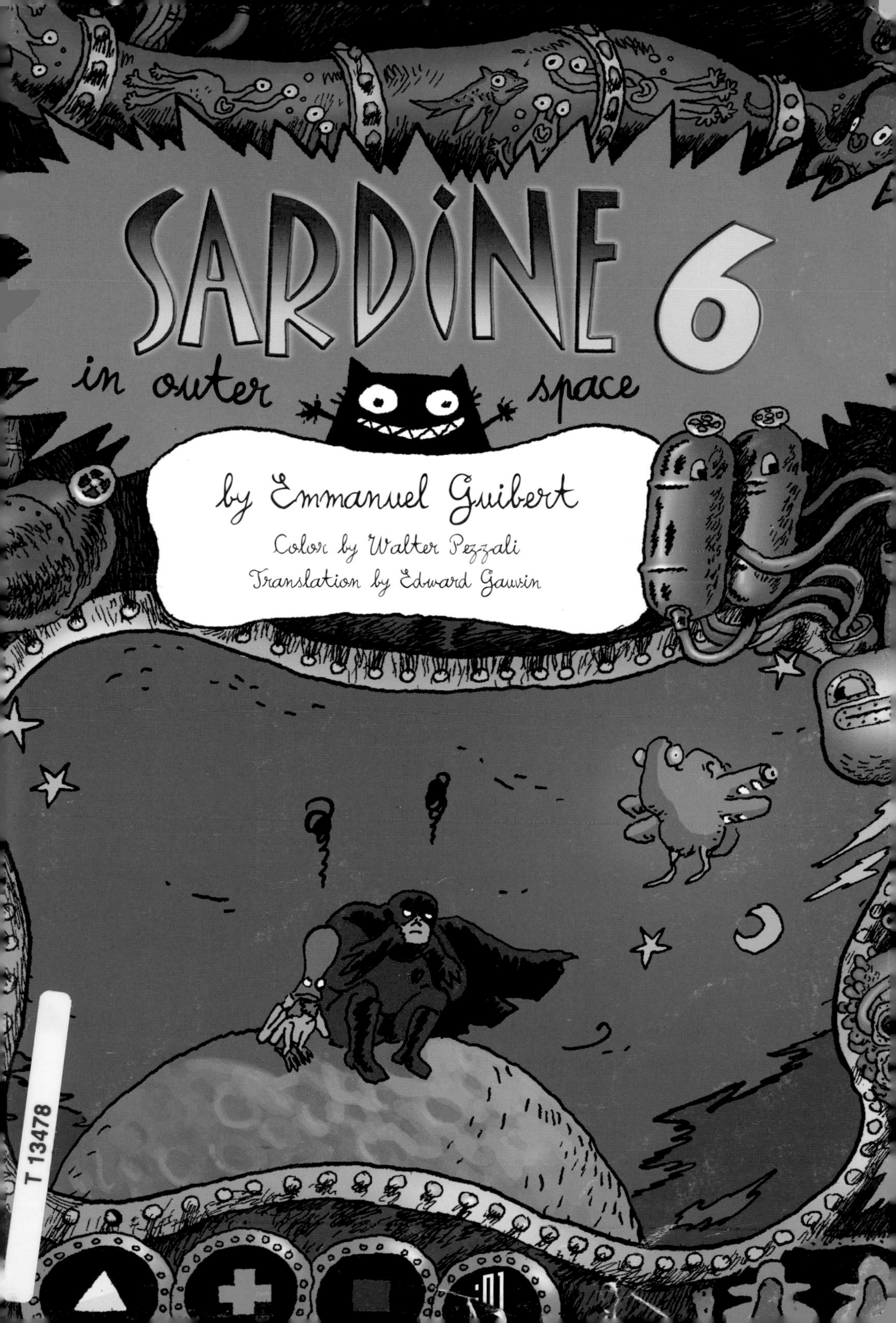
SARDINE 6
in outer space
by Emmanuel Guibert
Color by Walter Pezzali
Translation by Edward Gauvin

Contents

Umby the Cell Phone.............................3

Dumbo!....................................... 13

My Eye!....................................... 23

Going in Circles 33

Moon Pie....................................43

Robert Putto 53

Robot DJ 63

Milk Teeth................................... 73

Get Lost!.................................... 83

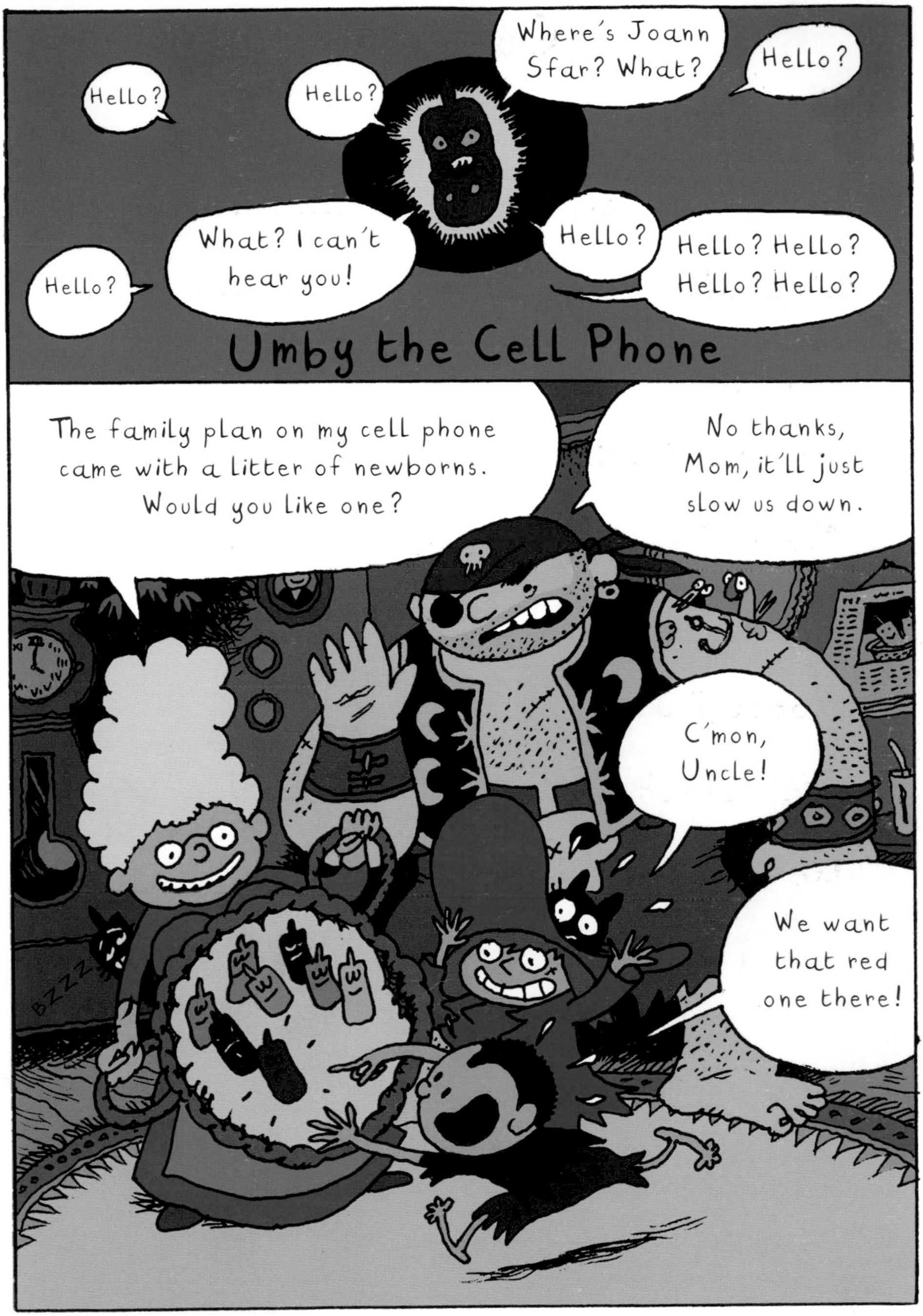

Hello?
Hello?
Where's Joann Sfar? What?
Hello?
Hello?
What? I can't hear you!
Hello?
Hello? Hello? Hello? Hello?
Umby the Cell Phone
The family plan on my cell phone came with a litter of newborns. Would you like one?
No thanks, Mom, it'll just slow us down.
C'mon, Uncle!
We want that red one there!
BZZZ

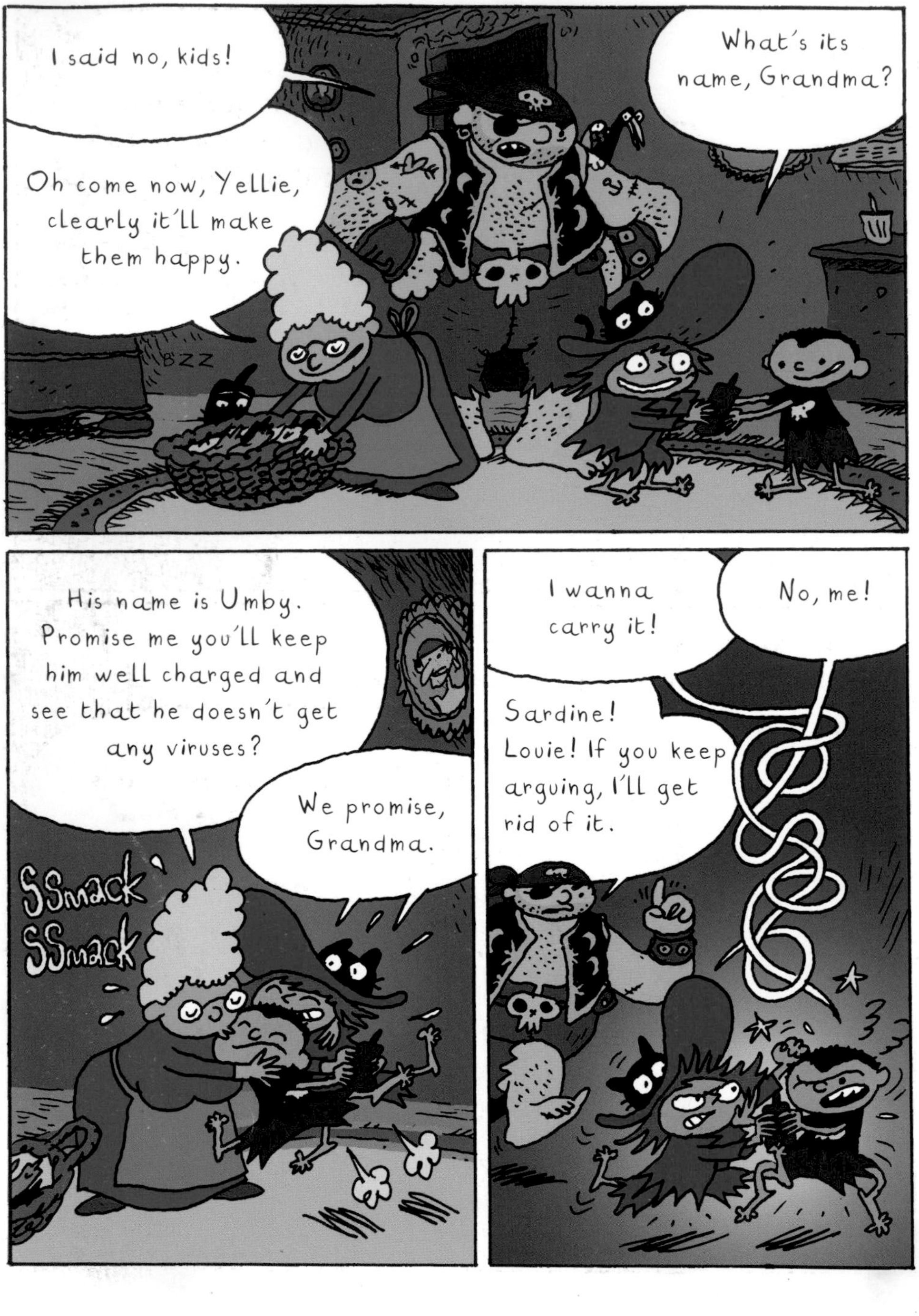
I said no, kids!
Oh come now, Yellie, clearly it'll make them happy.
What's its name, Grandma?
BZZ
His name is Umby. Promise me you'll keep him well charged and see that he doesn't get any viruses?
We promise, Grandma.
SSmack SSmack
I wanna carry it!
No, me!
Sardine! Louie! If you keep arguing, I'll get rid of it.

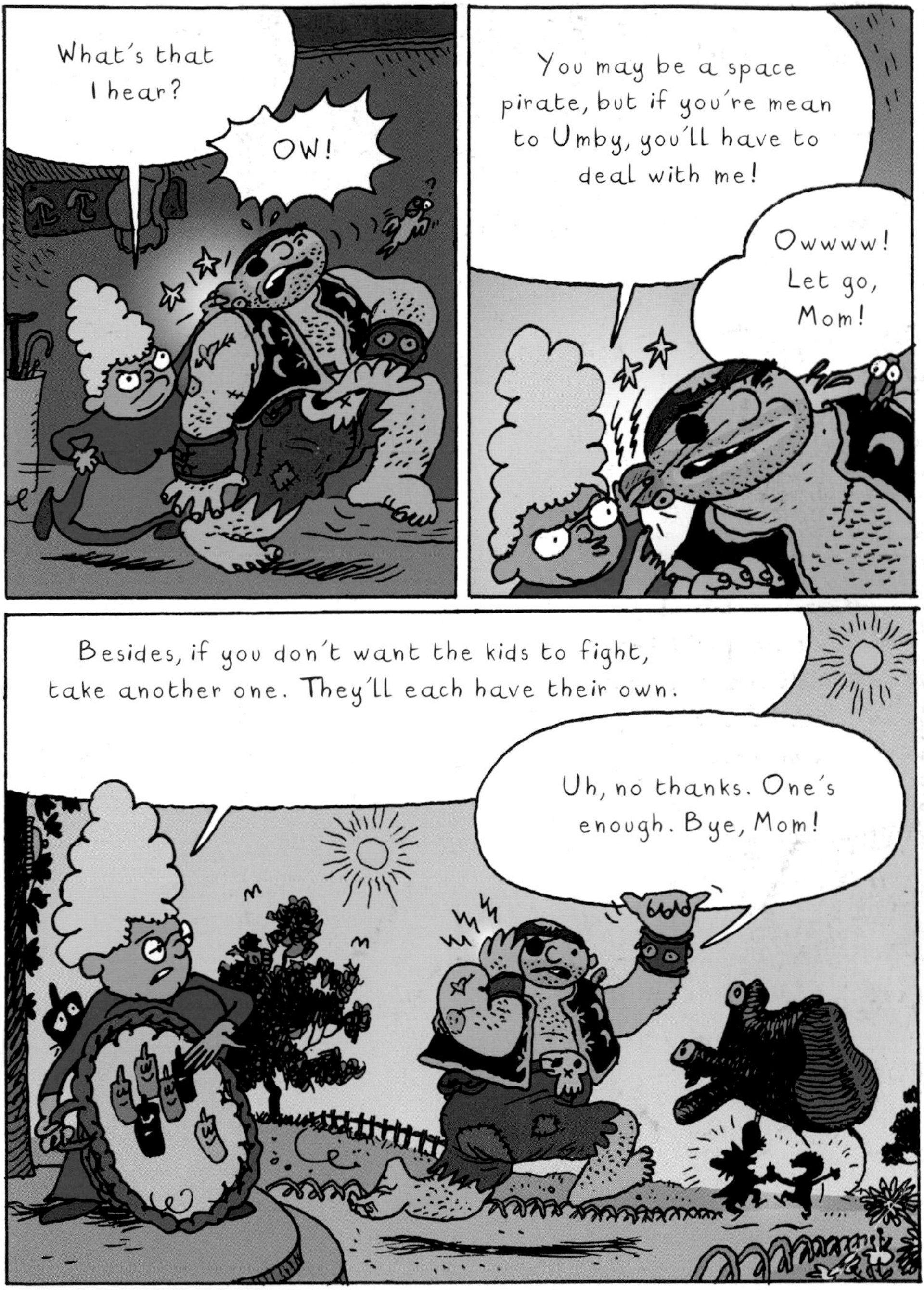
What's that I hear?
OW!
You may be a space pirate, but if you're mean to Umby, you'll have to deal with me!
Owwww! Let go, Mom!
Besides, if you don't want the kids to fight, take another one. They'll each have their own.
Uh, no thanks. One's enough. Bye, Mom!

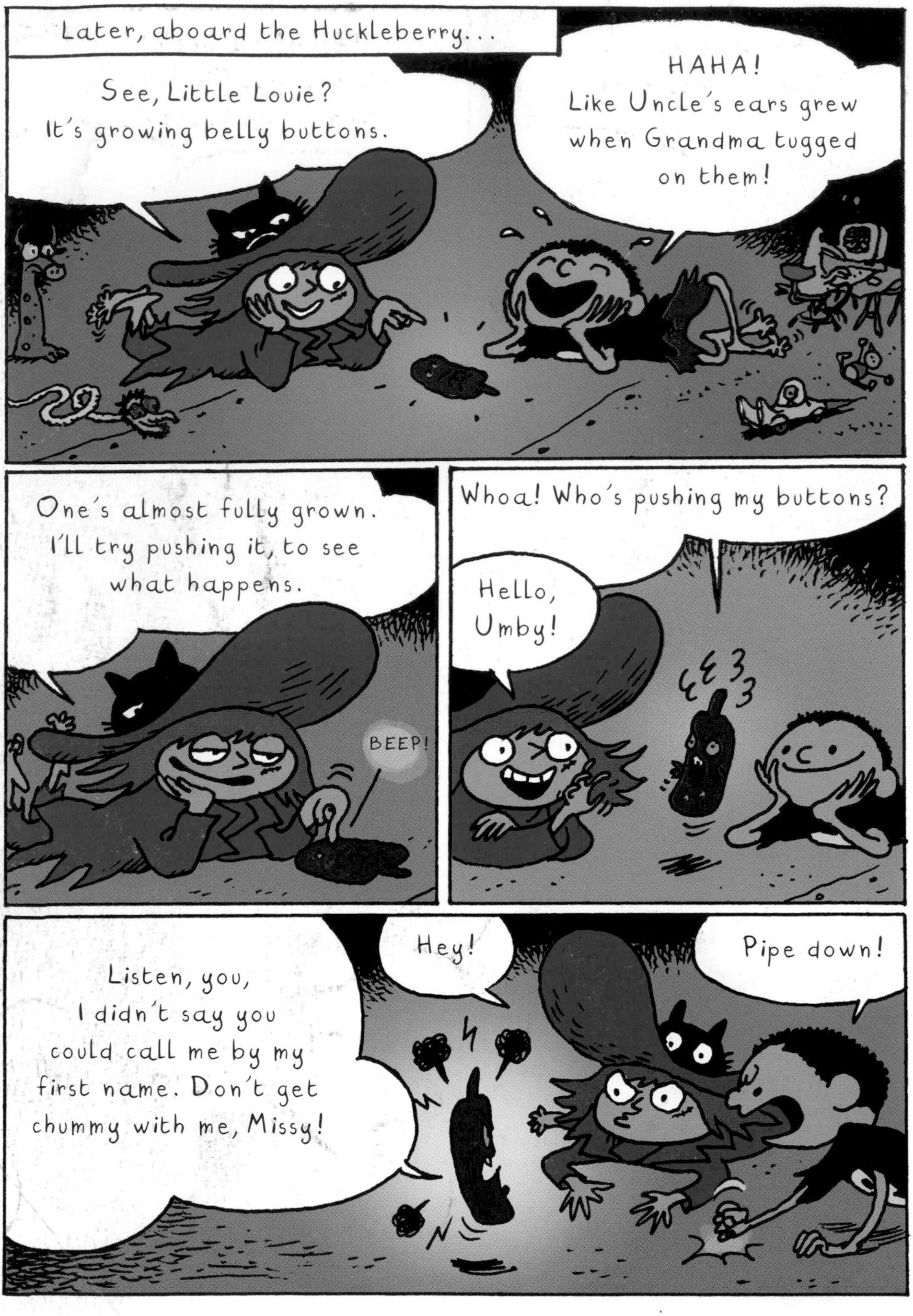
Later, aboard the Huckleberry...
See, Little Louie? It's growing belly buttons.
HAHA! Like Uncle's ears grew when Grandma tugged on them!
One's almost fully grown. I'll try pushing it, to see what happens.
BEEP!
Whoa! Who's pushing my buttons?
Hello, Umby!
Listen, you, I didn't say you could call me by my first name. Don't get chummy with me, Missy!
Hey!
Pipe down!

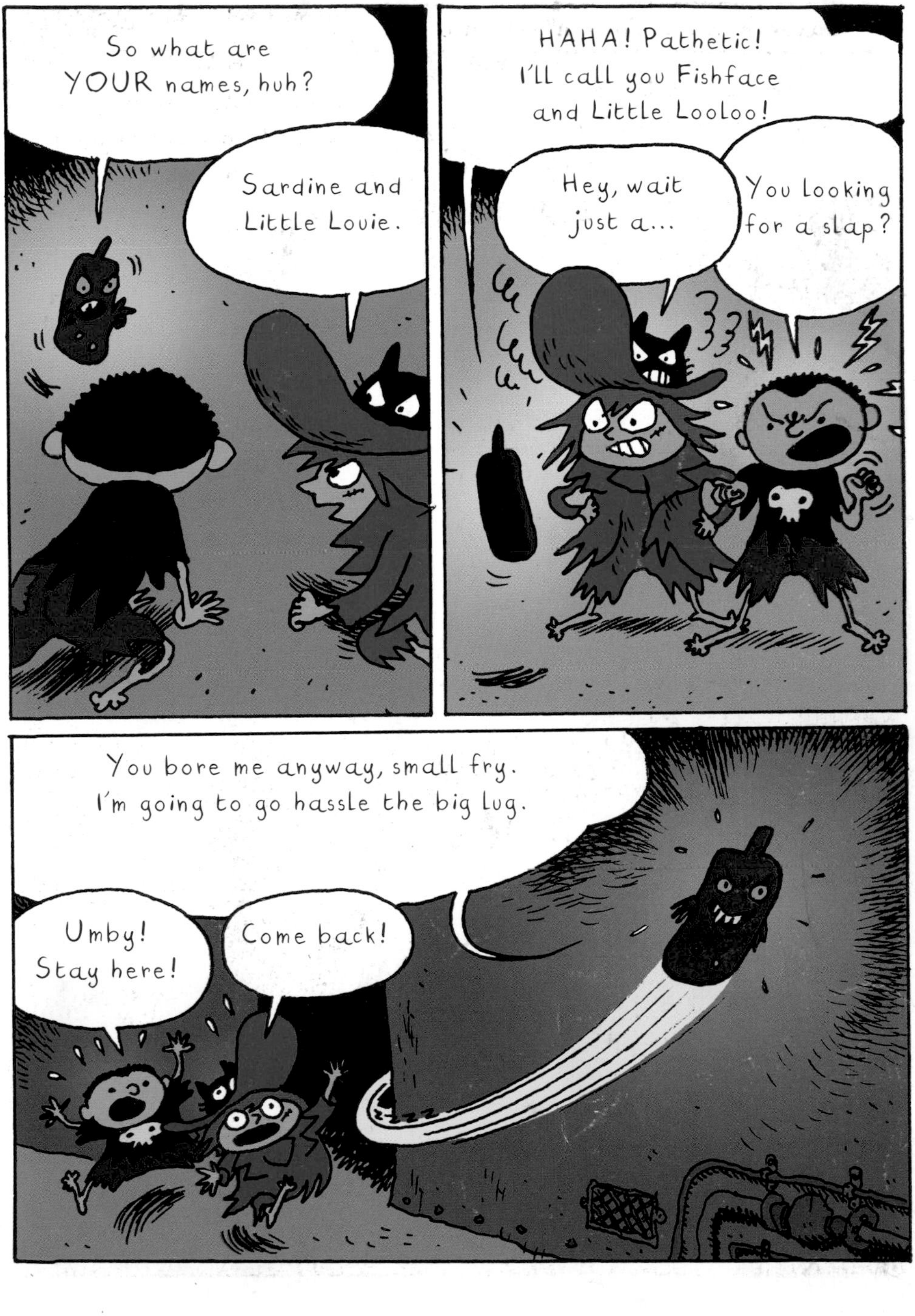

So what are YOUR names, huh?
Sardine and Little Louie.
HAHA! Pathetic! I'll call you Fishface and Little Looloo!
Hey, wait just a...
You looking for a slap?
You bore me anyway, small fry. I'm going to go hassle the big lug.
Umby! Stay here!
Come back!

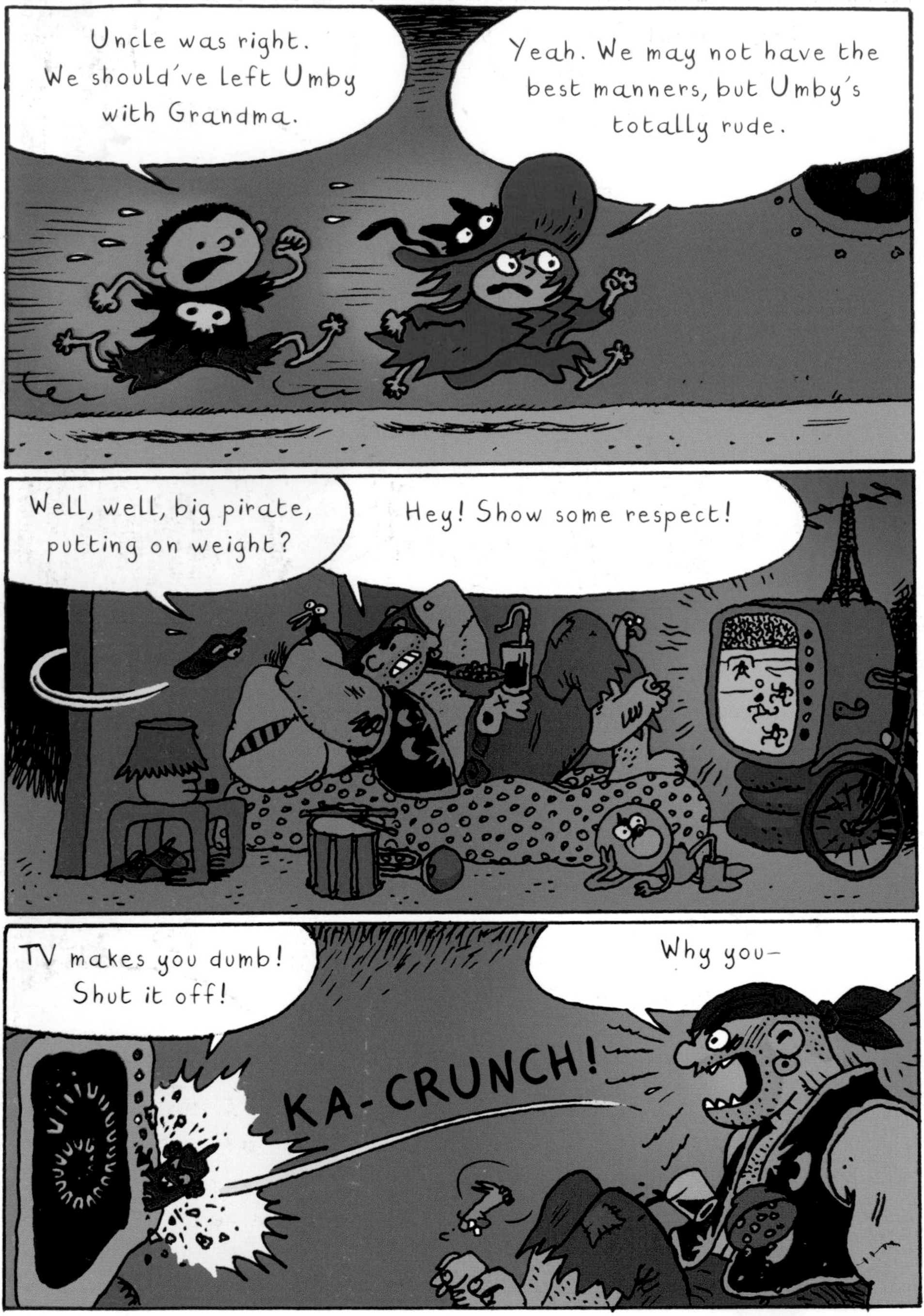
Uncle was right. We should've left Umby with Grandma.
Yeah. We may not have the best manners, but Umby's totally rude.
Well, well, big pirate, putting on weight?
Hey! Show some respect!
TV makes you dumb! Shut it off!
Why you-
KA-CRUNCH!

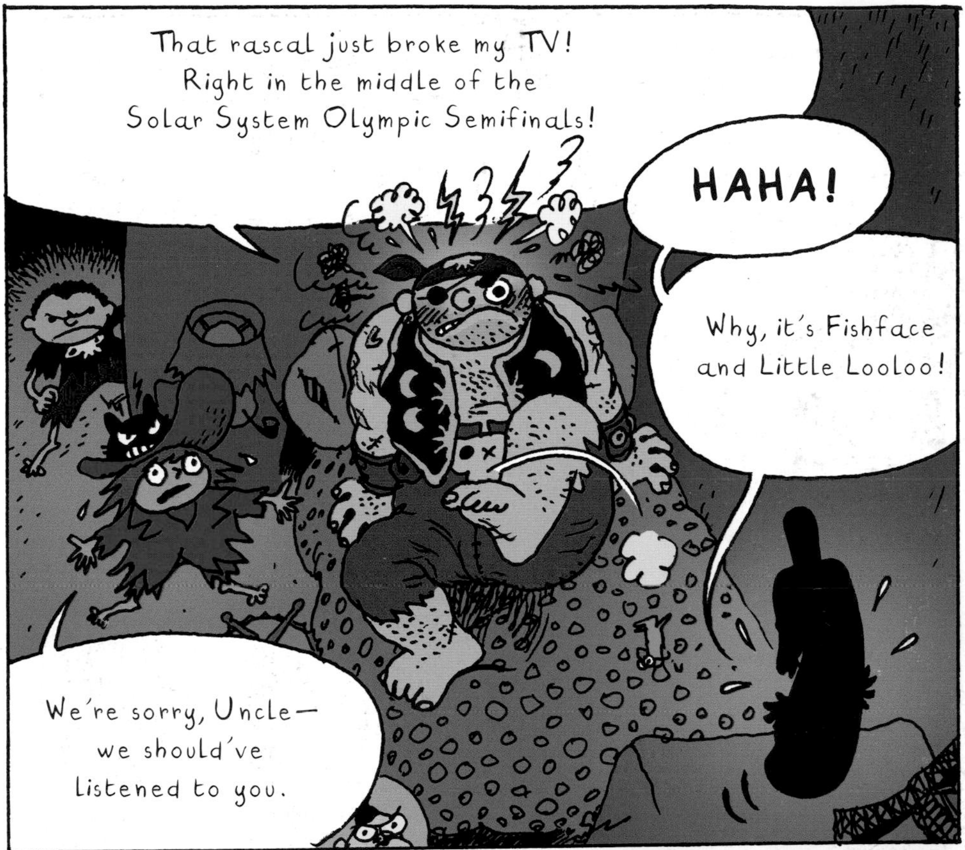
That rascal just broke my TV! Right in the middle of the Solar System Olympic Semifinals!
HAHA!
Why, it's Fishface and Little Looloo!
We're sorry, Uncle— we should've listened to you.

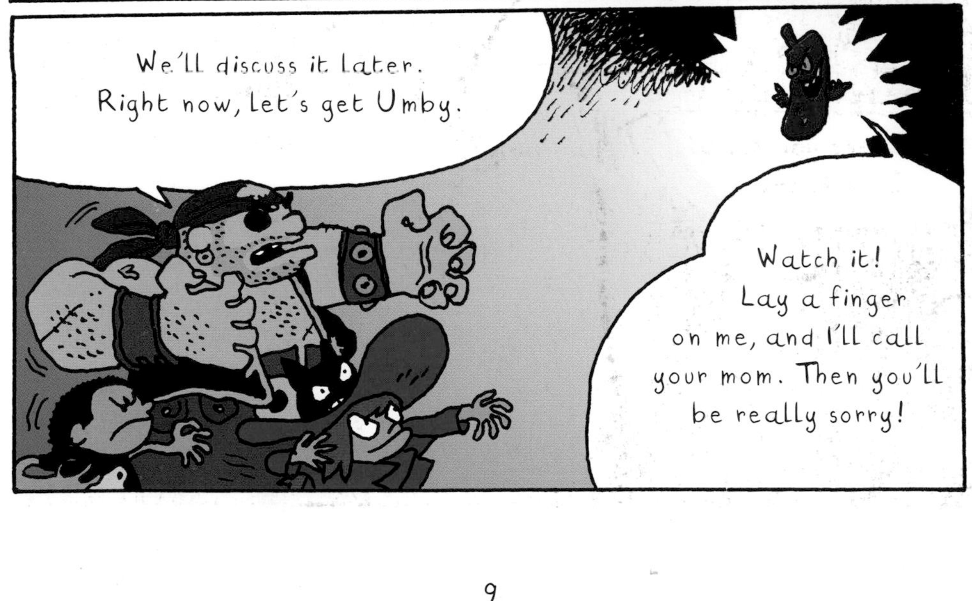
We'll discuss it later. Right now, let's get Umby.
Watch it! Lay a finger on me, and I'll call your mom. Then you'll be really sorry!

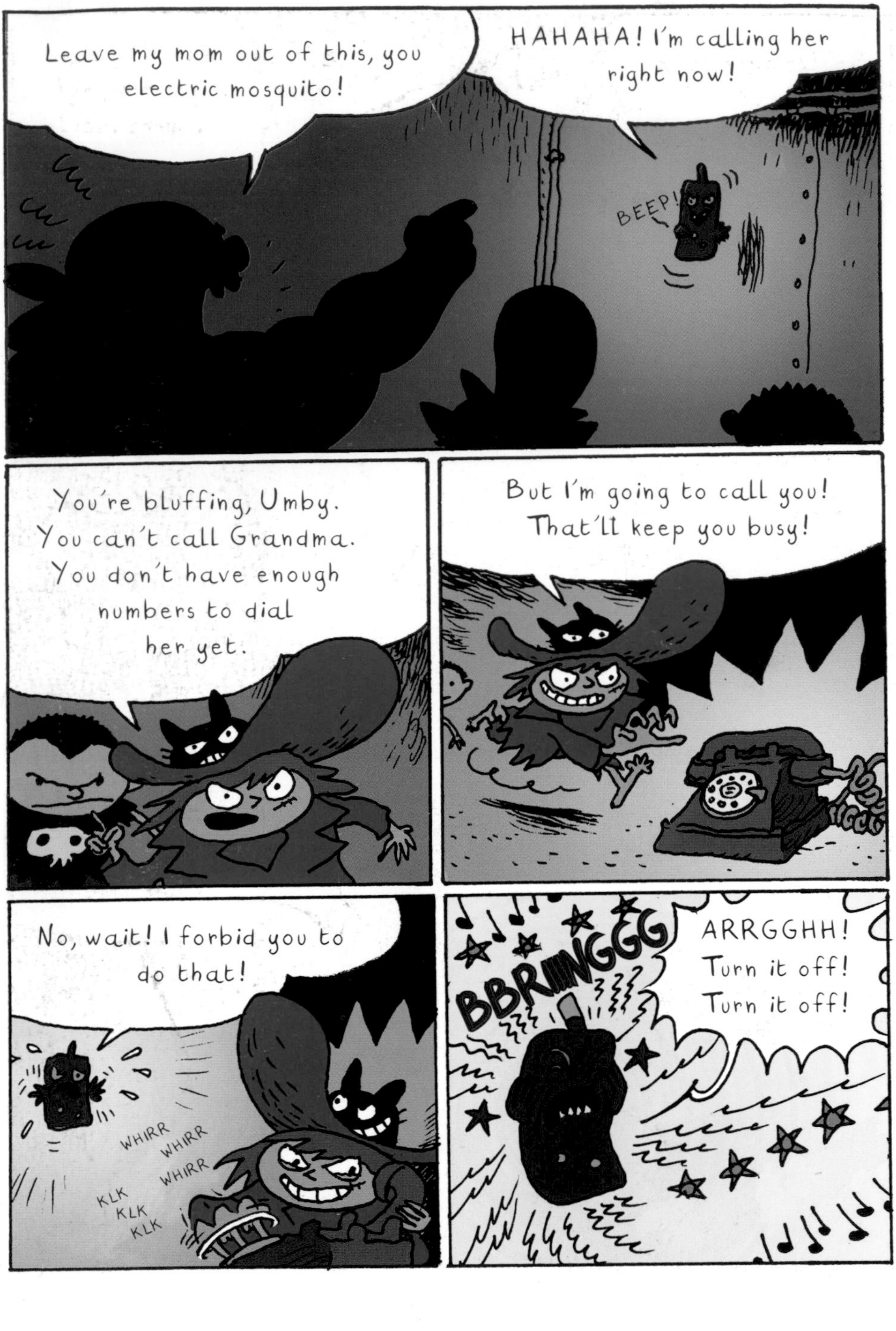
Leave my mom out of this, you electric mosquito!
HAHAHA! I'm calling her right now!
BEEP!
You're bluffing, Umby. You can't call Grandma. You don't have enough numbers to dial her yet.
But I'm going to call you! That'll keep you busy!
No, wait! I forbid you to do that!
WHIRR
WHIRR
WHIRR
KLK
KLK
KLK
BBRIIINGGG
ARRGGHH! Turn it off! Turn it off!

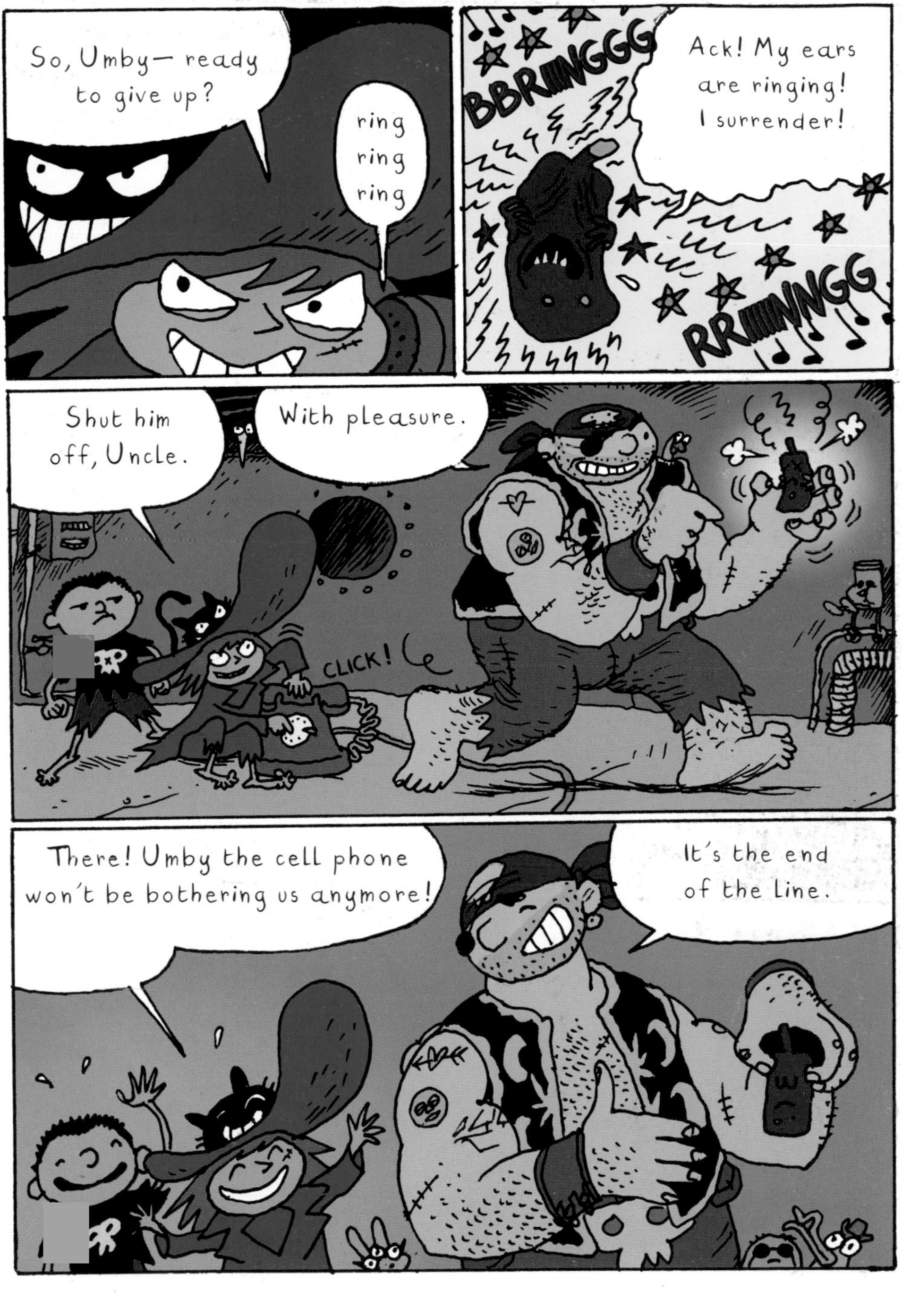

So, Umby— ready to give up?
ring ring ring
BBRIIINGGG
Ack! My ears are ringing! I surrender!
RRIIIINGG
Shut him off, Uncle.
With pleasure.
CLICK!
There! Umby the cell phone won't be bothering us anymore!
It's the end of the line.

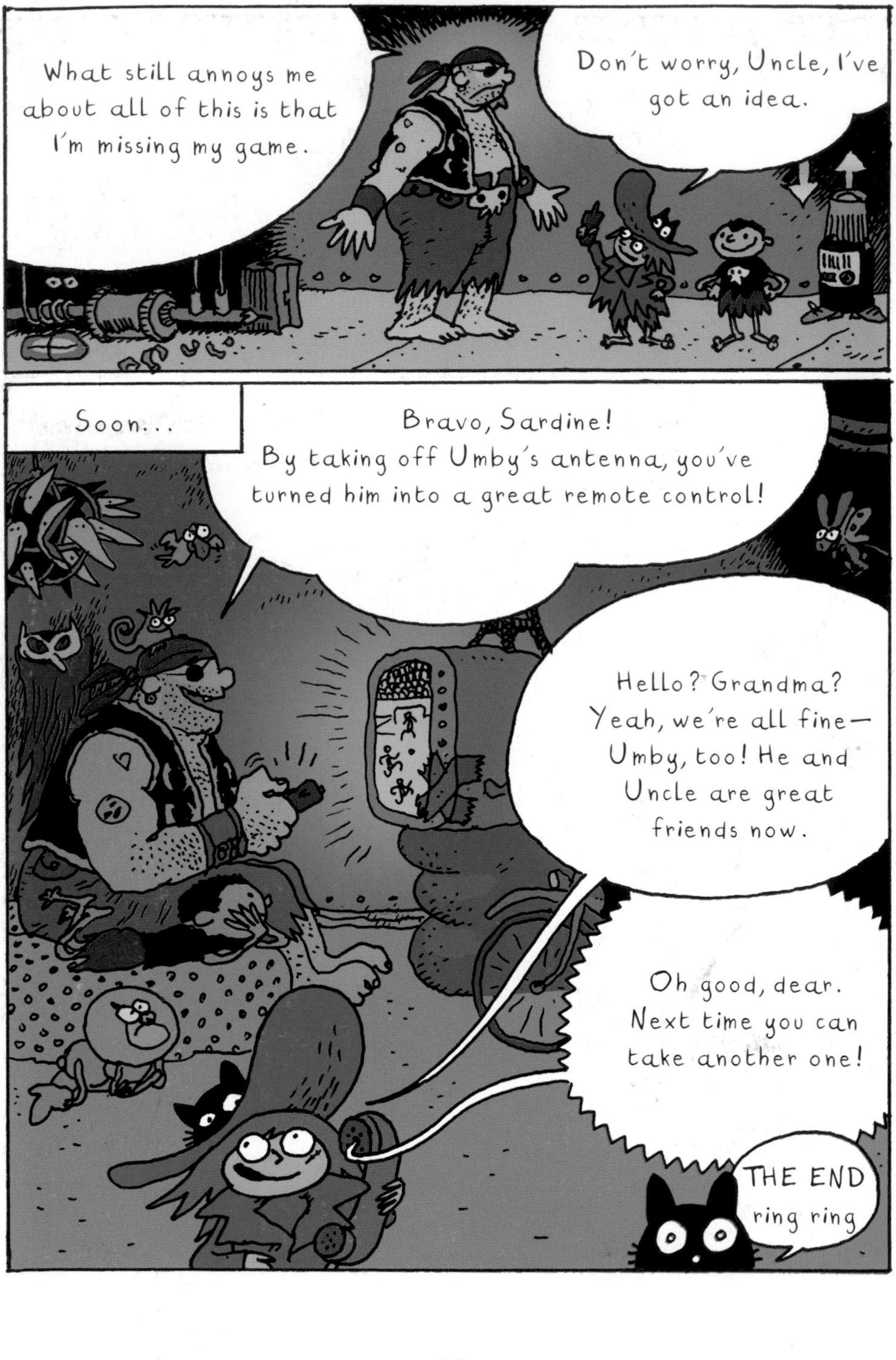
What still annoys me about all of this is that I'm missing my game.
Don't worry, Uncle, I've got an idea.
Soon...
Bravo, Sardine! By taking off Umby's antenna, you've turned him into a great remote control!
Hello? Grandma? Yeah, we're all fine— Umby, too! He and Uncle are great friends now.
Oh good, dear. Next time you can take another one!
THE END
ring ring

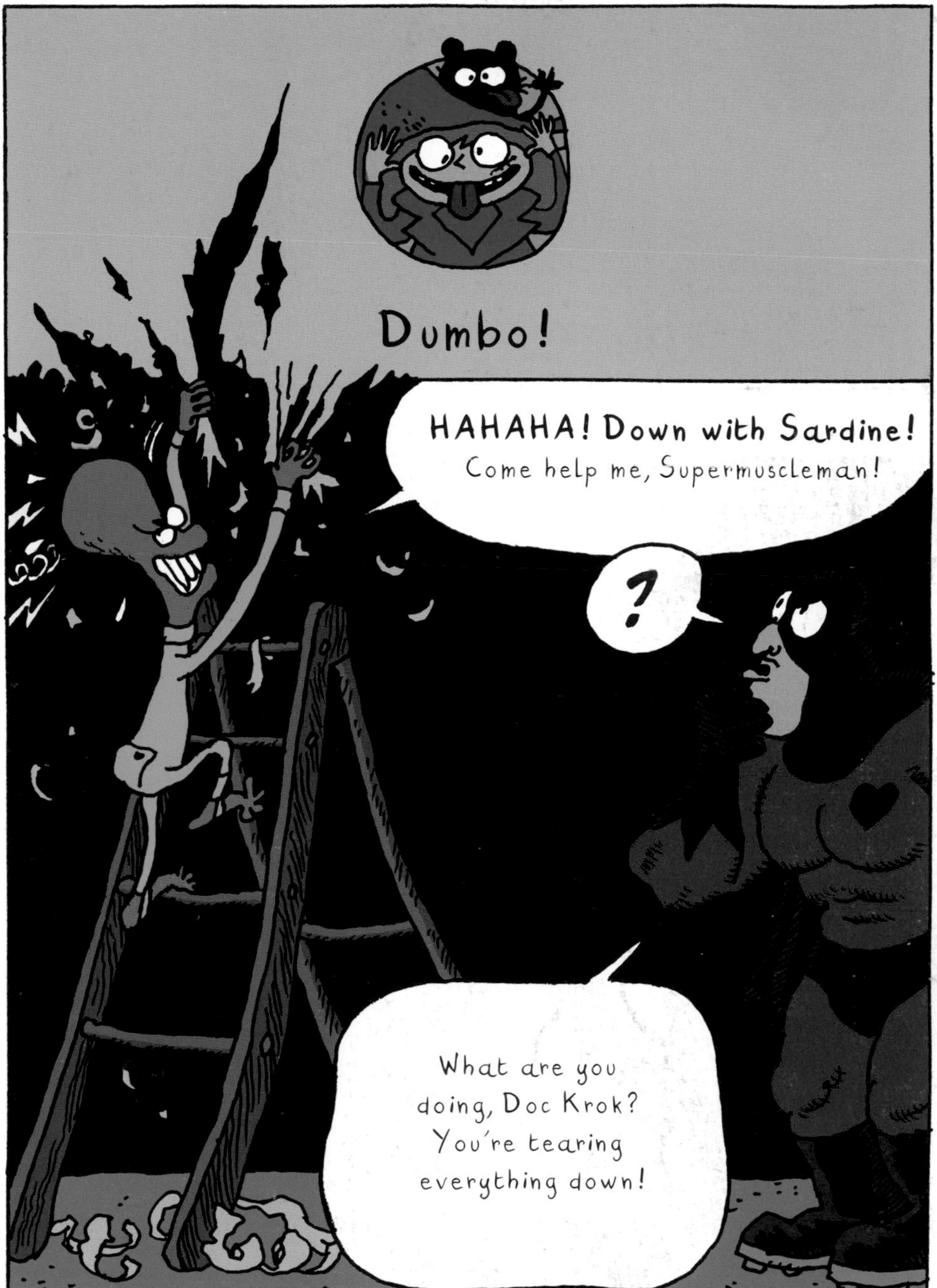
Dumbo!
HAHAHA! Down with Sardine! Come help me, Supermuscleman!
?
What are you doing, Doc Krok? You're tearing everything down!

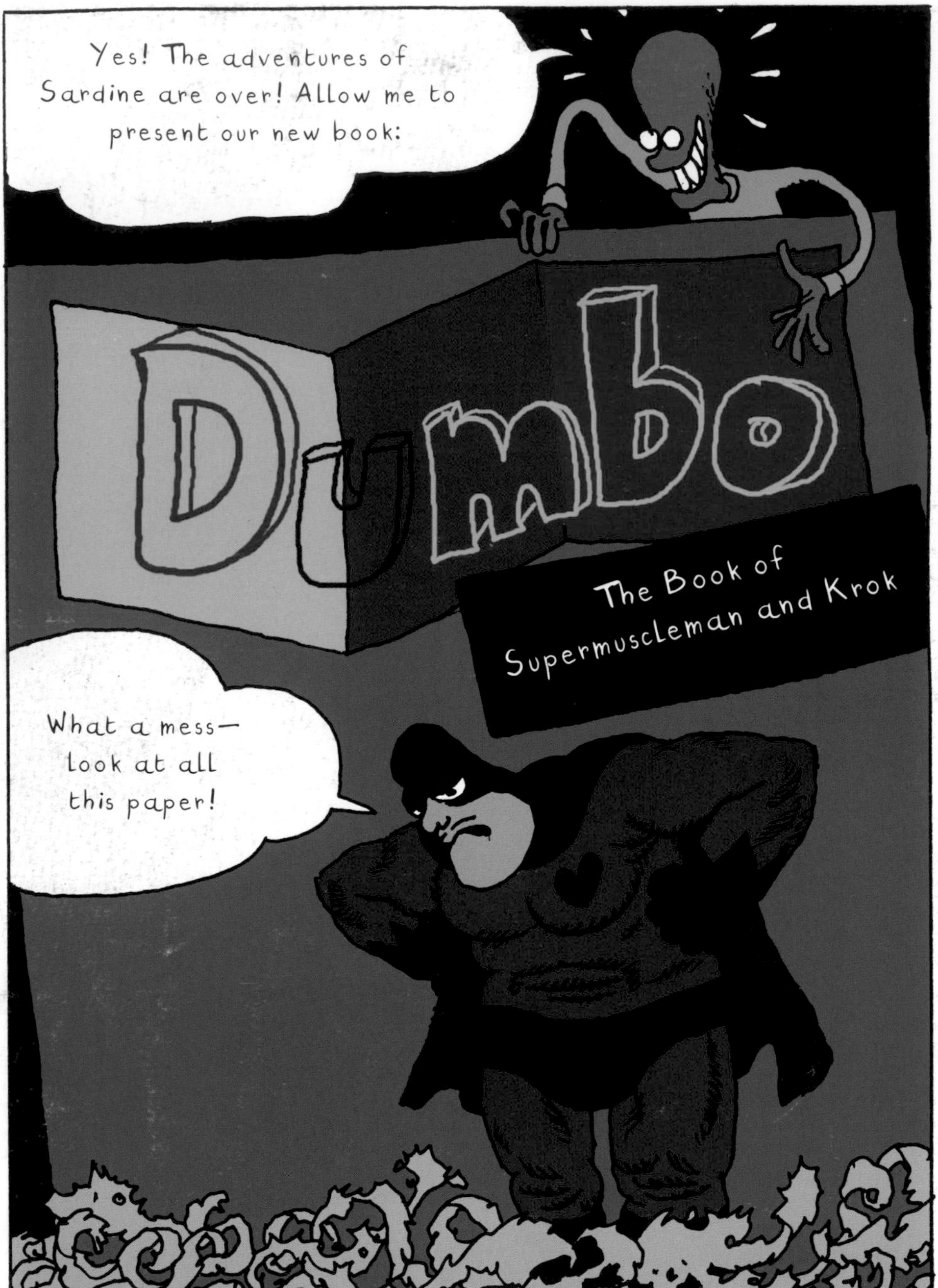
Yes! The adventures of Sardine are over! Allow me to present our new book:
Dumbo
The Book of Supermuscleman and Krok
What a mess— look at all this paper!

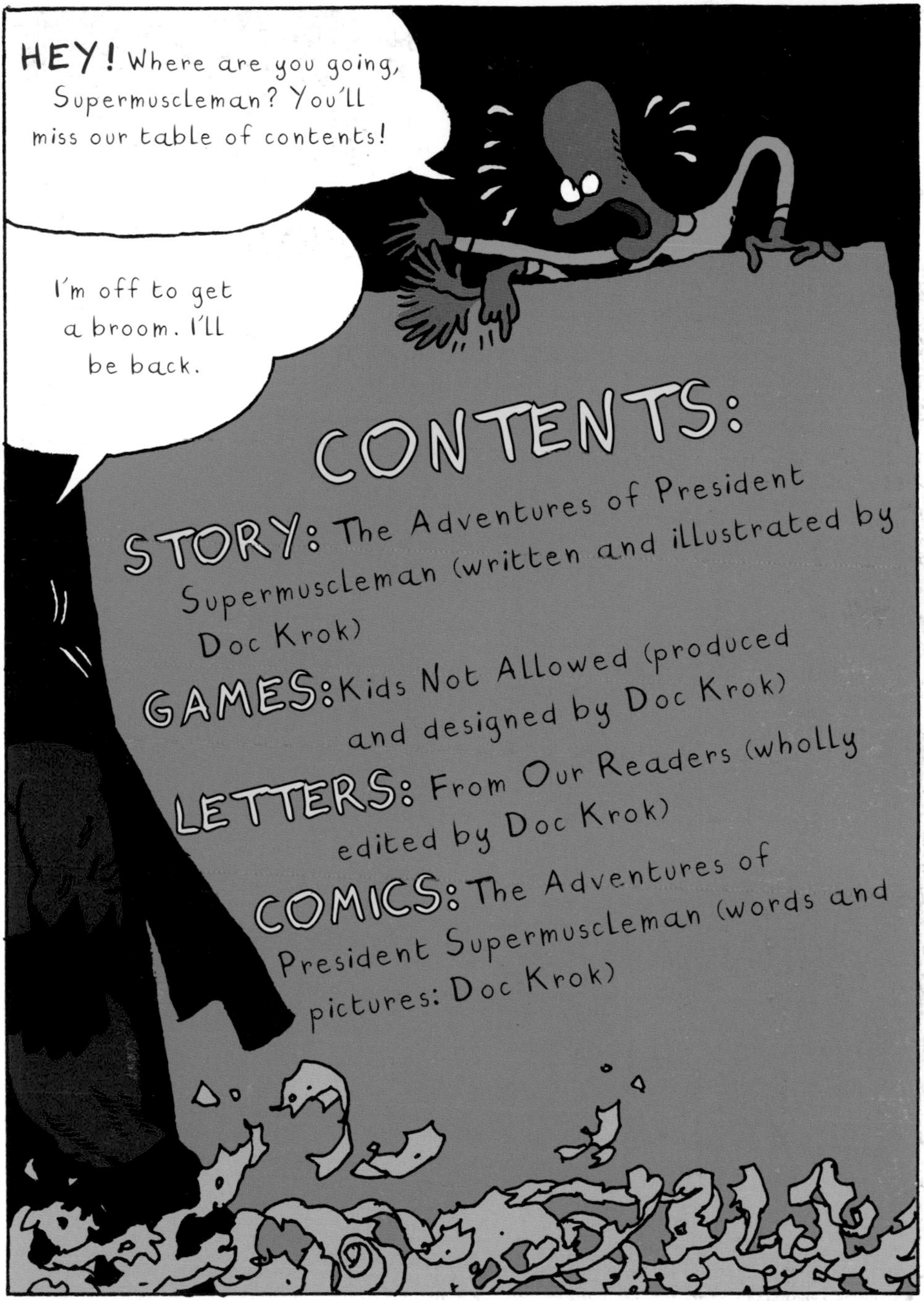
HEY! Where are you going, Supermuscleman? You'll miss our table of contents!
I'm off to get a broom. I'll be back.
CONTENTS:
STORY: The Adventures of President Supermuscleman (written and illustrated by Doc Krok)
GAMES: Kids Not Allowed (produced and designed by Doc Krok)
LETTERS: From Our Readers (wholly edited by Doc Krok)
COMICS: The Adventures of President Supermuscleman (words and pictures: Doc Krok)

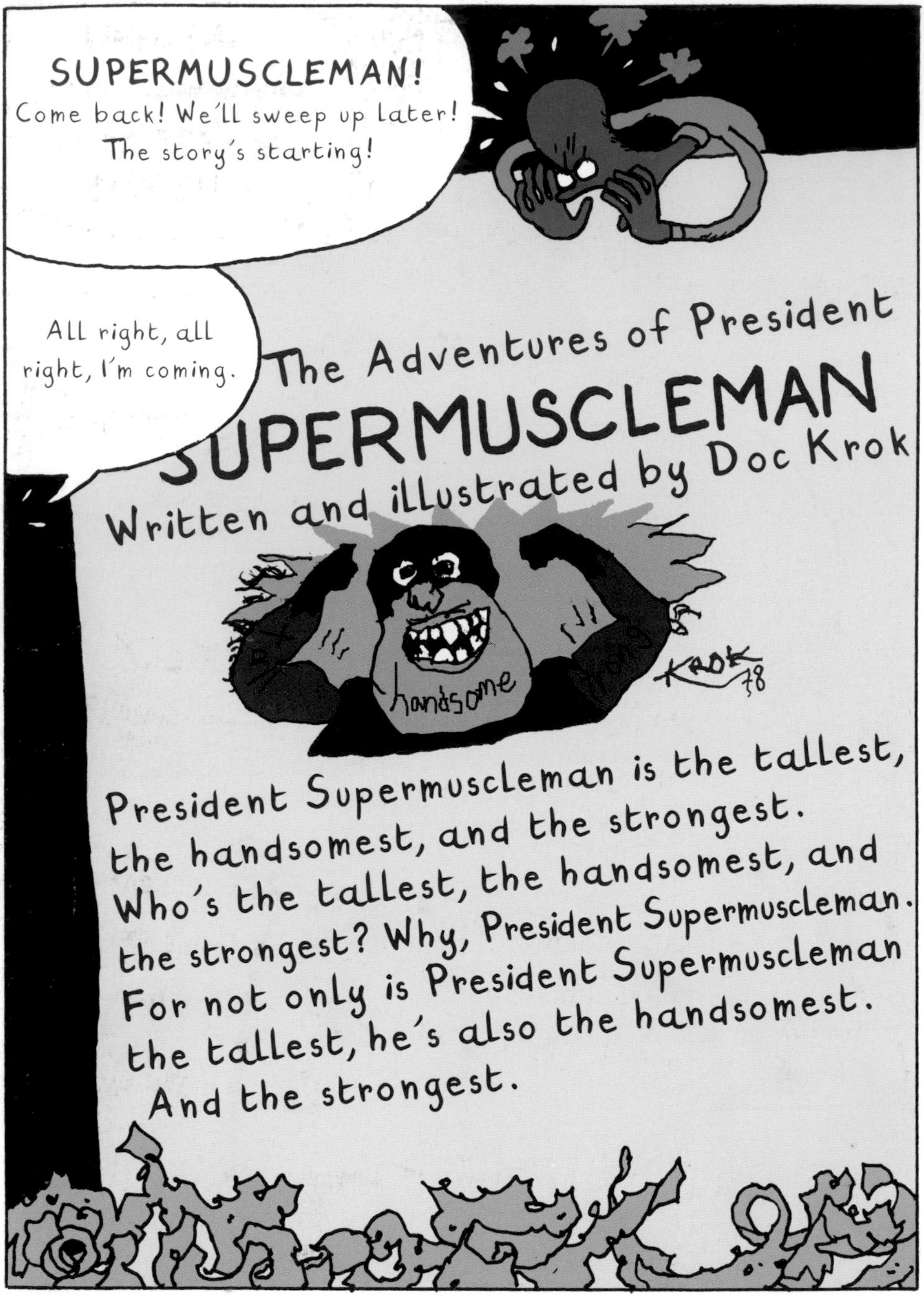
SUPERMUSCLEMAN! Come back! We'll sweep up later! The story's starting!
All right, all right, I'm coming.
The Adventures of President SUPERMUSCLEMAN
Written and illustrated by Doc Krok
handsome
KROK 78
President Supermuscleman is the tallest, the handsomest, and the strongest. Who's the tallest, the handsomest, and the strongest? Why, President Supermuscleman. For not only is President Supermuscleman the tallest, he's also the handsomest. And the strongest.

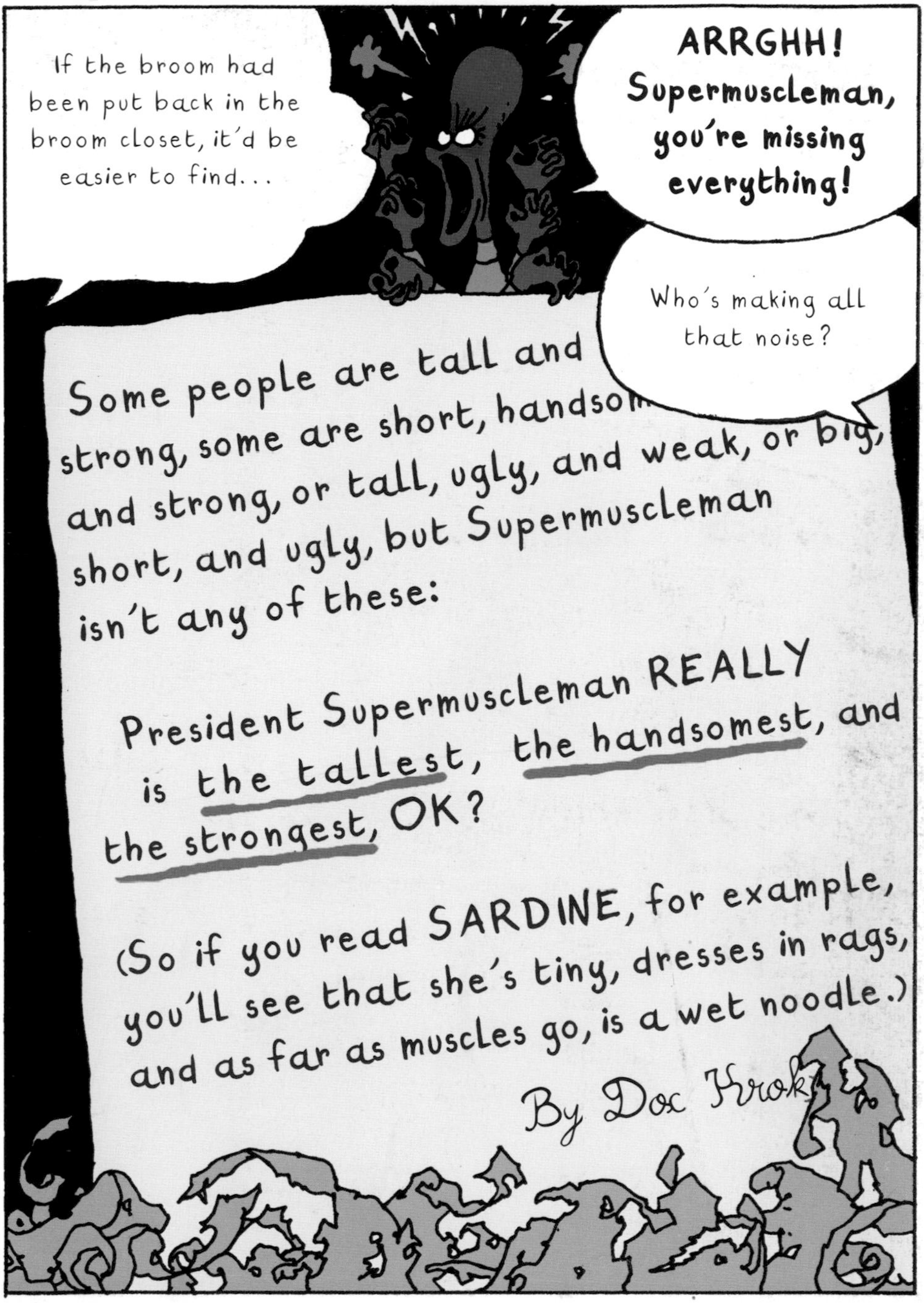
If the broom had been put back in the broom closet, it'd be easier to find...
ARRGHH! Supermuscleman, you're missing everything!
Who's making all that noise?
Some people are tall and
strong, some are short, handso
and strong, or tall, ugly, and weak, or big,
short, and ugly, but Supermuscleman
isn't any of these:
President Supermuscleman REALLY is the tallest, the handsomest, and the strongest, OK?
(So if you read SARDINE, for example, you'll see that she's tiny, dresses in rags, and as far as muscles go, is a wet noodle.)
By Doc Krok

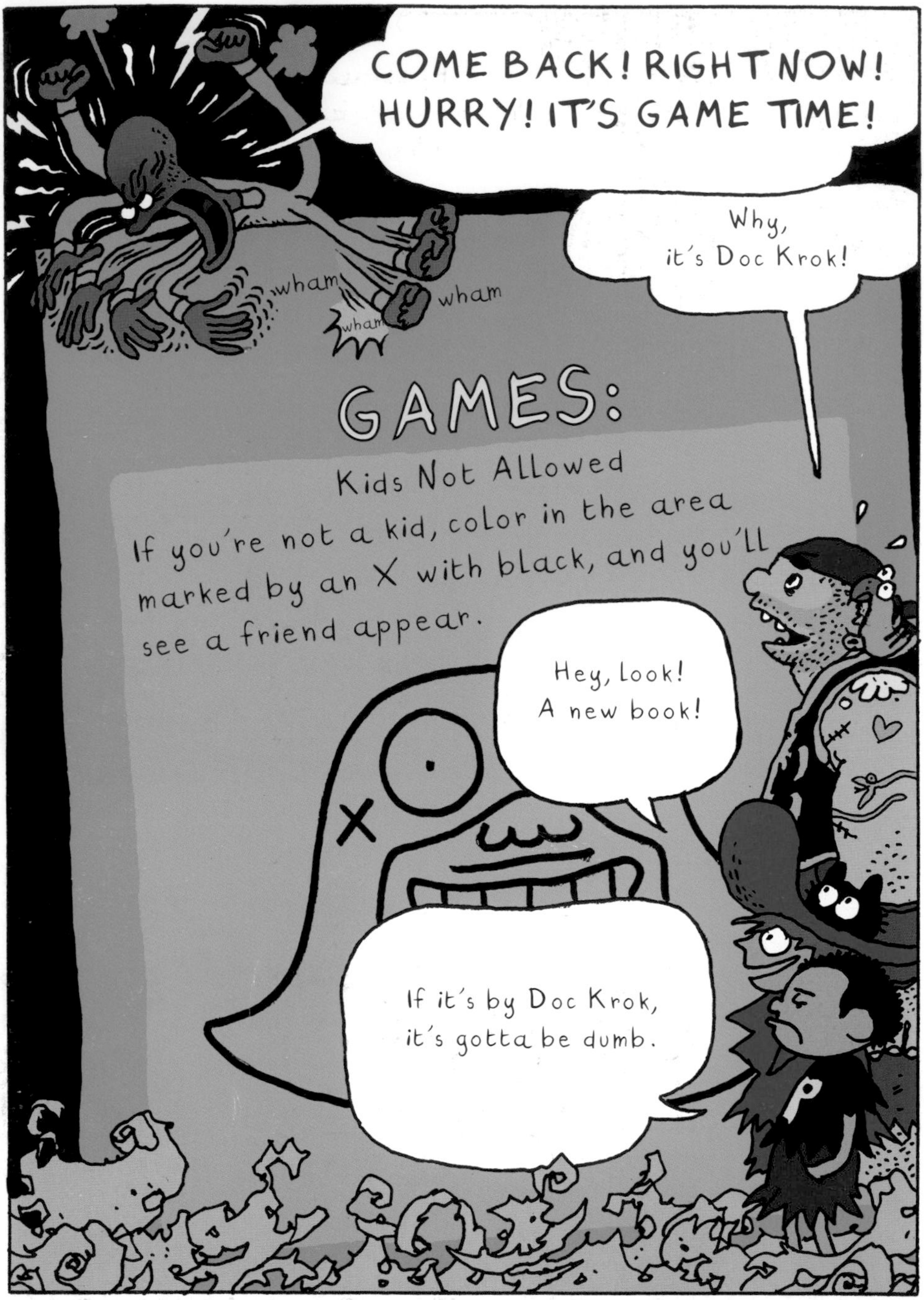
COME BACK! RIGHT NOW! HURRY! IT'S GAME TIME!
wham
wham
wham
Why, it's Doc Krok!
GAMES:
Kids Not Allowed
If you're not a kid, color in the area marked by an X with black, and you'll see a friend appear.
Hey, look! A new book!
If it's by Doc Krok, it's gotta be dumb.

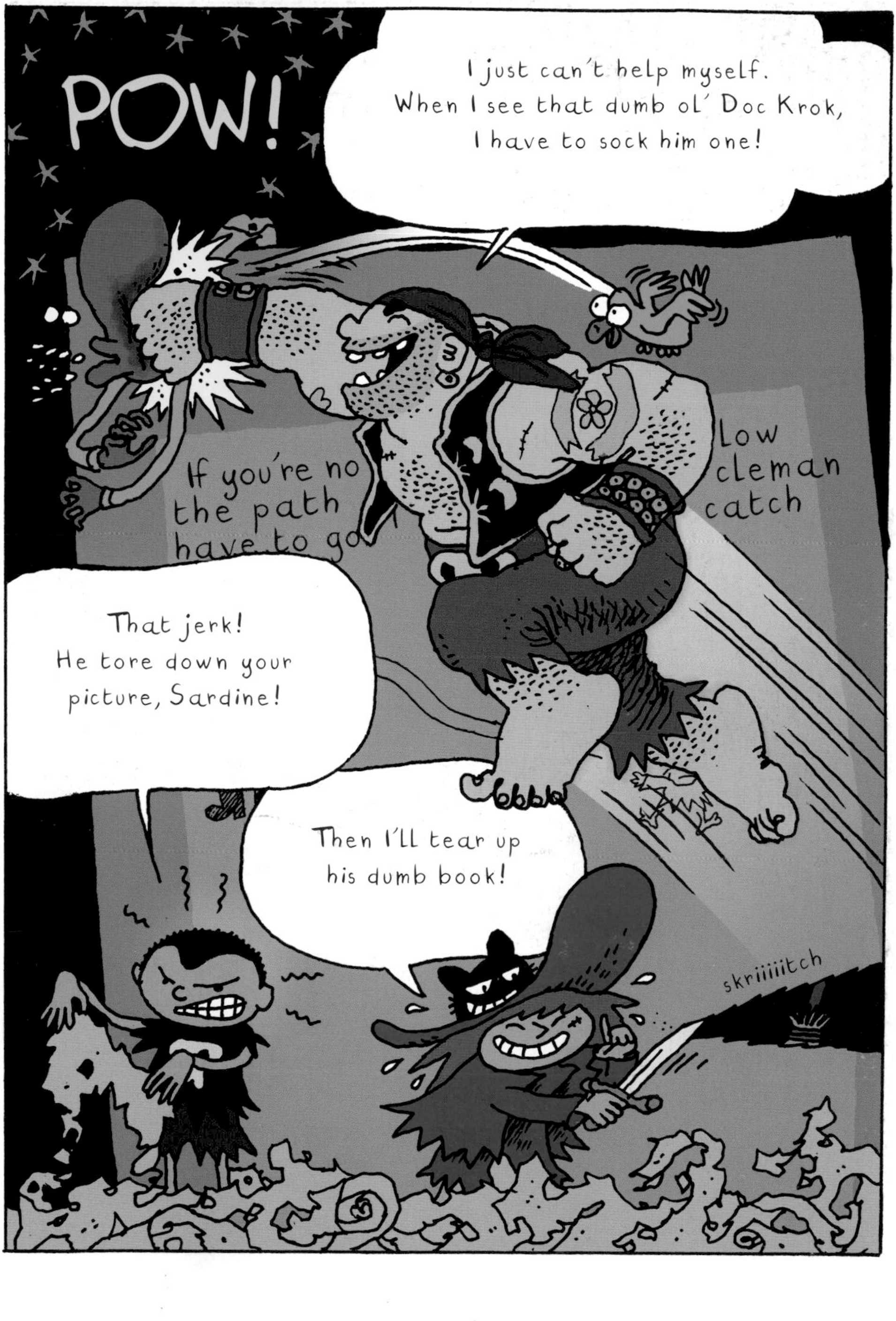
POW!
I just can't help myself. When I see that dumb ol' Doc Krok, I have to sock him one!
If you're no the path have to go
Low cleman catch
That jerk! He tore down your picture, Sardine!
Then I'll tear up his dumb book!
skriiiiitch

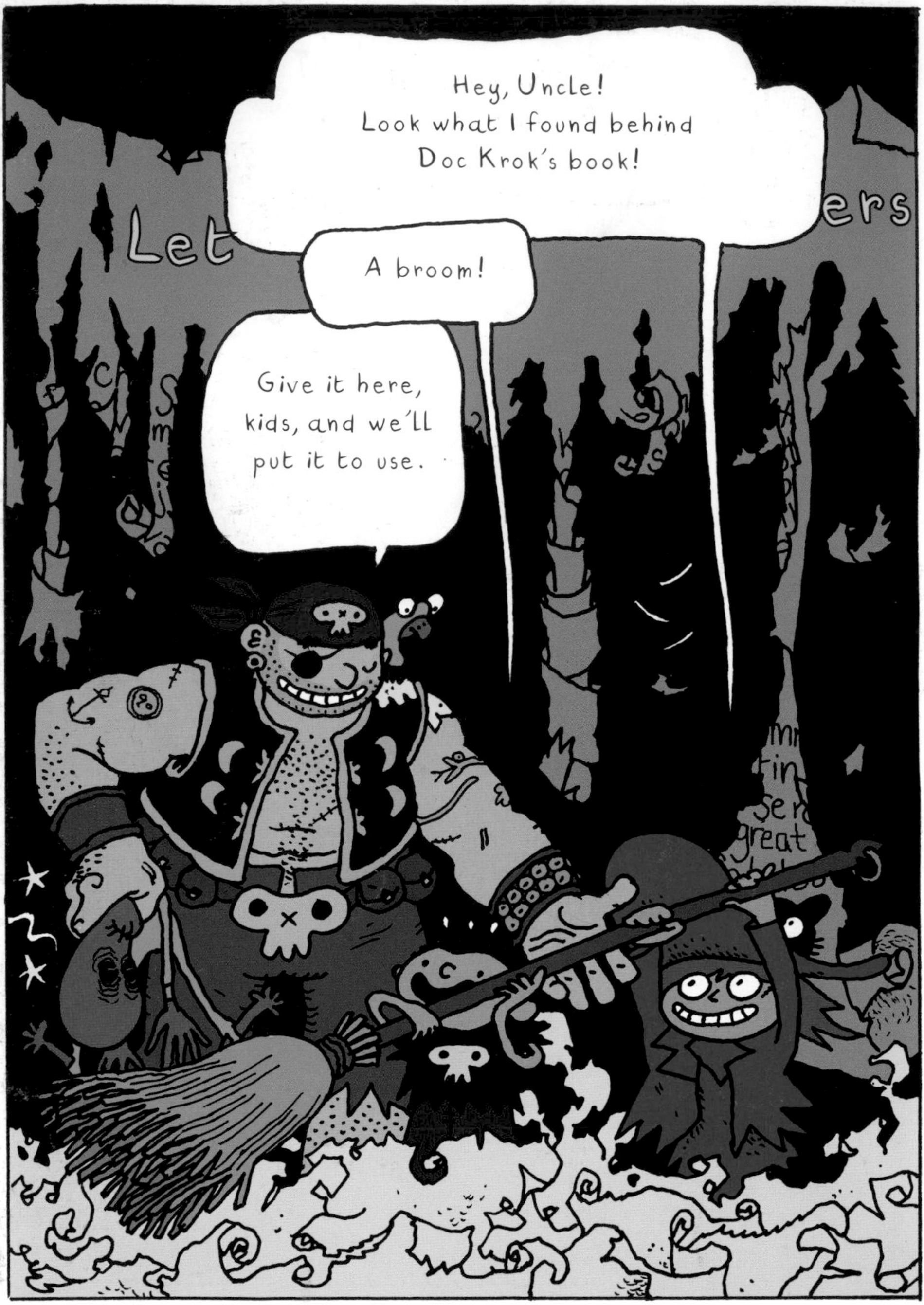
Hey, Uncle! Look what I found behind Doc Krok's book!
A broom!
Give it here, kids, and we'll put it to use.

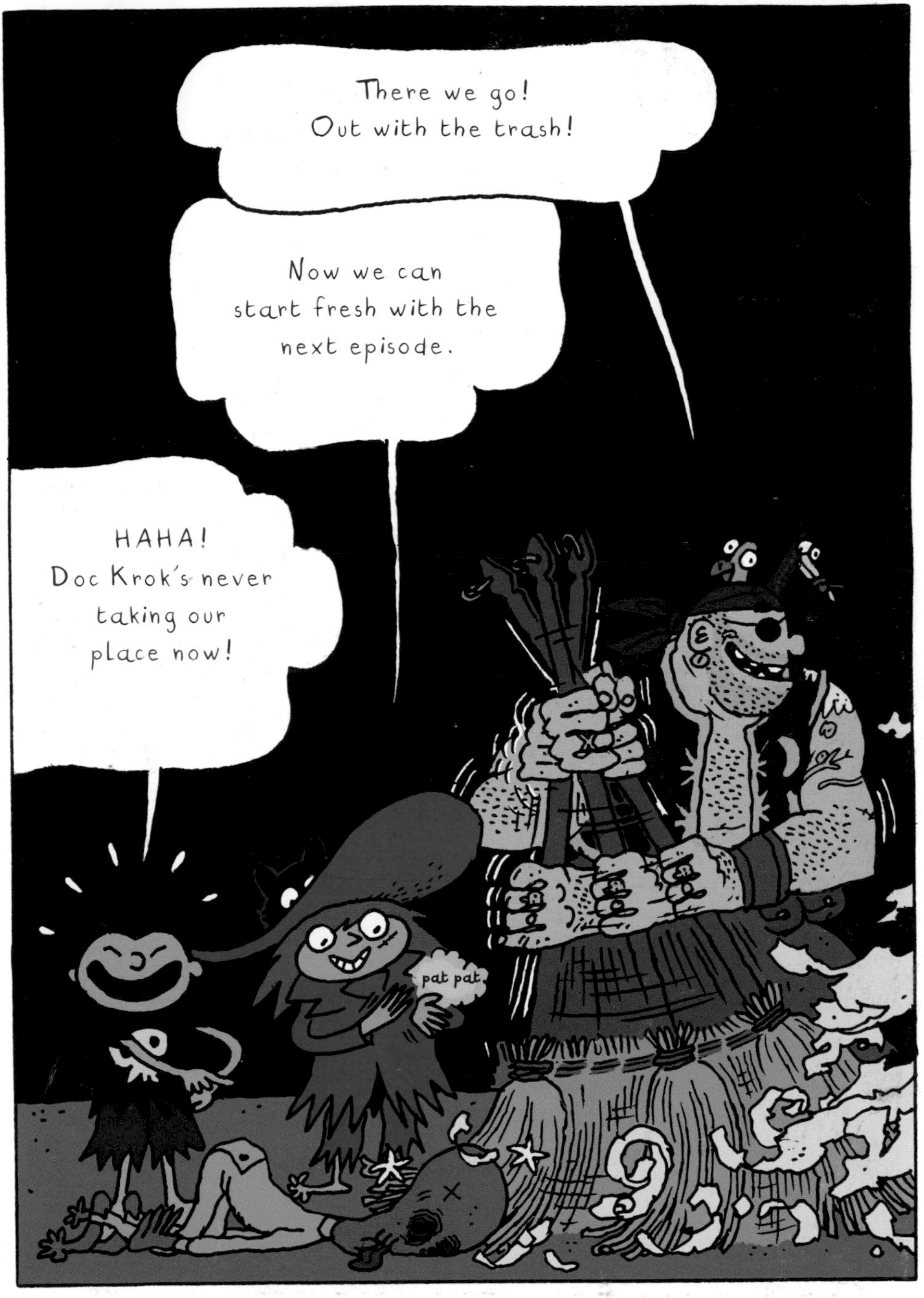
There we go! Out with the trash!
Now we can start fresh with the next episode.
HAHA! Doc Krok's never taking our place now!
pat pat

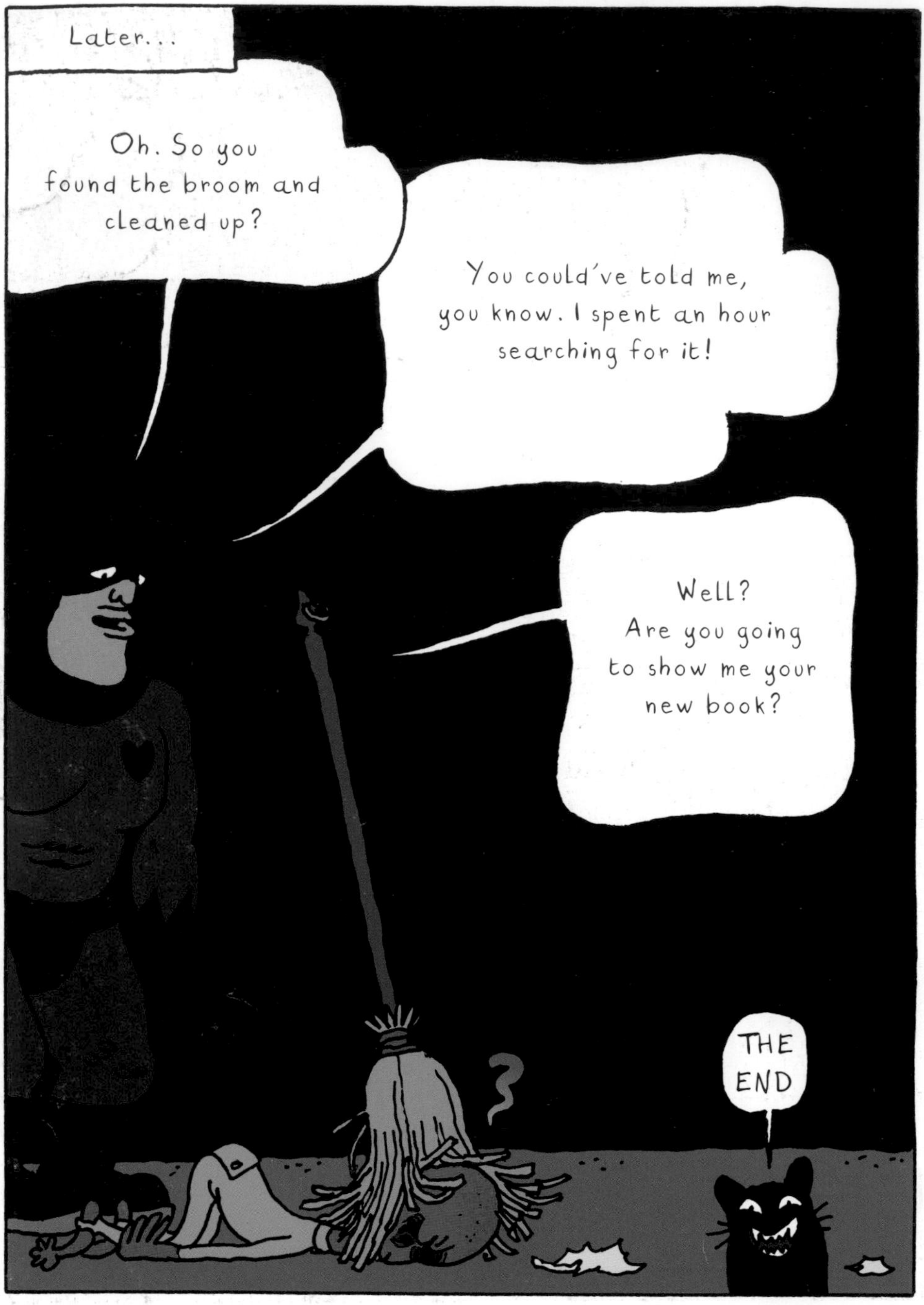
Later...
Oh. So you found the broom and cleaned up?
You could've told me, you know. I spent an hour searching for it!
Well? Are you going to show me your new book?
THE END

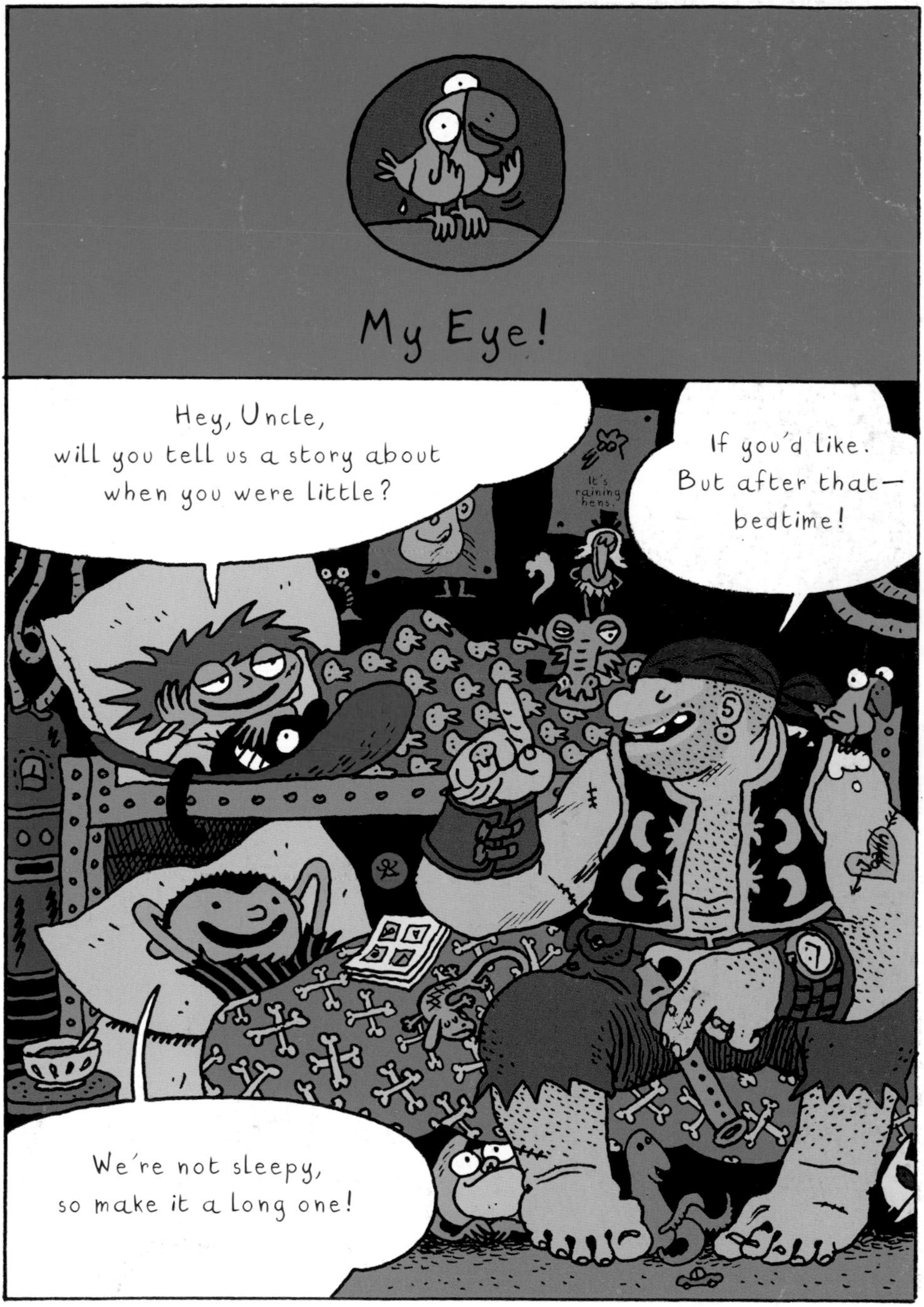
My Eye!
Hey, Uncle, will you tell us a story about when you were little?
It's raining hens.
If you'd like. But after that—bedtime!
We're not sleepy, so make it a long one!

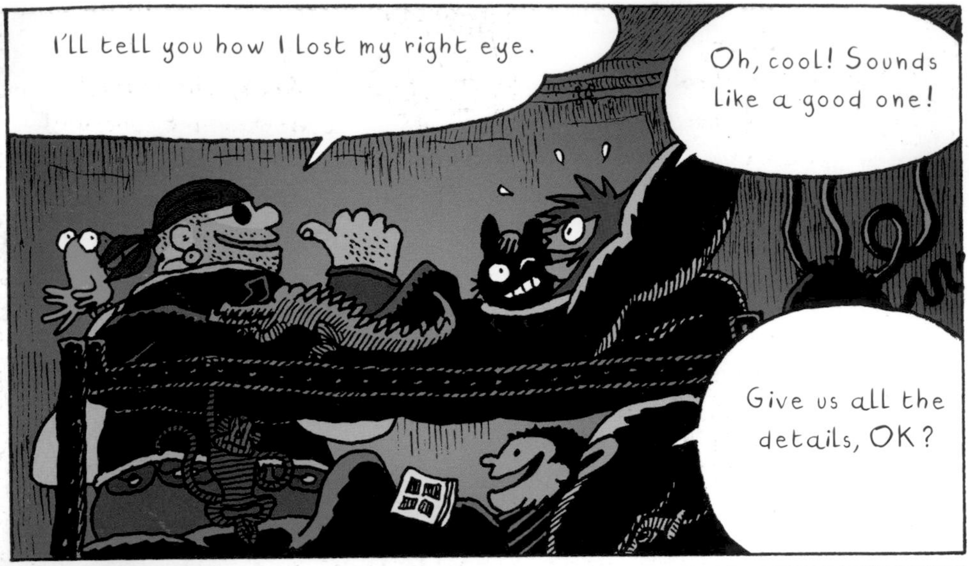
I'll tell you how I lost my right eye.
Oh, cool! Sounds like a good one!
Give us all the details, OK?

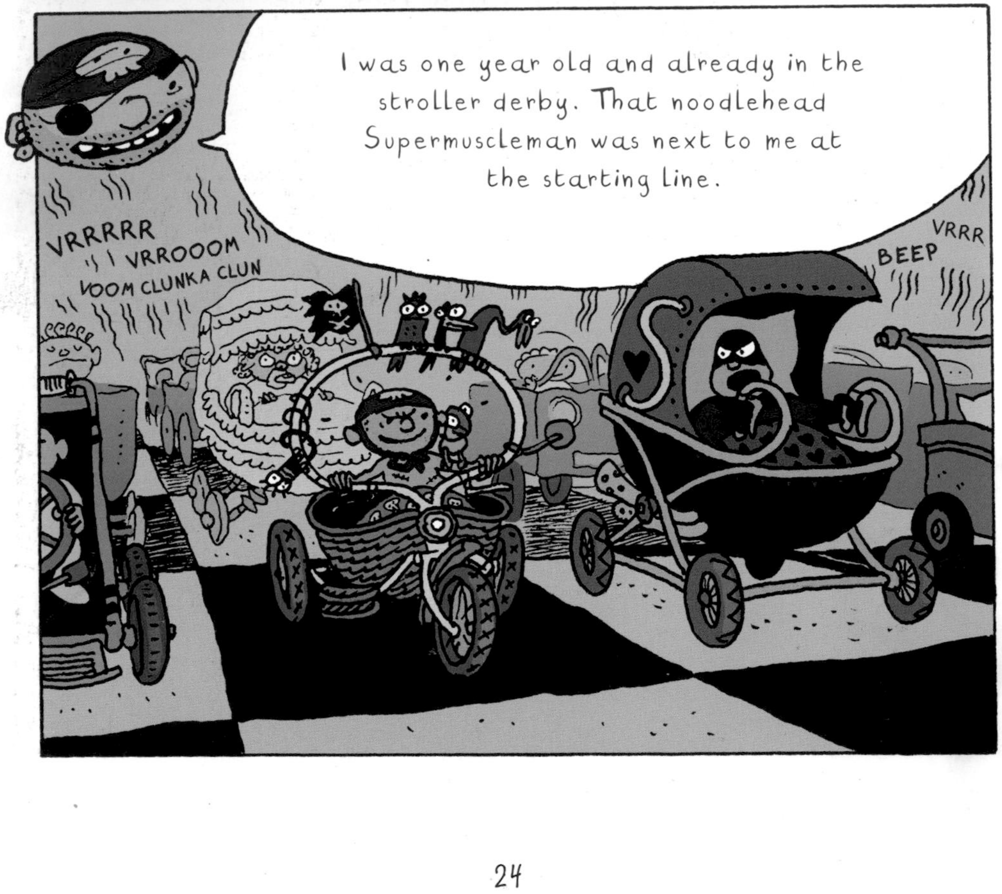
I was one year old and already in the stroller derby. That noodlehead Supermuscleman was next to me at the starting line.
VRRRRR
VRROOOM
VOOM CLUNKA CLUN
BEEP
VRRR

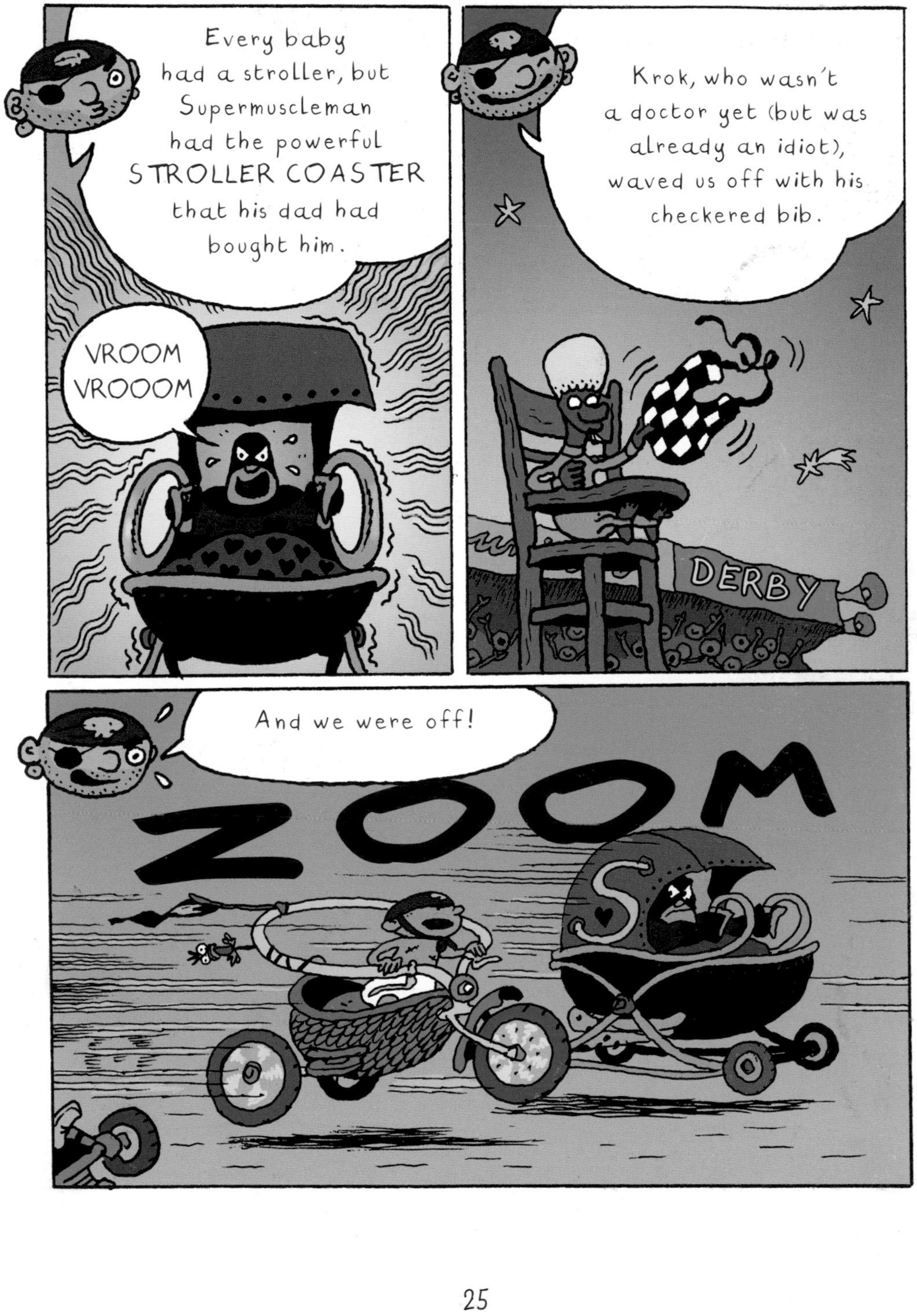
Every baby had a stroller, but Supermuscleman had the powerful STROLLER COASTER that his dad had bought him.
VROOM VROOOM
Krok, who wasn't a doctor yet (but was already an idiot), waved us off with his checkered bib.
DERBY
And we were off!
ZOOM

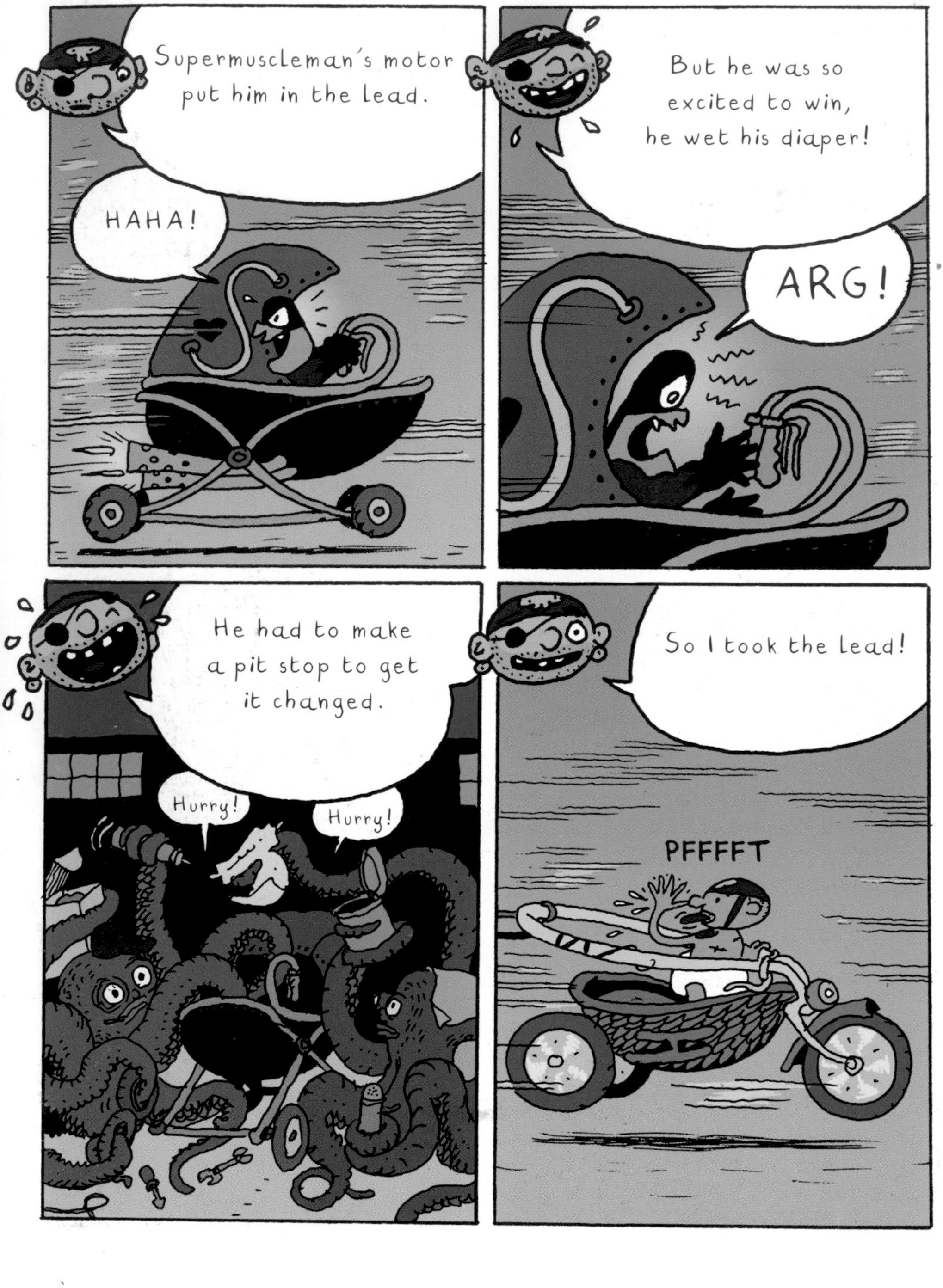
Supermuscleman's motor put him in the lead.
HAHA!
But he was so excited to win, he wet his diaper!
ARG!
He had to make a pit stop to get it changed.
Hurry!
Hurry!
So I took the lead!
PFFFFT

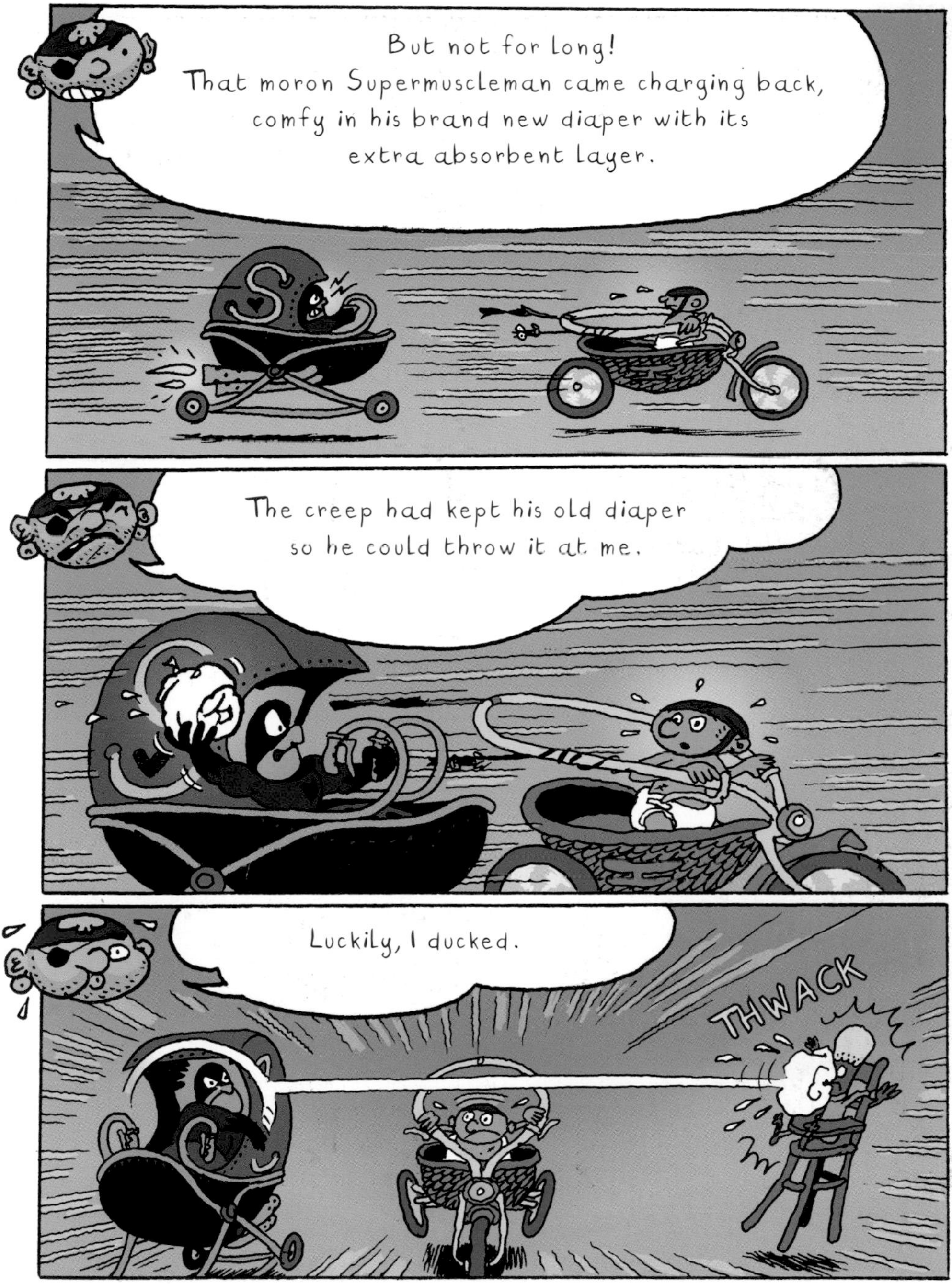
But not for long!
That moron Supermuscleman came charging back, comfy in his brand new diaper with its extra absorbent layer.
The creep had kept his old diaper so he could throw it at me.
Luckily, I ducked.
THWACK

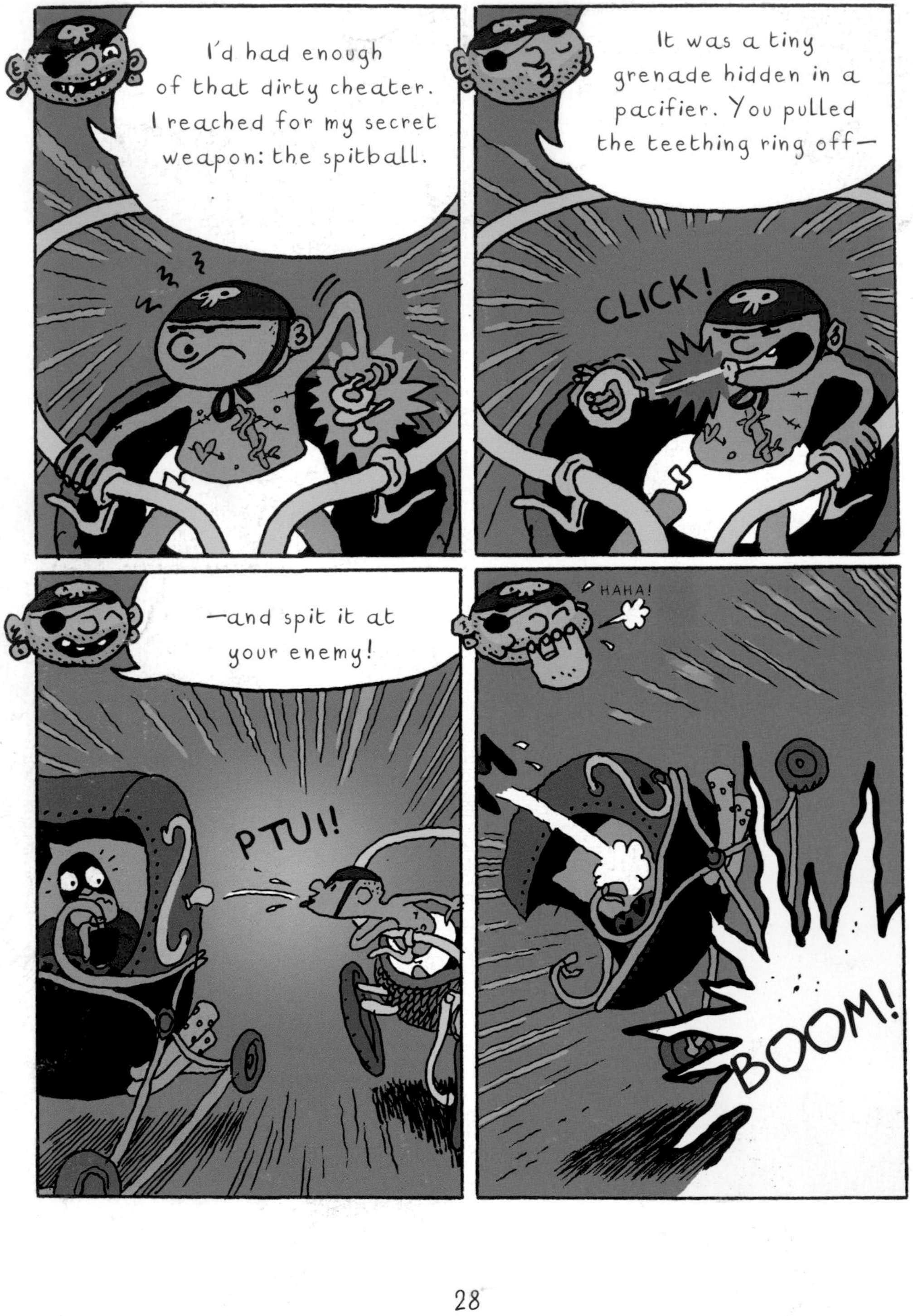
I'd had enough of that dirty cheater. I reached for my secret weapon: the spitball.
It was a tiny grenade hidden in a pacifier. You pulled the teething ring off—
CLICK!
—and spit it at your enemy!
PTUI!
HAHA!
BOOM!

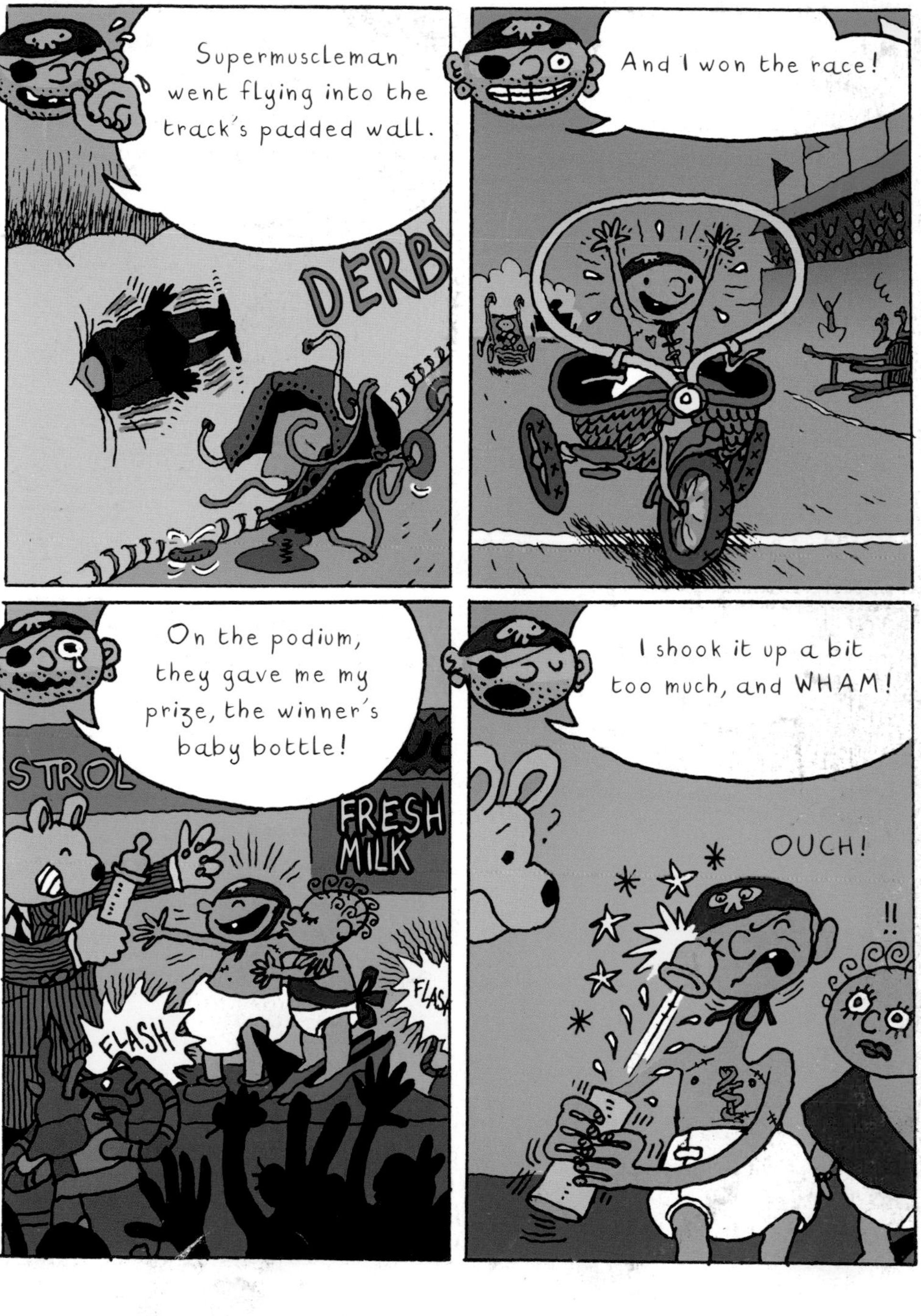
Supermuscleman went flying into the track's padded wall.
DERB
And I won the race!
On the podium, they gave me my prize, the winner's baby bottle!
STROL
FRESH MILK
FLASH
FLASH
I shook it up a bit too much, and WHAM!
OUCH!
!!

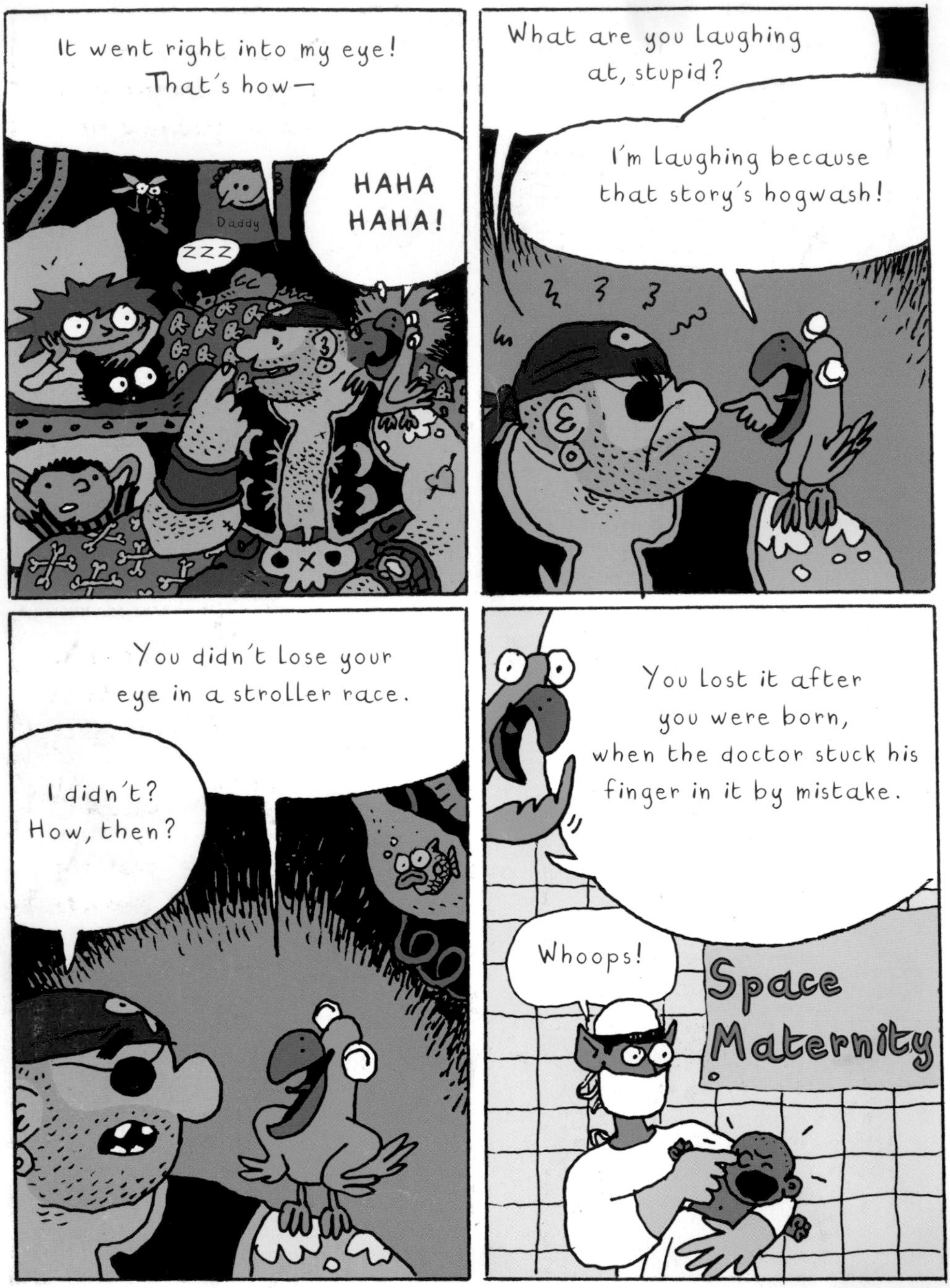
It went right into my eye! That's how—
HAHA HAHA!
Daddy
ZZZ
What are you laughing at, stupid?
I'm laughing because that story's hogwash!
You didn't lose your eye in a stroller race.
I didn't? How, then?
You lost it after you were born, when the doctor stuck his finger in it by mistake.
Whoops!
Space Maternity

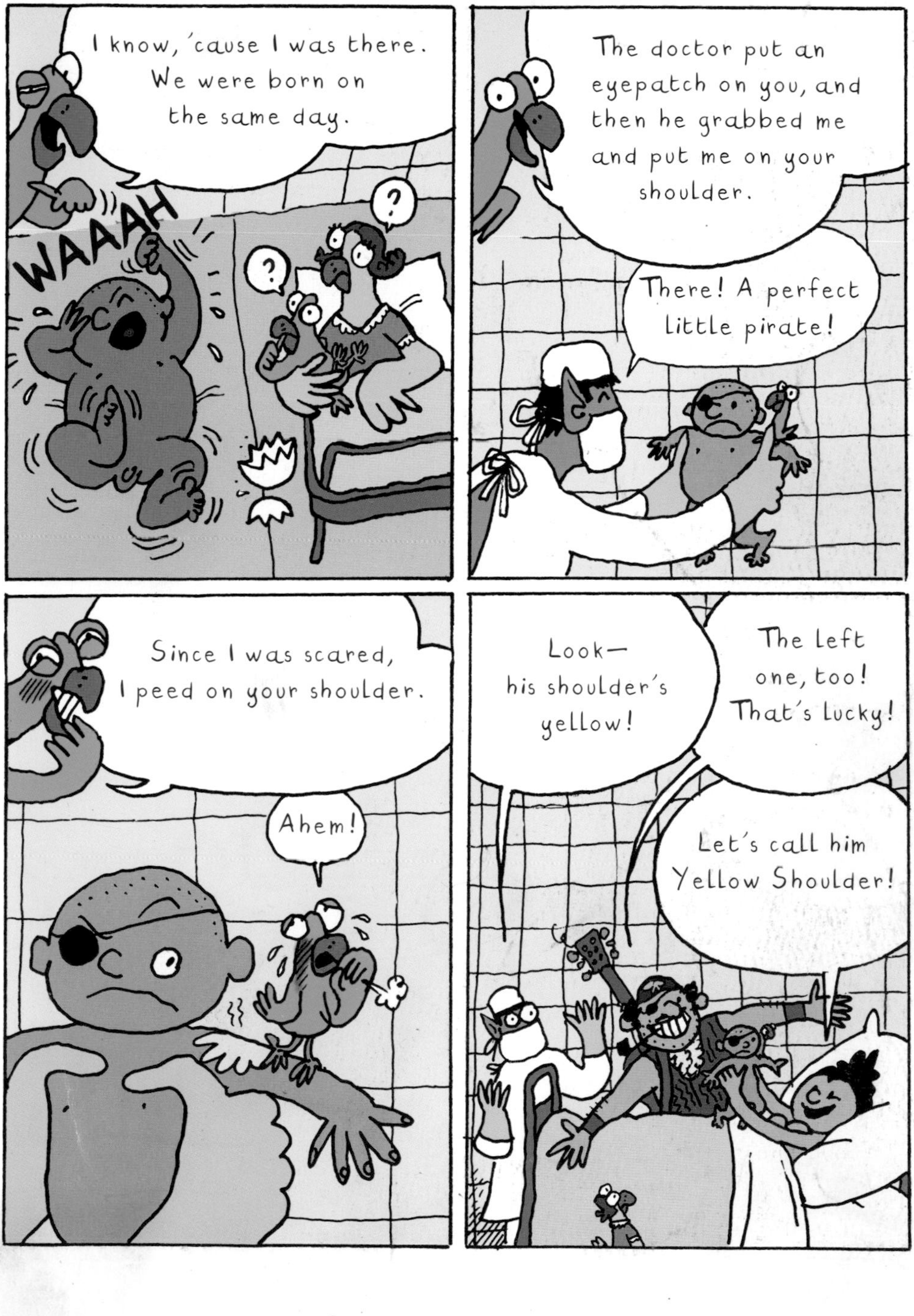
I know, 'cause I was there. We were born on the same day.
WAAAH
?
?
The doctor put an eyepatch on you, and then he grabbed me and put me on your shoulder.
There! A perfect little pirate!
Since I was scared, I peed on your shoulder.
Ahem!
Look— his shoulder's yellow!
The left one, too! That's lucky!
Let's call him Yellow Shoulder!

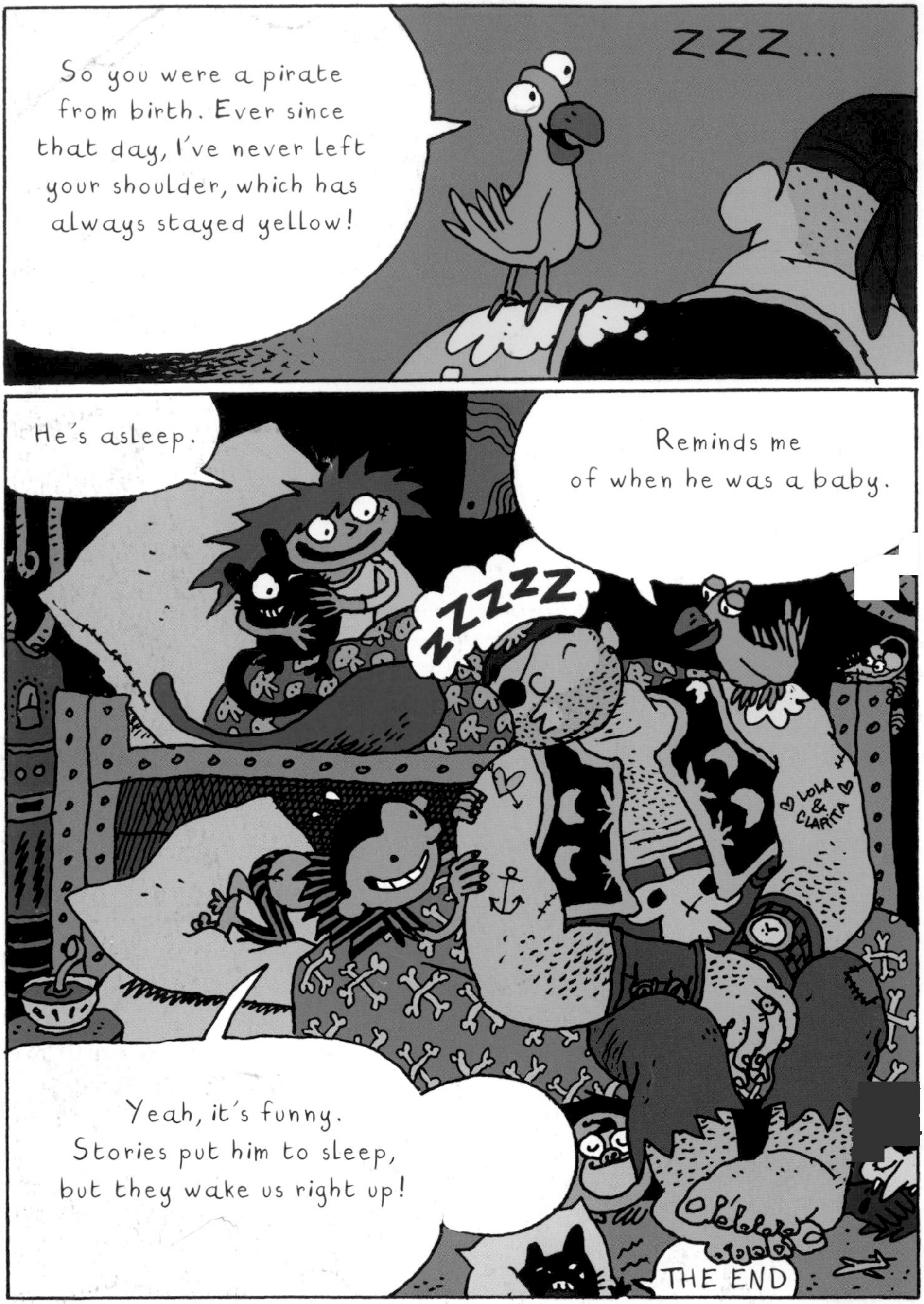
So you were a pirate from birth. Ever since that day, I've never left your shoulder, which has always stayed yellow!
ZZZ...
He's asleep.
Reminds me of when he was a baby.
ZZZZZ
LOLA & CLARITA
Yeah, it's funny. Stories put him to sleep, but they wake us right up!
THE END

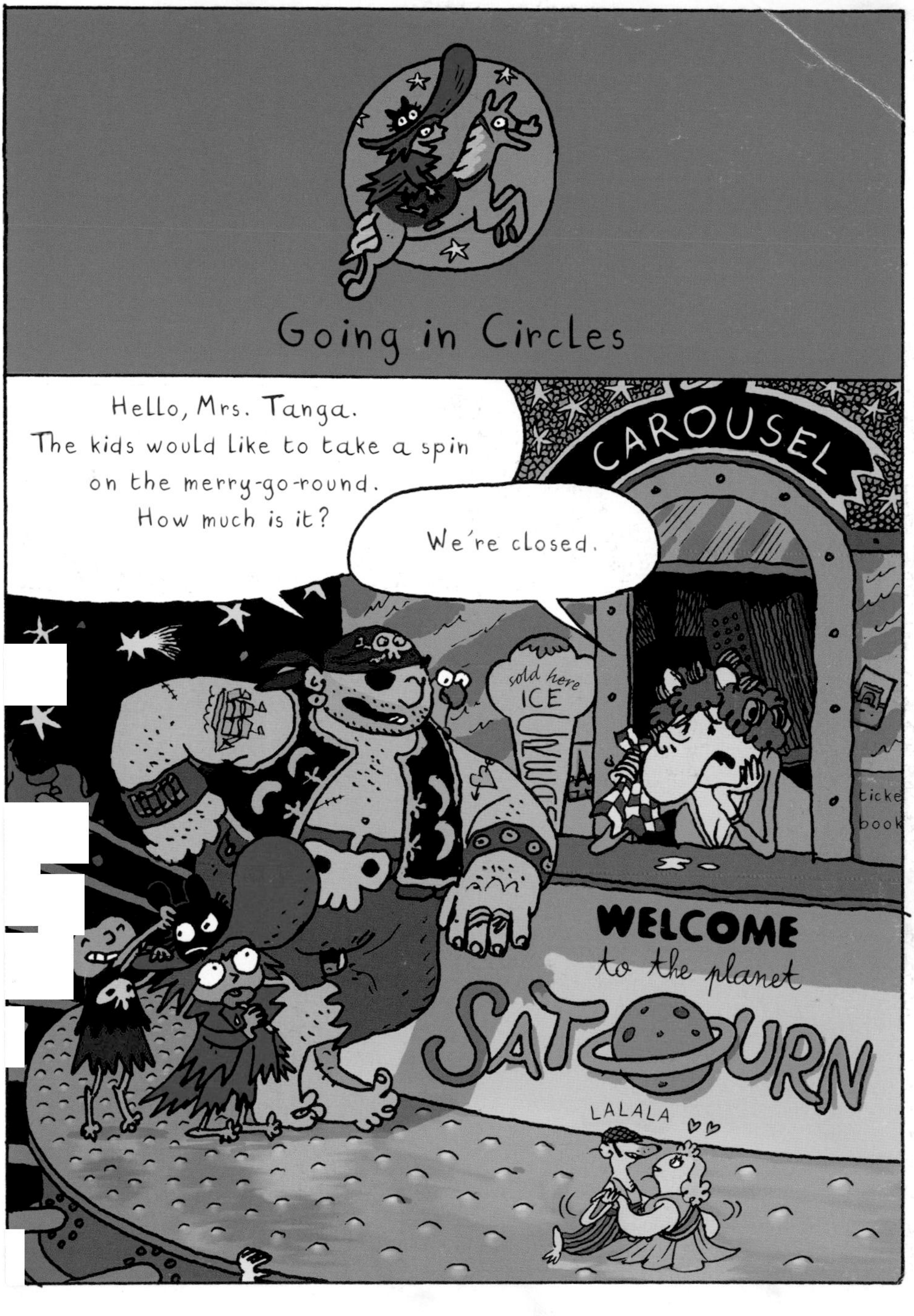
Going in Circles
Hello, Mrs. Tanga.
The kids would like to take a spin
on the merry-go-round.
How much is it?
We're closed.
CAROUSEL
sold here
ICE
WELCOME
to the planet
SATURN
LALALA

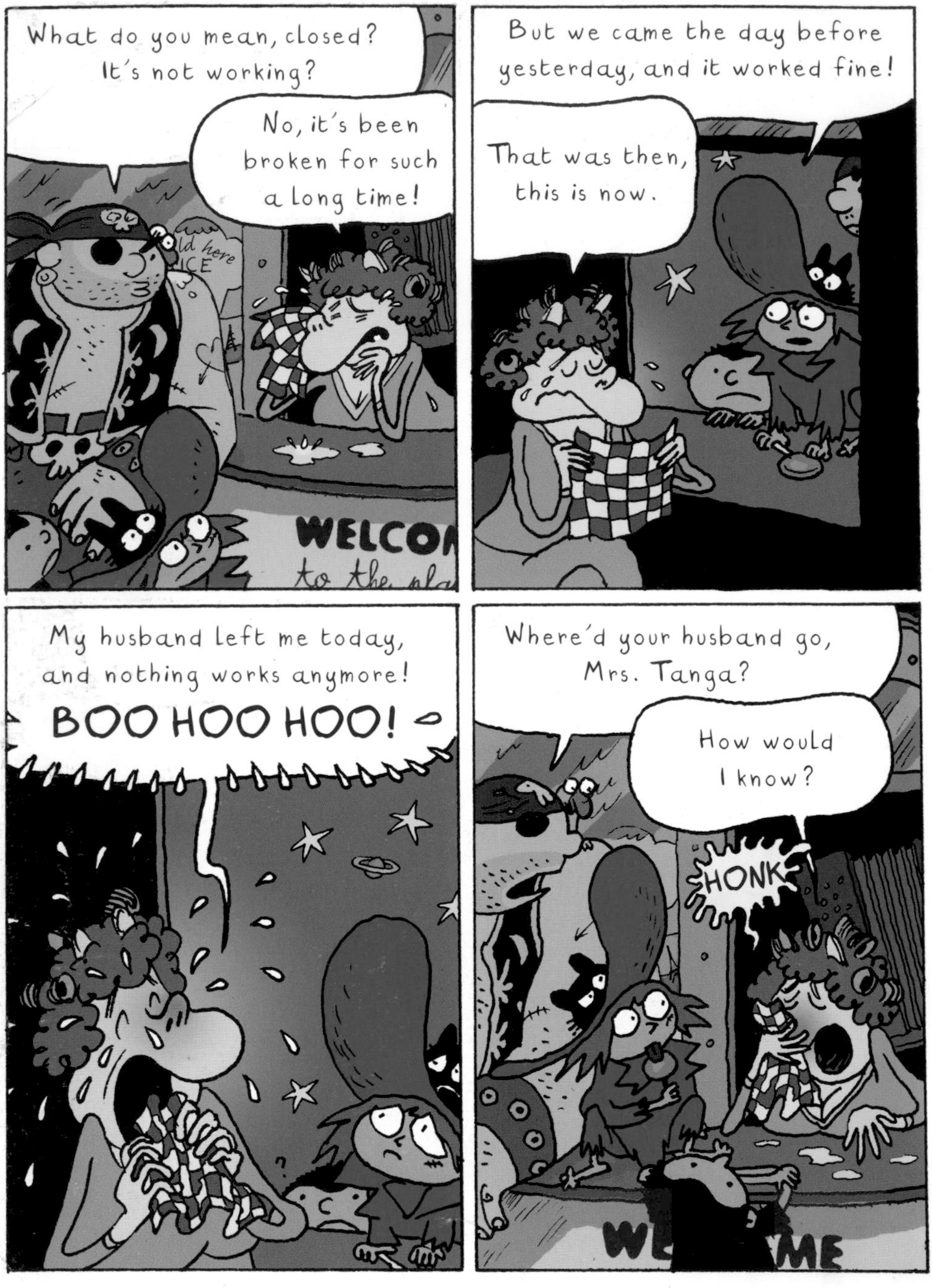

What do you mean, closed? It's not working?
No, it's been broken for such a long time!
WELCOM
But we came the day before yesterday, and it worked fine!
That was then, this is now.
My husband left me today, and nothing works anymore!
BOO HOO HOO!
Where'd your husband go, Mrs. Tanga?
How would I know?
HONK

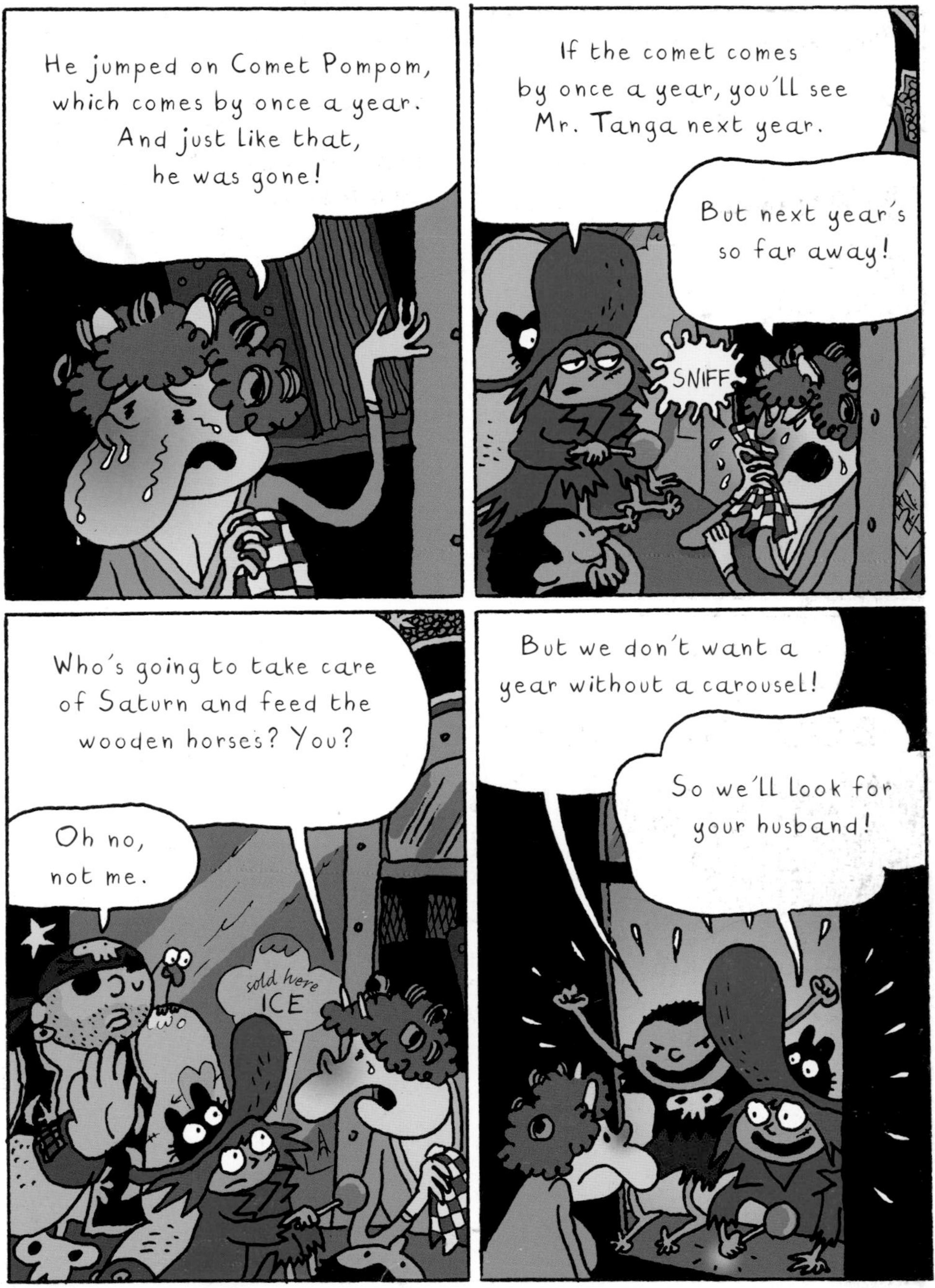
He jumped on Comet Pompom, which comes by once a year. And just like that, he was gone!
If the comet comes by once a year, you'll see Mr. Tanga next year.
But next year's so far away!
SNIFF
Who's going to take care of Saturn and feed the wooden horses? You?
Oh no, not me.
sold here ICE
But we don't want a year without a carousel!
So we'll look for your husband!

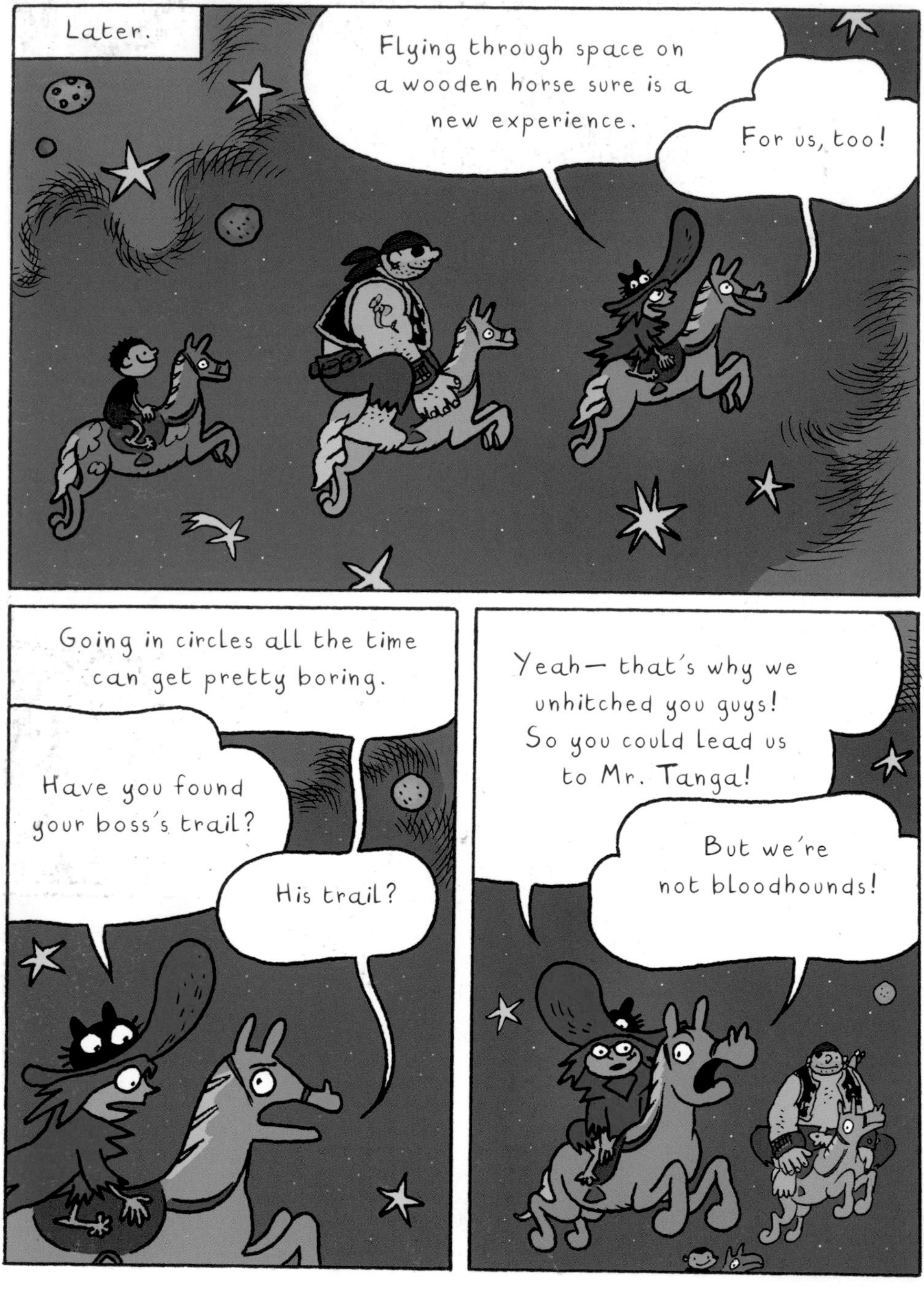
Later.
Flying through space on a wooden horse sure is a new experience.
For us, too!
Going in circles all the time can get pretty boring.
Have you found your boss's trail?
His trail?
Yeah— that's why we unhitched you guys! So you could lead us to Mr. Tanga!
But we're not bloodhounds!

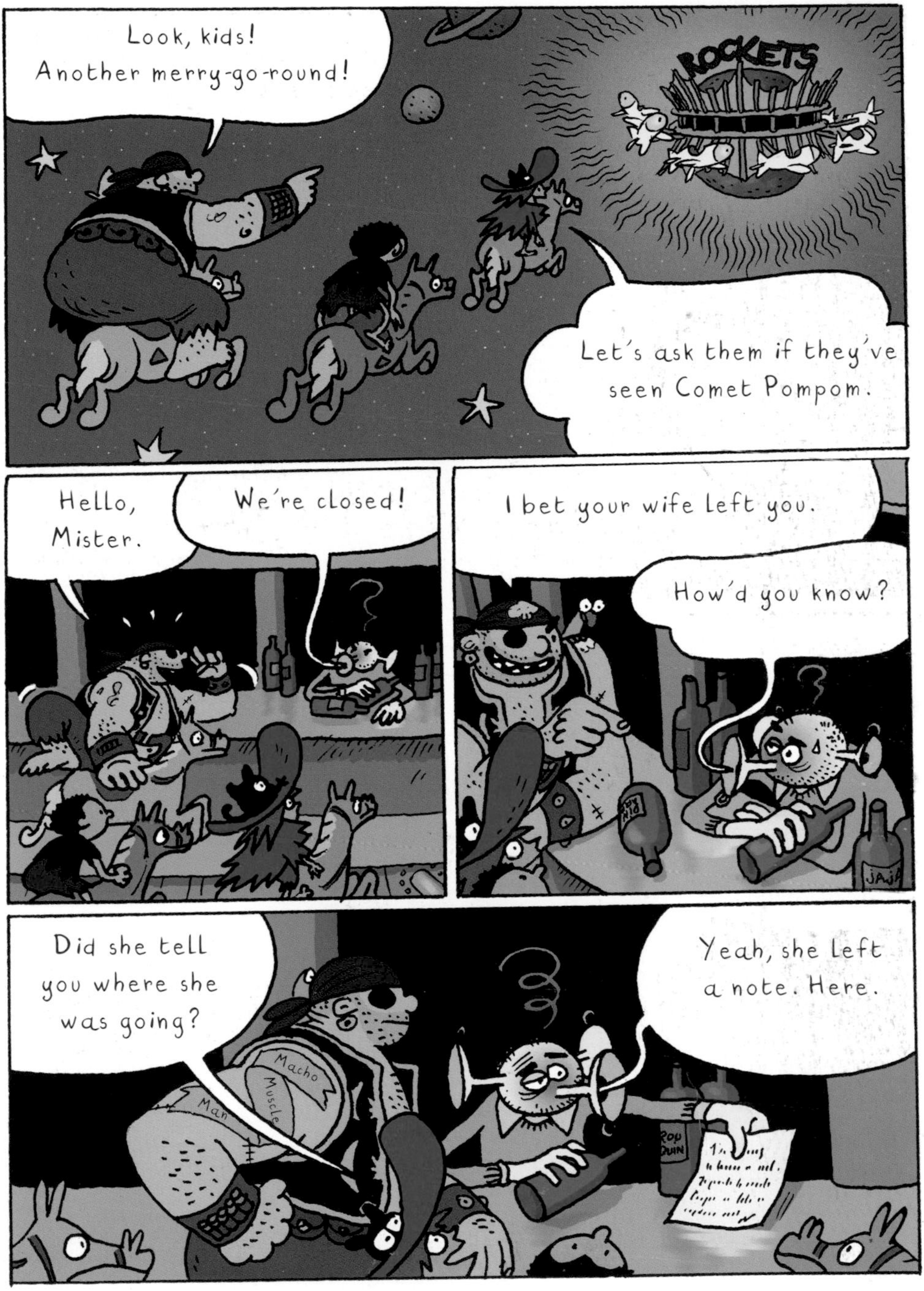
Look, kids! Another merry-go-round!
ROCKETS
Let's ask them if they've seen Comet Pompom.
Hello, Mister.
We're closed!
I bet your wife left you.
How'd you know?
Did she tell you where she was going?
Macho
Muscle
Man
Yeah, she left a note. Here.

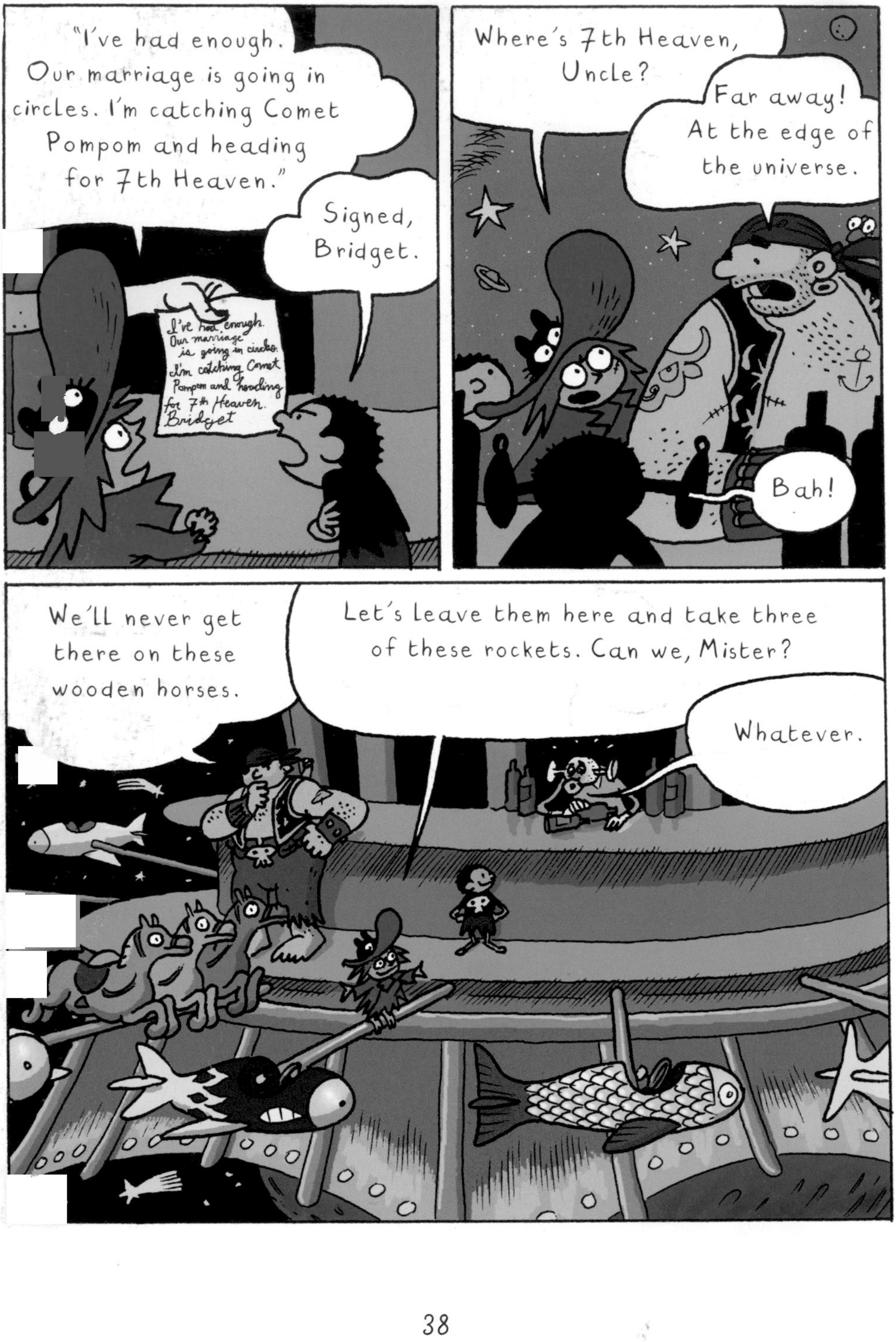
"I've had enough. Our marriage is going in circles. I'm catching Comet Pompom and heading for 7th Heaven."
Signed, Bridget.
Where's 7th Heaven, Uncle?
Far away! At the edge of the universe.
Bah!
We'll never get there on these wooden horses.
Let's leave them here and take three of these rockets. Can we, Mister?
Whatever.

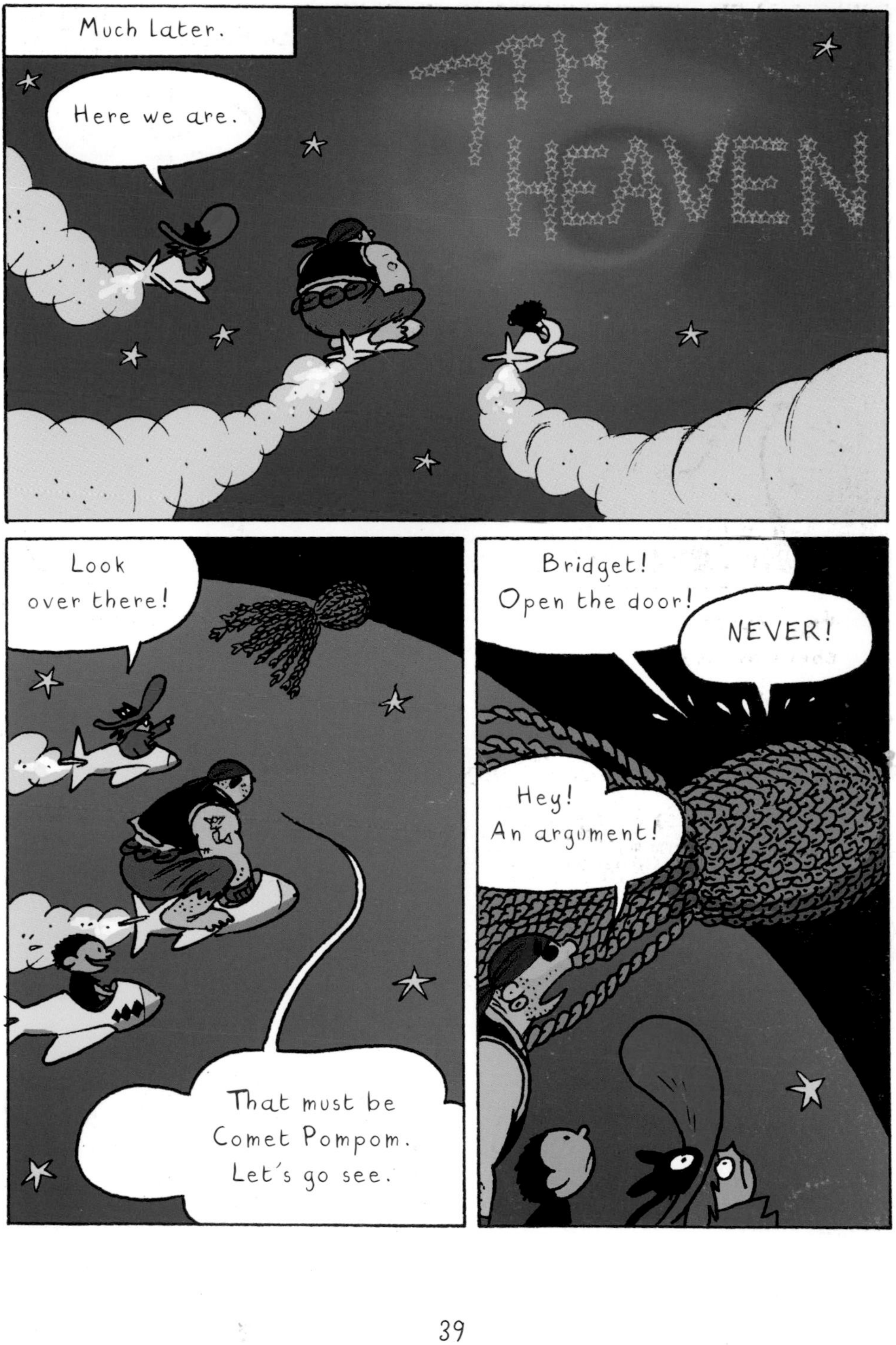
Much later.
7TH HEAVEN
Here we are.
Look over there!
That must be Comet Pompom. Let's go see.
Bridget! Open the door!
NEVER!
Hey! An argument!

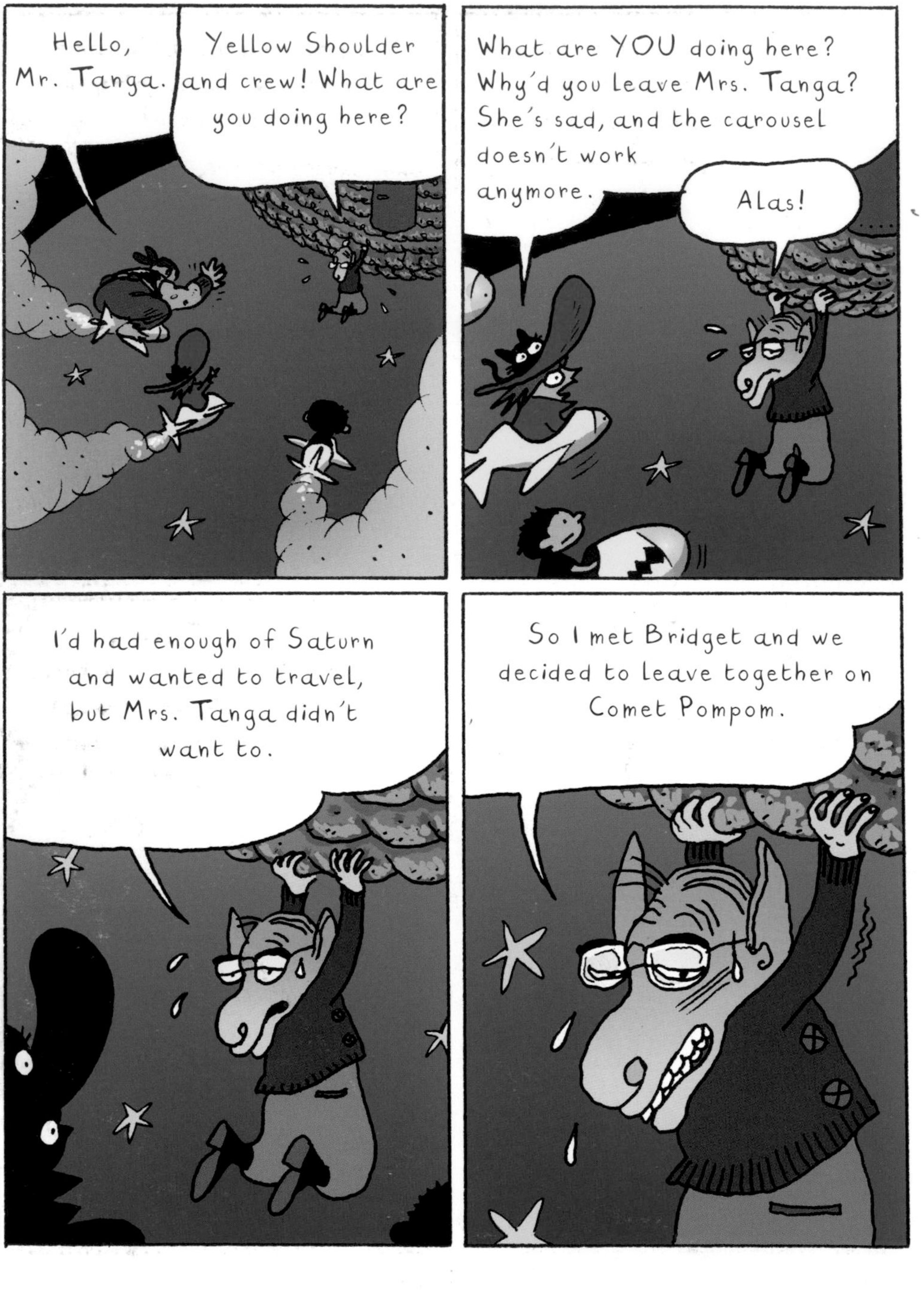
Hello, Mr. Tanga.
Yellow Shoulder and crew! What are you doing here?
What are YOU doing here? Why'd you leave Mrs. Tanga? She's sad, and the carousel doesn't work anymore.
Alas!
I'd had enough of Saturn and wanted to travel, but Mrs. Tanga didn't want to.
So I met Bridget and we decided to leave together on Comet Pompom.

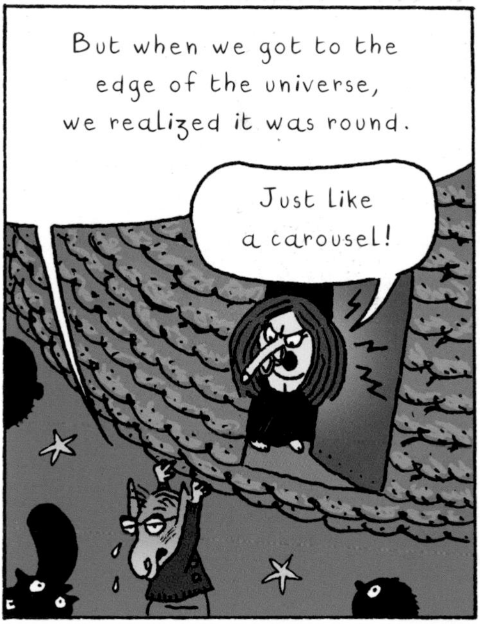
But when we got to the edge of the universe, we realized it was round.
Just like a carousel!
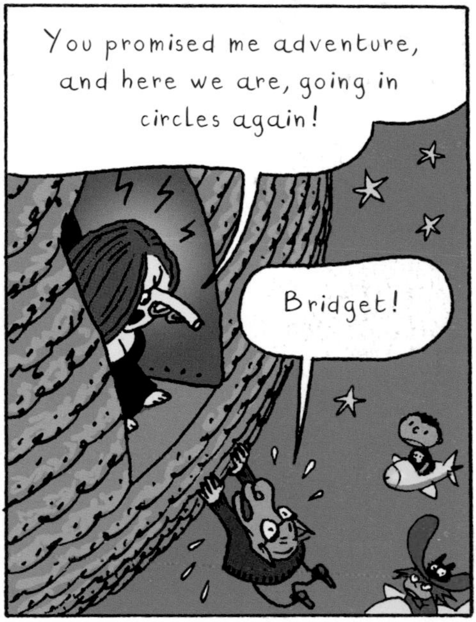
You promised me adventure, and here we are, going in circles again!
Bridget!
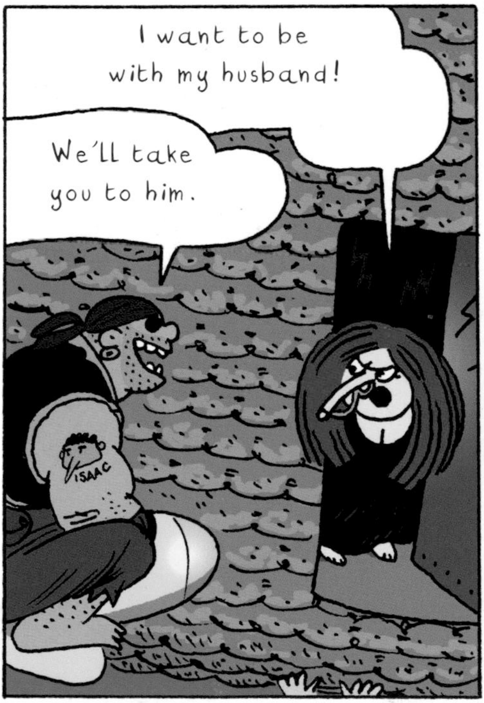
I want to be with my husband!
We'll take you to him.
ISAAC
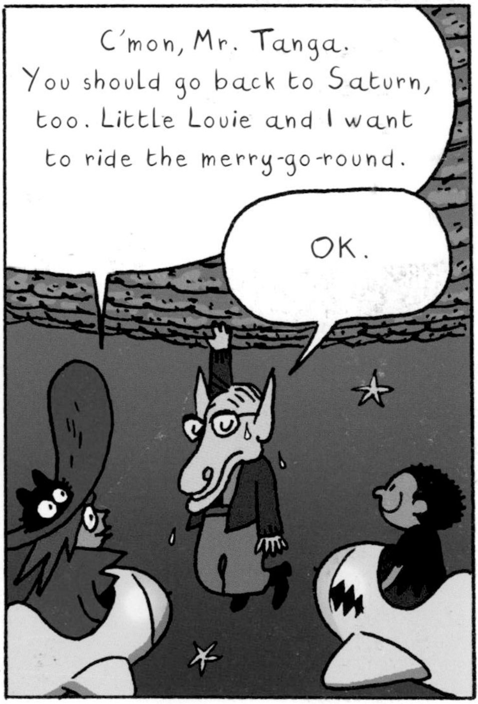
C'mon, Mr. Tanga. You should go back to Saturn, too. Little Louie and I want to ride the merry-go-round.
OK.

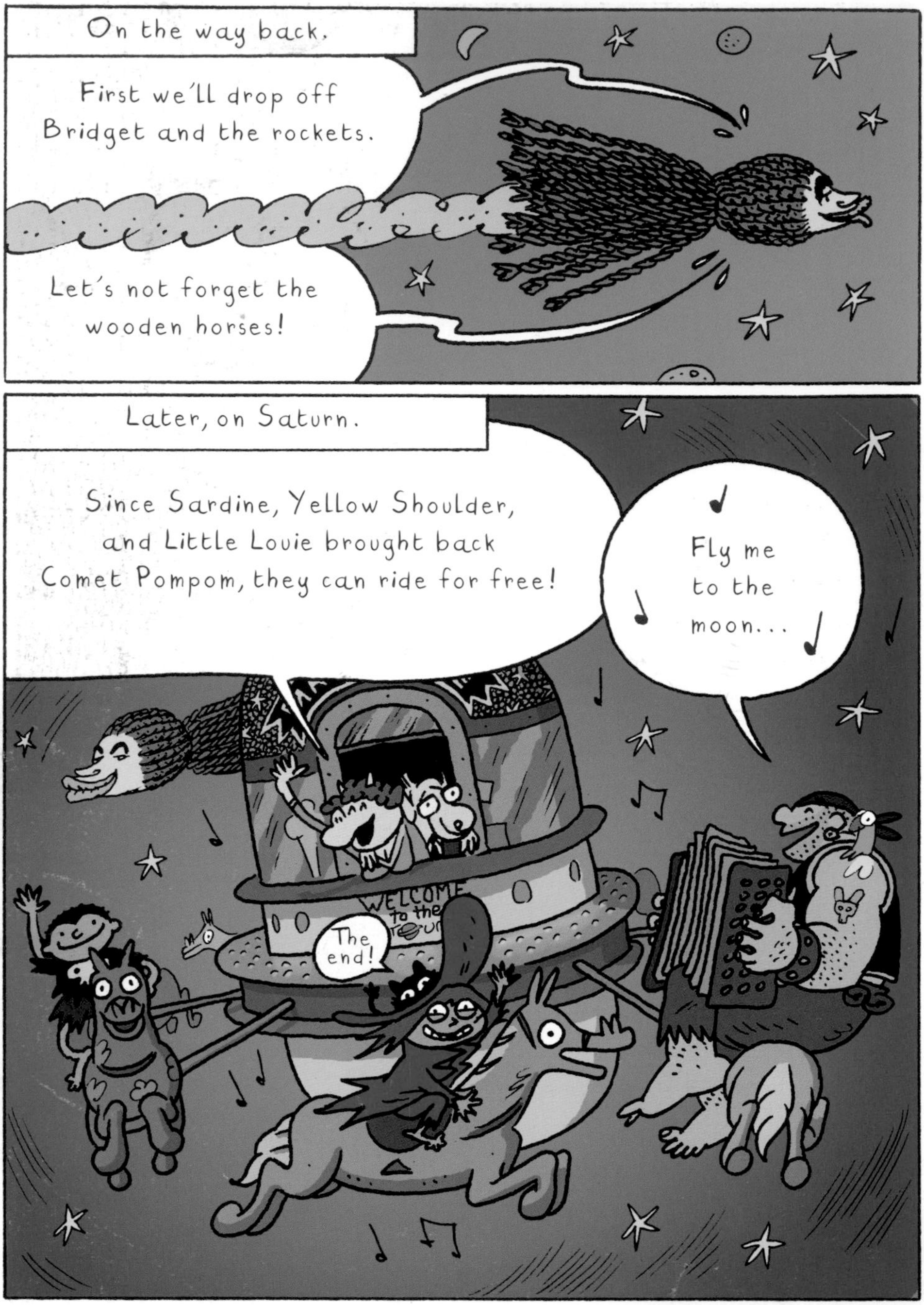
On the way back.
First we'll drop off Bridget and the rockets.
Let's not forget the wooden horses!
Later, on Saturn.
Since Sardine, Yellow Shoulder, and Little Louie brought back Comet Pompom, they can ride for free!
Fly me to the moon...
The end!

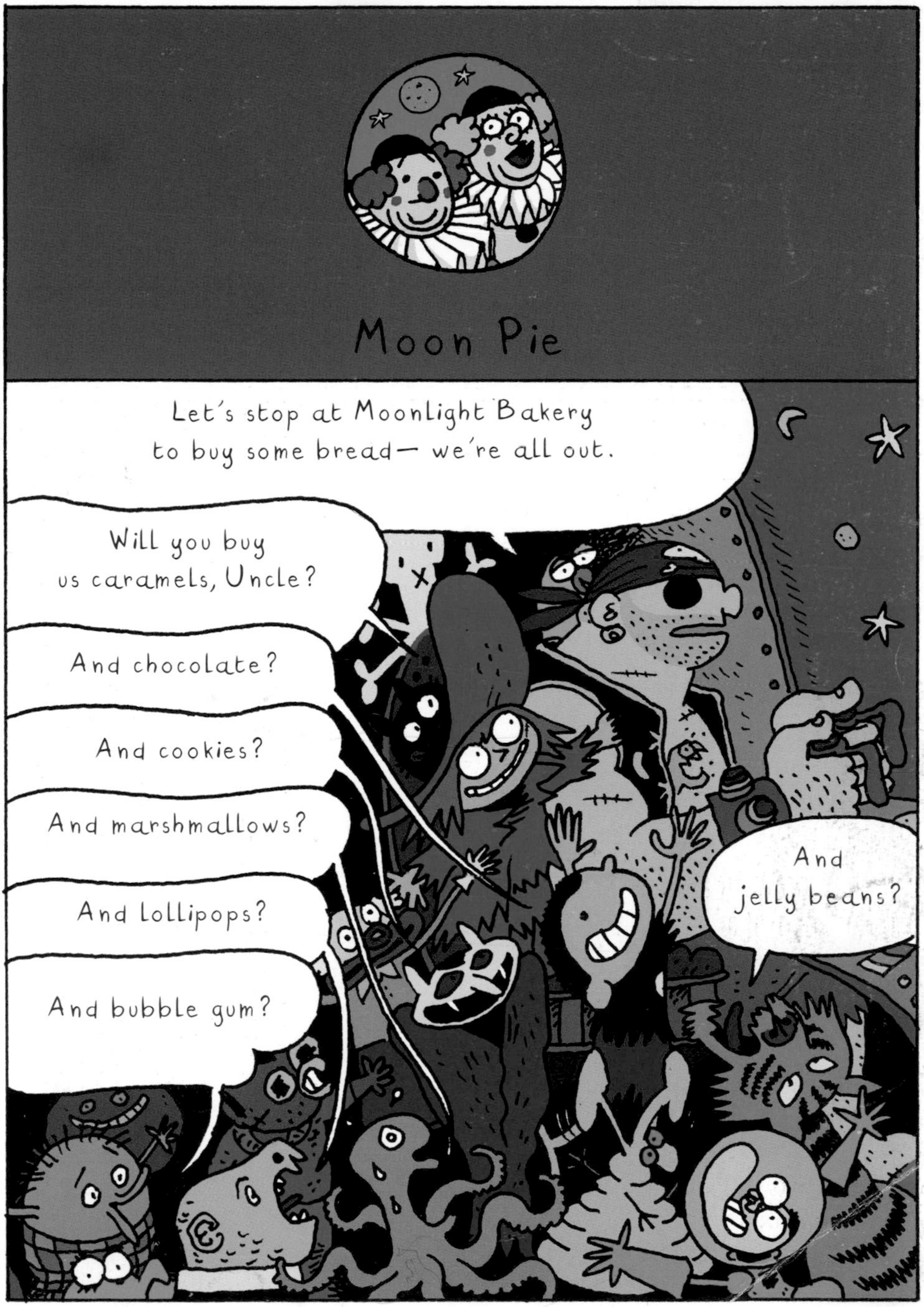
Moon Pie
Let's stop at Moonlight Bakery to buy some bread— we're all out.
Will you buy us caramels, Uncle?
And chocolate?
And cookies?
And marshmallows?
And lollipops?
And bubble gum?
And jelly beans?

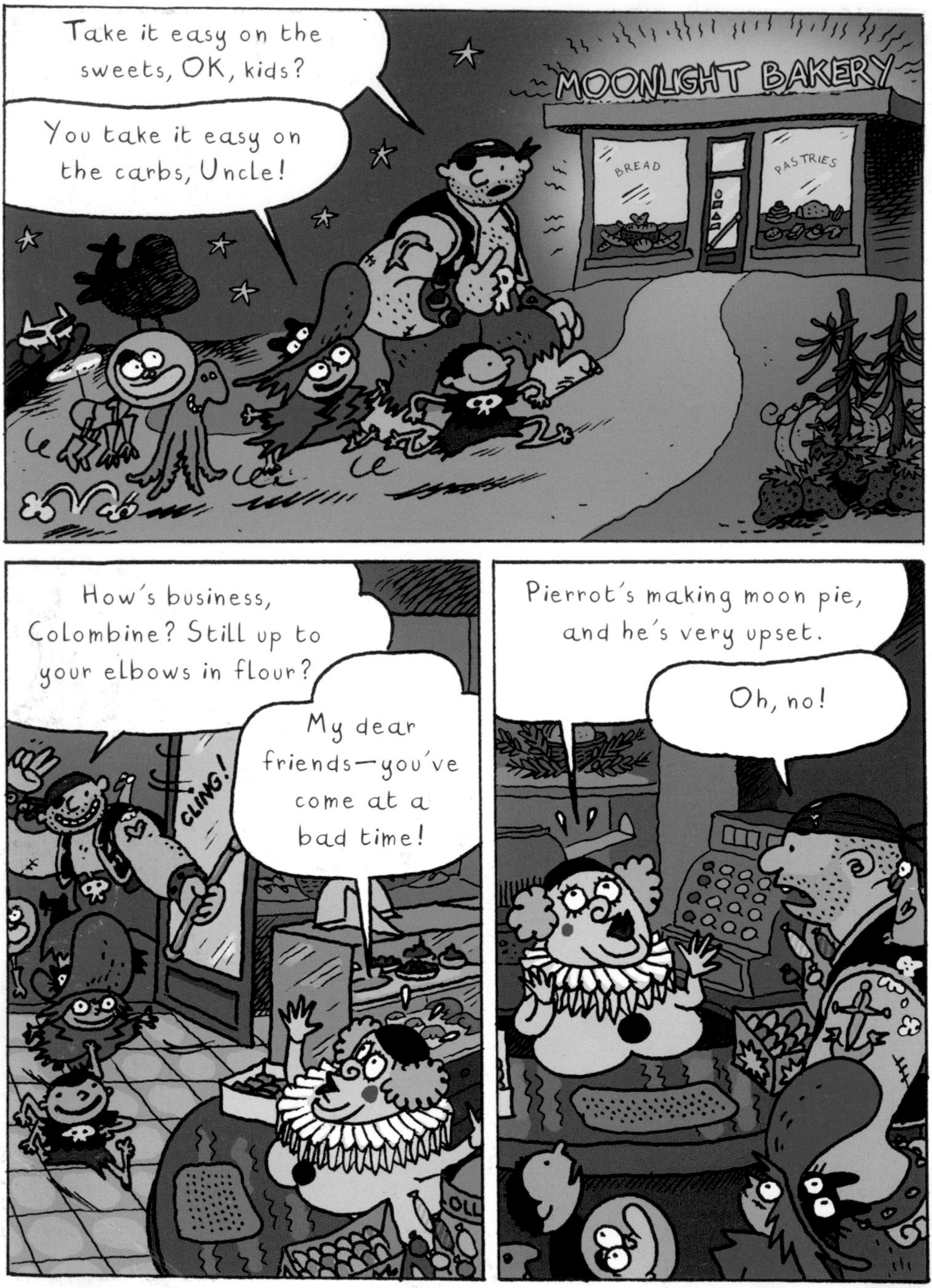
Take it easy on the sweets, OK, kids?
You take it easy on the carbs, Uncle!
MOONLIGHT BAKERY
BREAD
PASTRIES
How's business, Colombine? Still up to your elbows in flour?
CLING!
My dear friends—you've come at a bad time!
Pierrot's making moon pie, and he's very upset.
Oh, no!

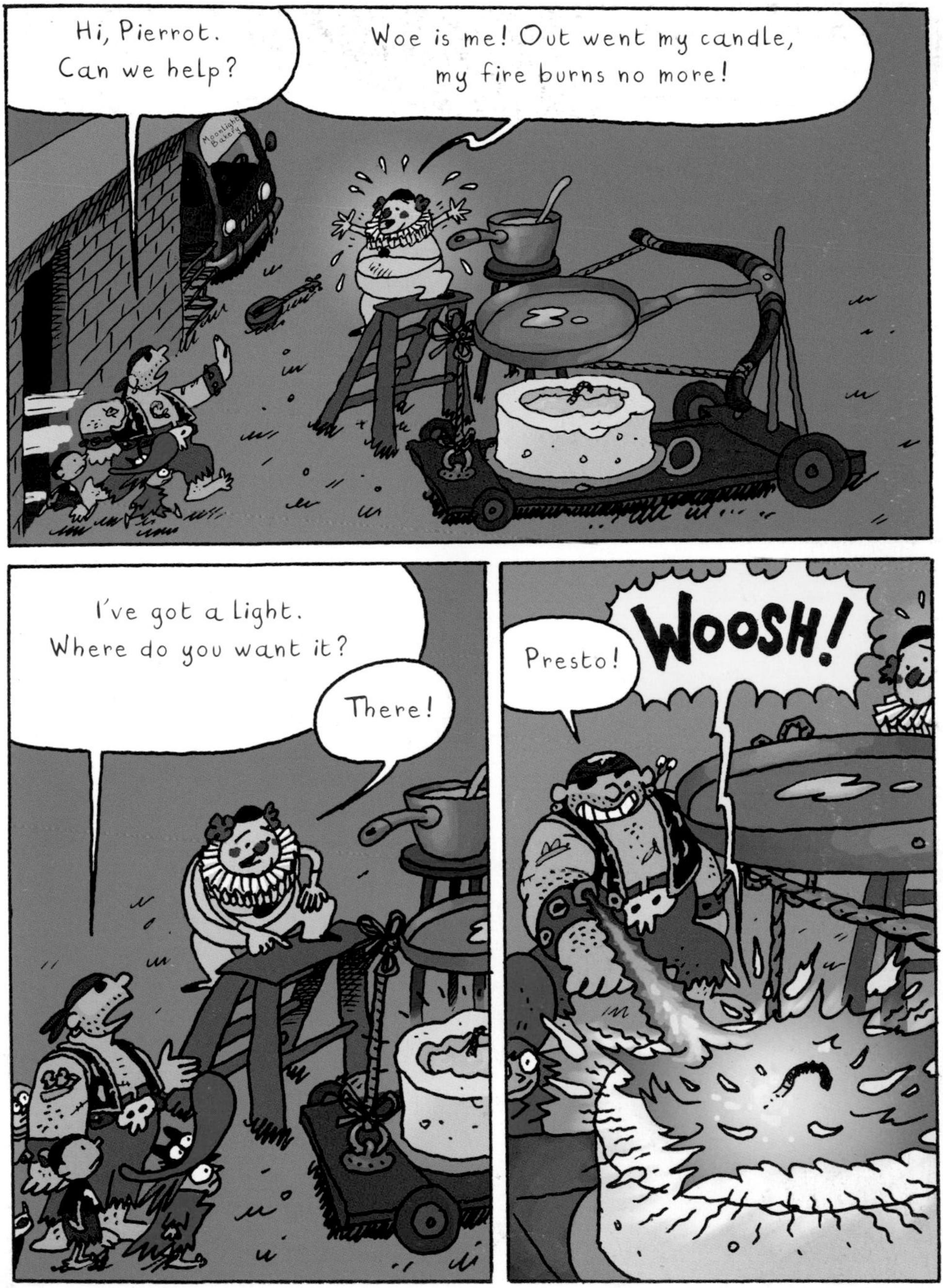
Hi, Pierrot.
Can we help?
Woe is me! Out went my candle,
my fire burns no more!
Moonlight Bakery
I've got a light.
Where do you want it?
There!
Presto!
WOOSH!

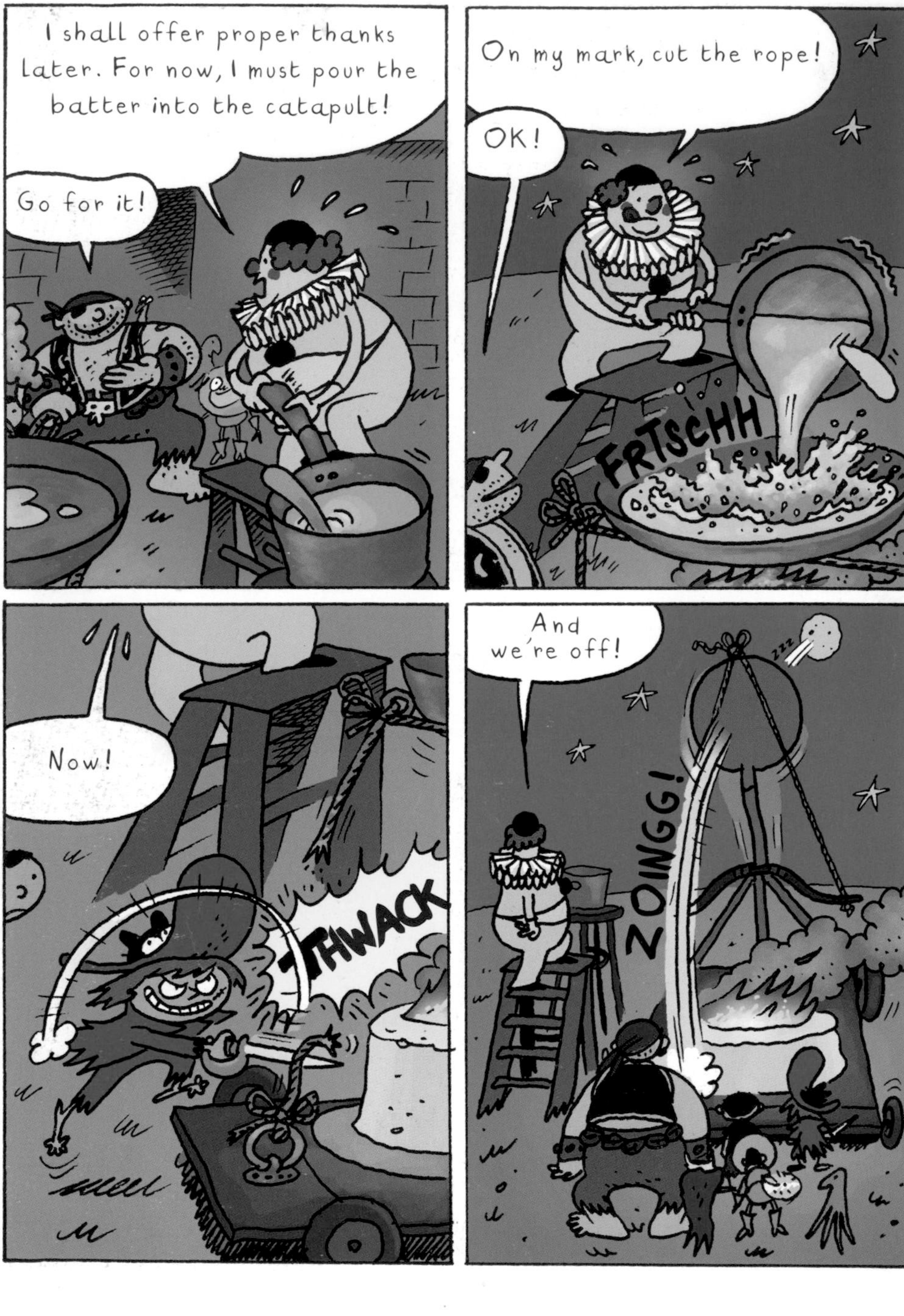
I shall offer proper thanks later. For now, I must pour the batter into the catapult!
Go for it!
On my mark, cut the rope!
OK!
FRTSCHH
Now!
THWACK
And we're off!
ZOINGG!

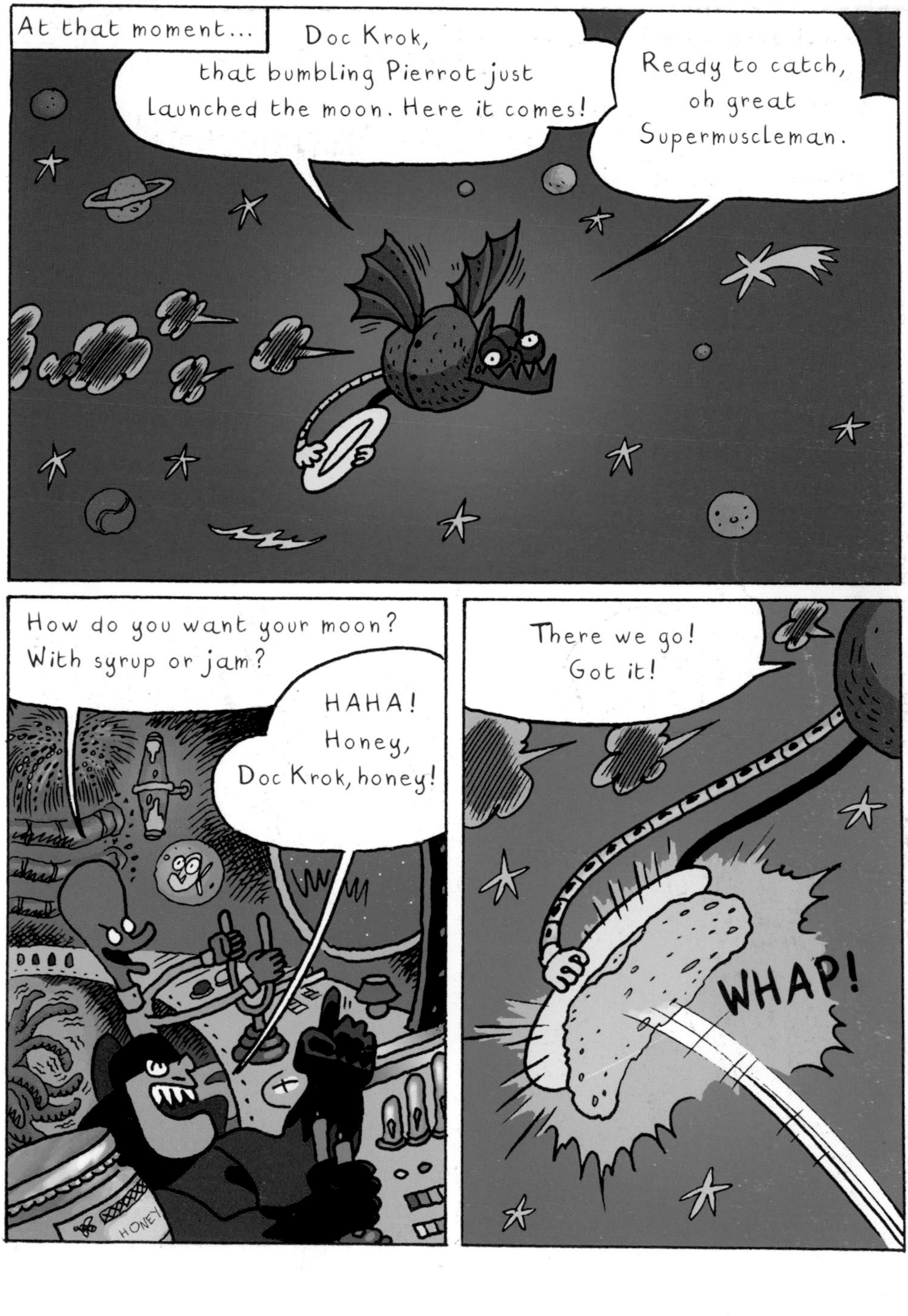
At that moment...
Doc Krok, that bumbling Pierrot just launched the moon. Here it comes!
Ready to catch, oh great Supermuscleman.
How do you want your moon? With syrup or jam?
HAHA! Honey, Doc Krok, honey!
HONEY
There we go! Got it!
WHAP!

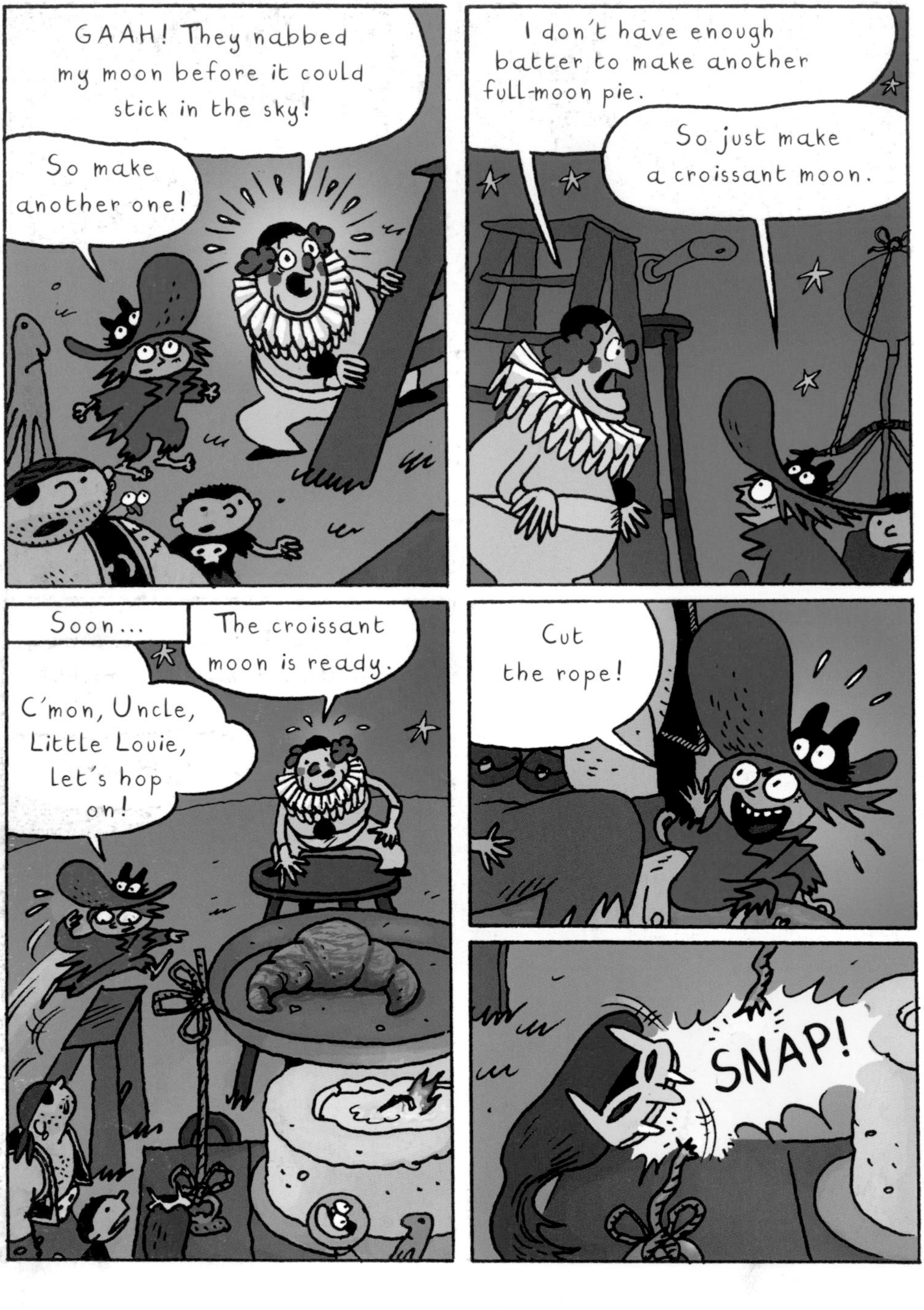
GAAH! They nabbed my moon before it could stick in the sky!
So make another one!
I don't have enough batter to make another full-moon pie.
So just make a croissant moon.
Soon...
The croissant moon is ready.
C'mon, Uncle, Little Louie, let's hop on!
Cut the rope!
SNAP!

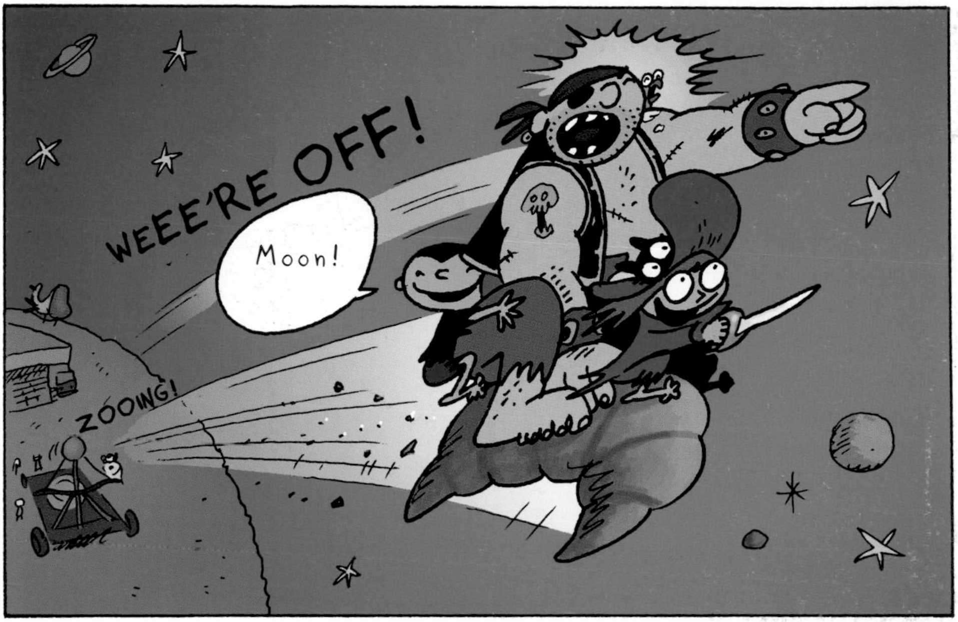
WEEE'RE OFF!
Moon!
ZOOMING!

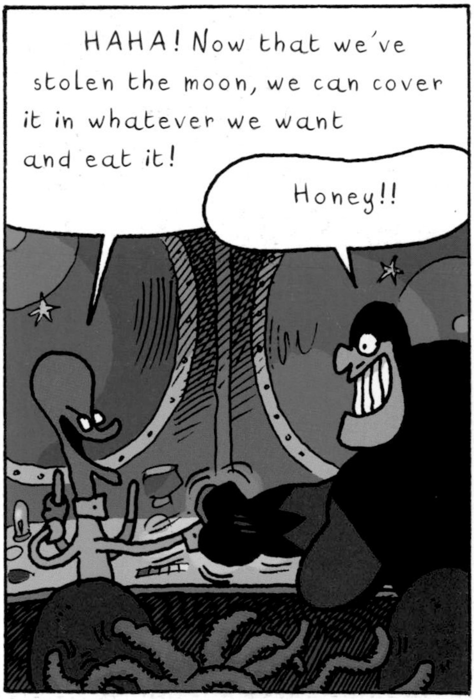
HAHA! Now that we've stolen the moon, we can cover it in whatever we want and eat it!
Honey!!

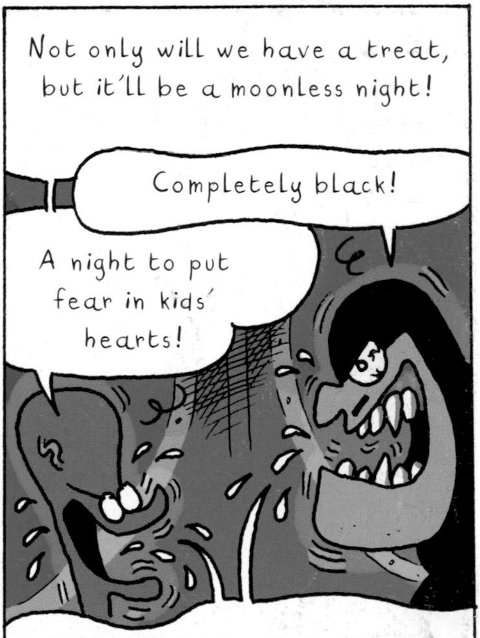
Not only will we have a treat, but it'll be a moonless night!
Completely black!
A night to put fear in kids' hearts!
HAHAHA

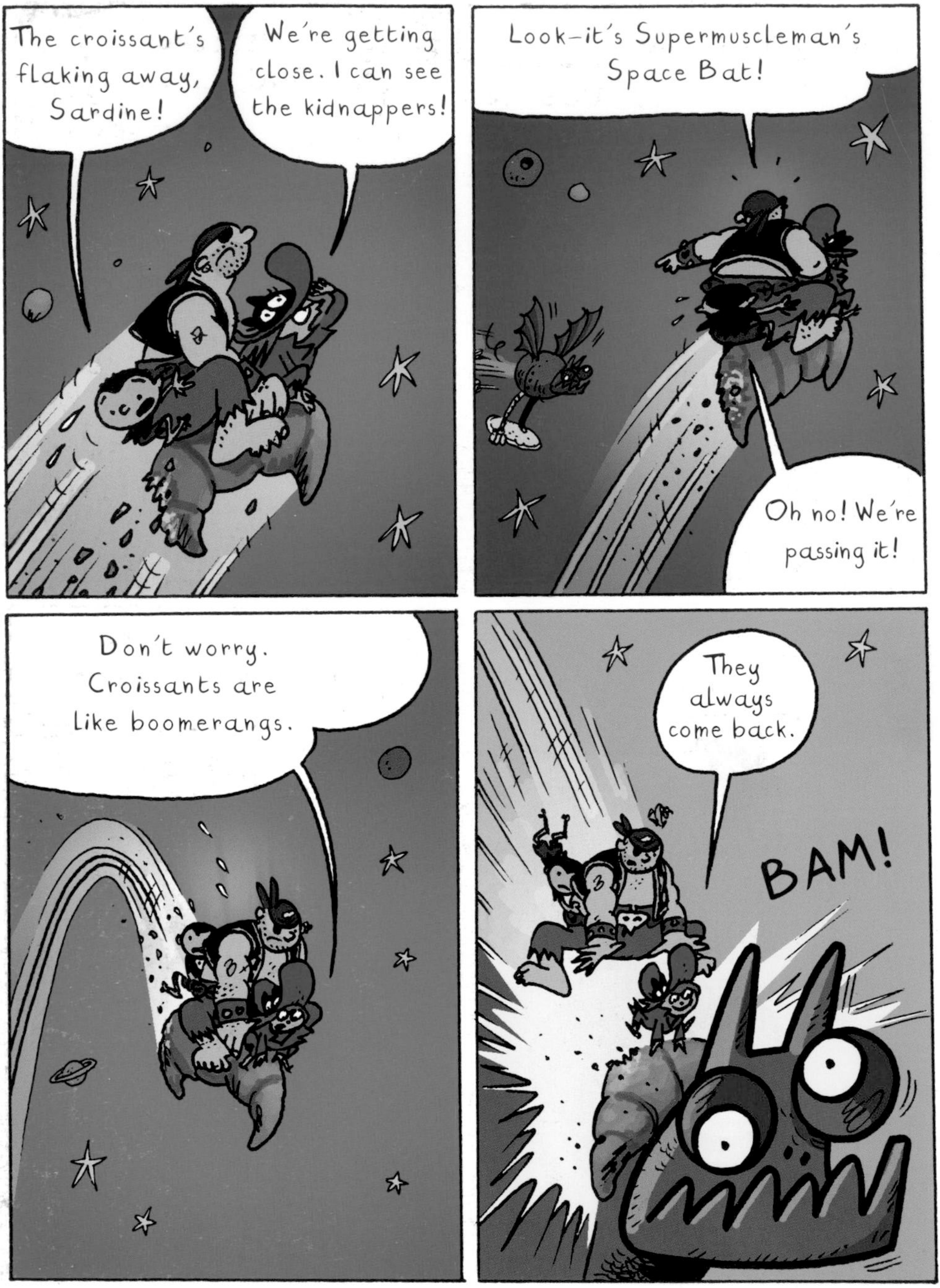
The croissant's flaking away, Sardine!
We're getting close. I can see the kidnappers!
Look–it's Supermuscleman's Space Bat!
Oh no! We're passing it!
Don't worry. Croissants are like boomerangs.
They always come back.
BAM!

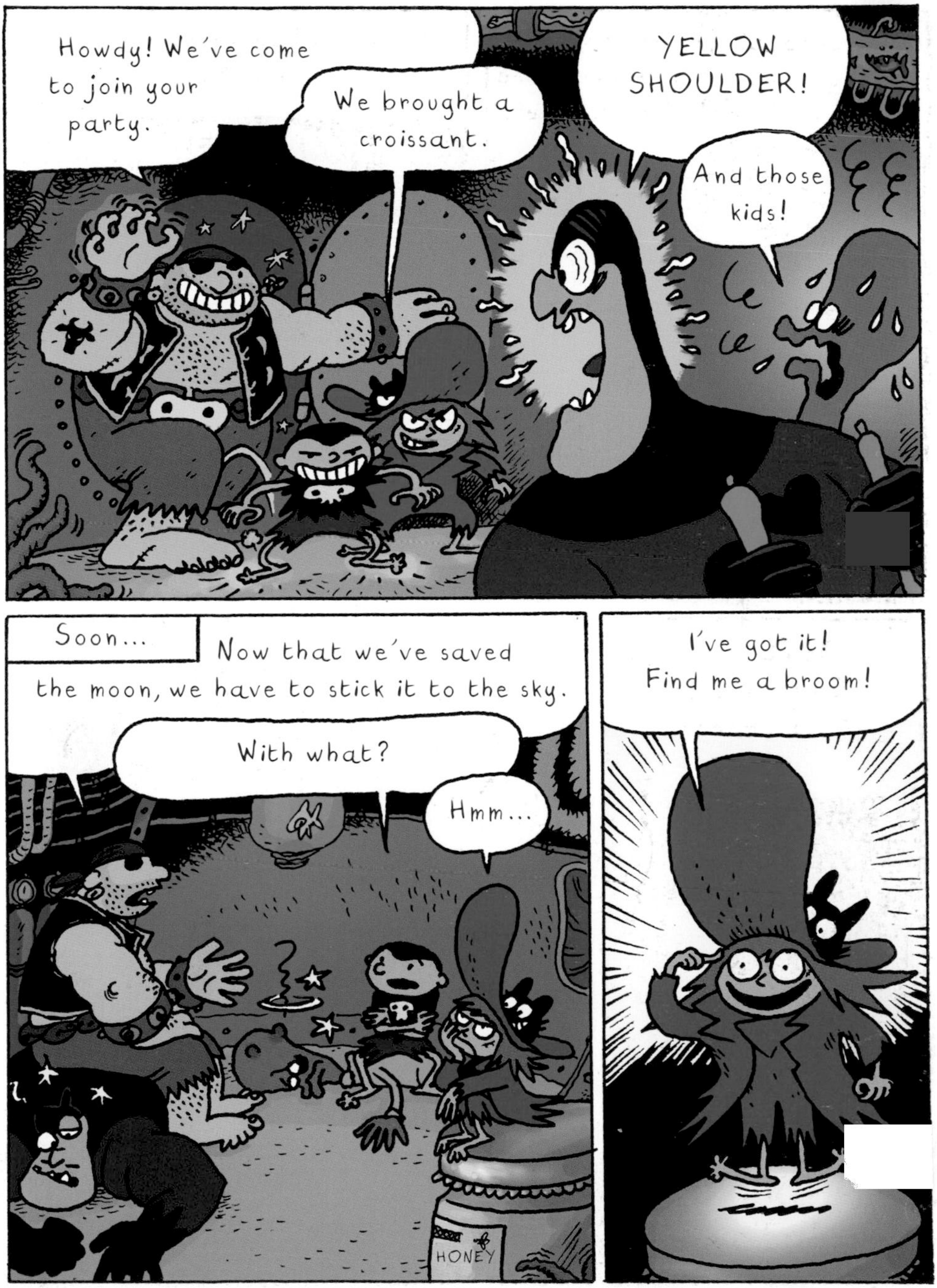
Howdy! We've come to join your party.
We brought a croissant.
YELLOW SHOULDER!
And those kids!
Soon...
Now that we've saved the moon, we have to stick it to the sky.
With what?
Hmm...
HONEY
I've got it! Find me a broom!

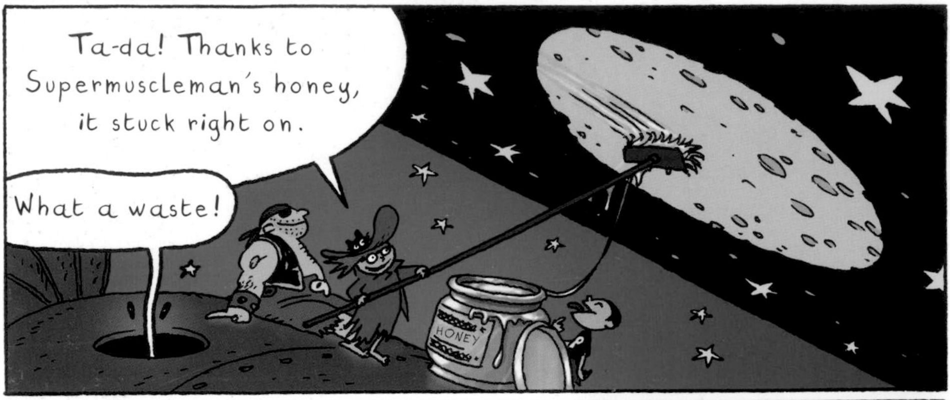
Ta-da! Thanks to Supermuscleman's honey, it stuck right on.
What a waste!
HONEY

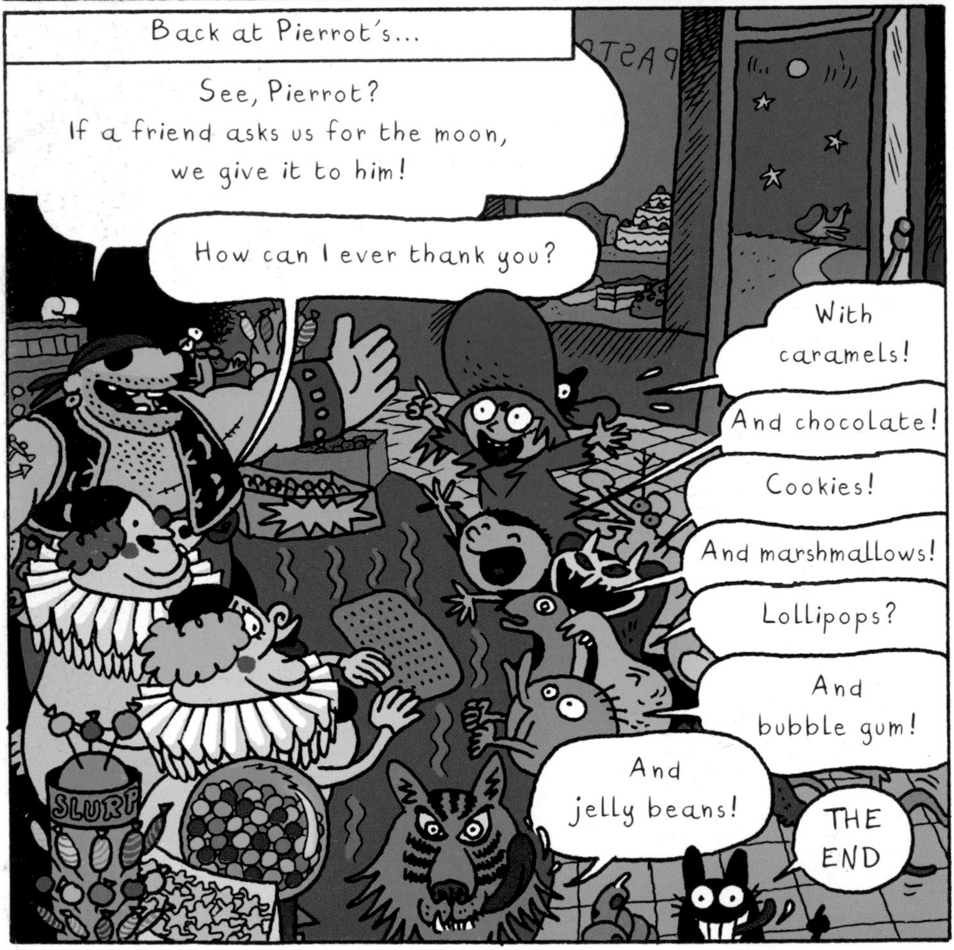
Back at Pierrot's...
See, Pierrot? If a friend asks us for the moon, we give it to him!
How can I ever thank you?
With caramels!
And chocolate!
Cookies!
And marshmallows!
Lollipops?
And bubble gum!
And jelly beans!
THE END
SLURP

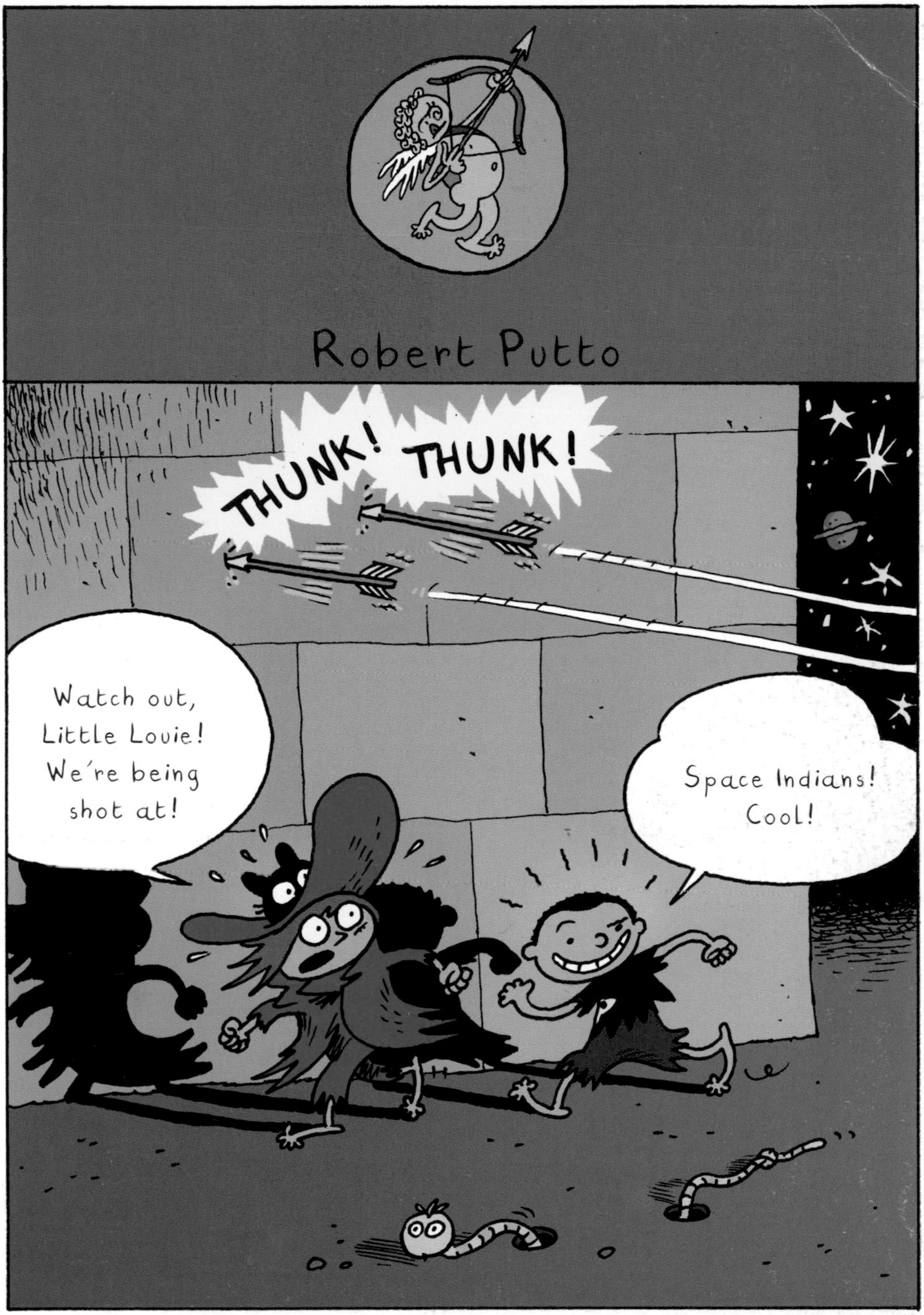
Robert Putto
THUNK! THUNK!
Watch out, Little Louie! We're being shot at!
Space Indians! Cool!

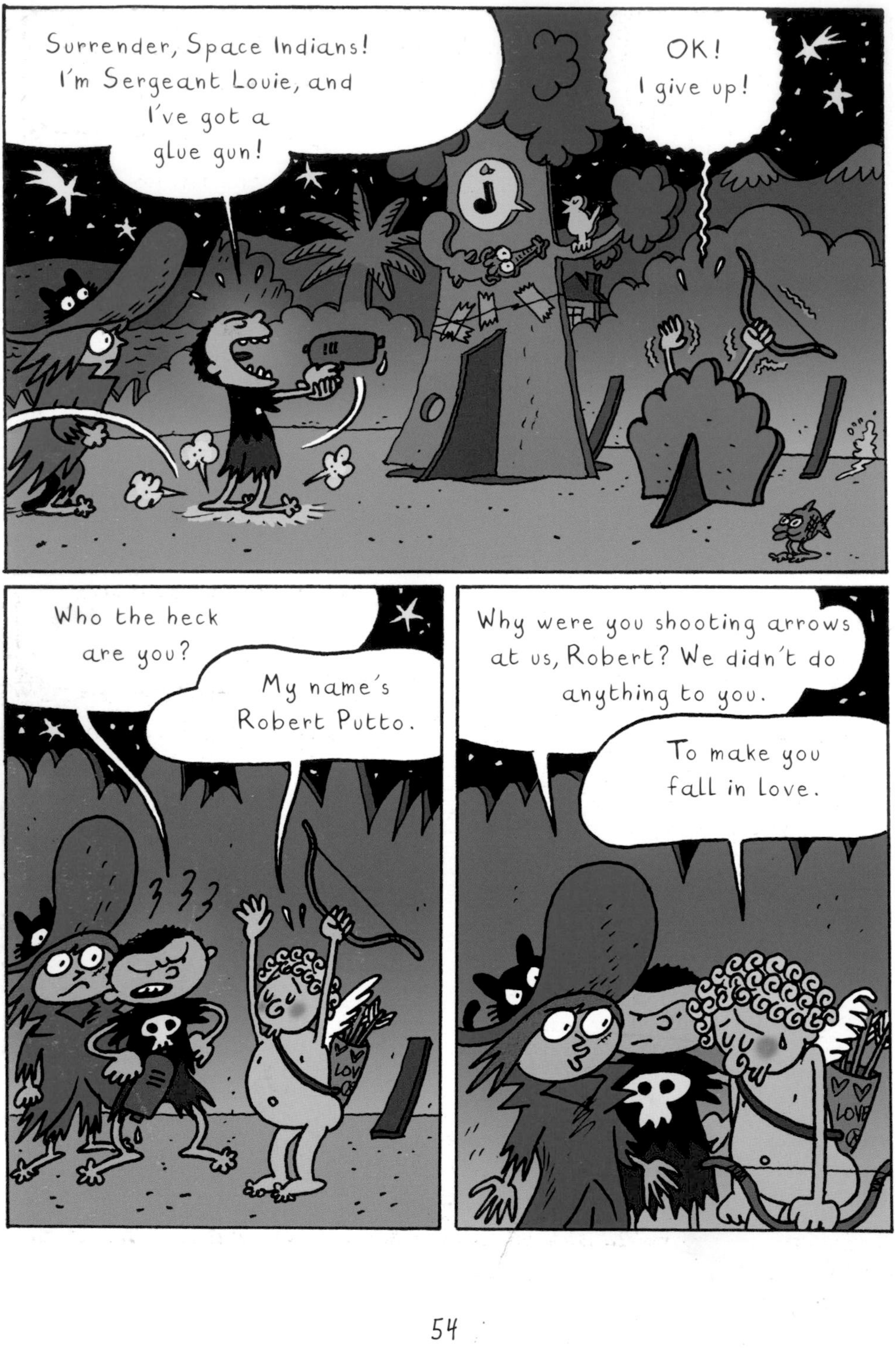
Surrender, Space Indians! I'm Sergeant Louie, and I've got a glue gun!
OK! I give up!
Who the heck are you?
My name's Robert Putto.
Why were you shooting arrows at us, Robert? We didn't do anything to you.
To make you fall in love.

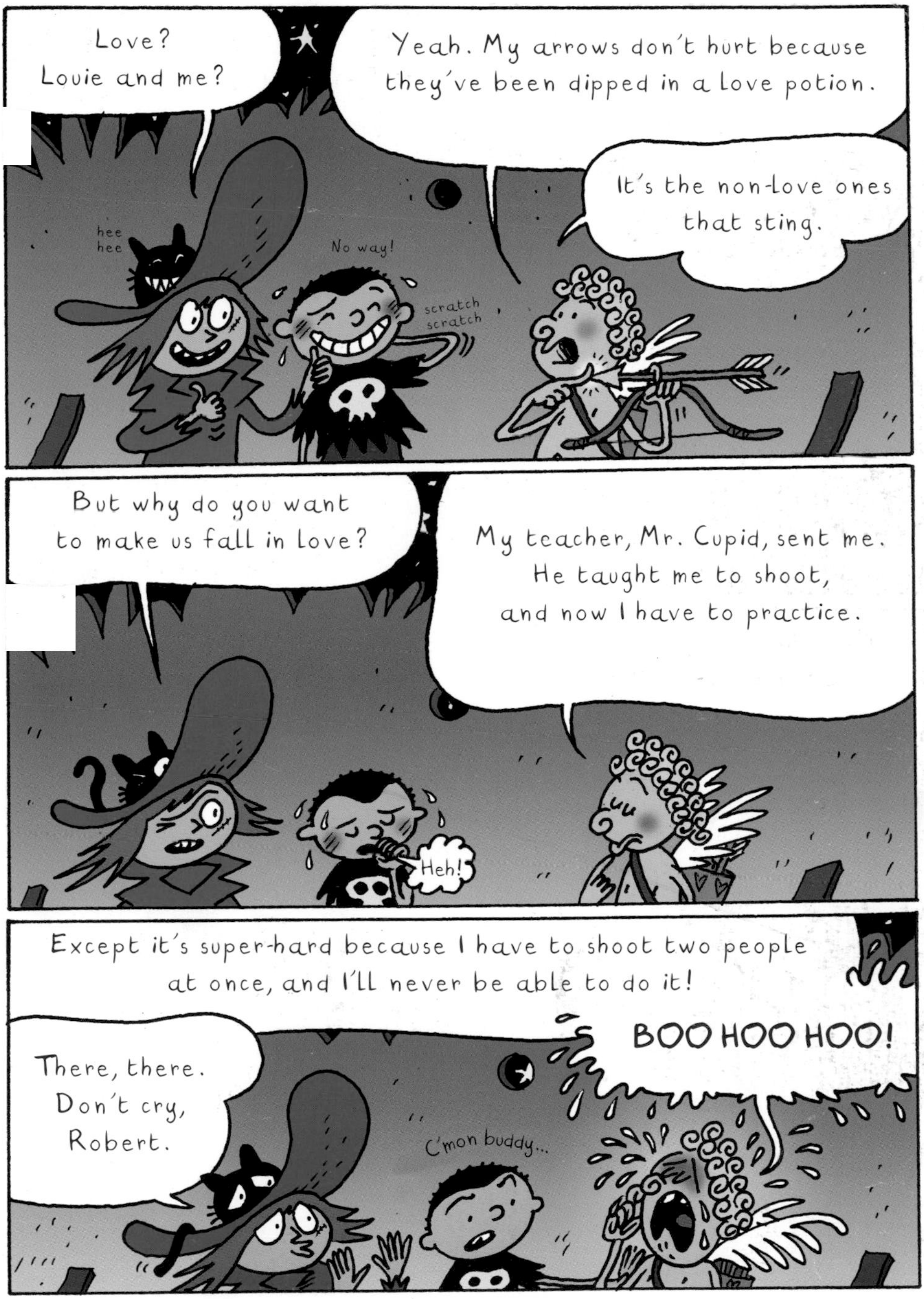
Love?
Louie and me?
Yeah. My arrows don't hurt because they've been dipped in a love potion.
It's the non-love ones that sting.
hee hee
No way!
scratch scratch
But why do you want to make us fall in love?
My teacher, Mr. Cupid, sent me. He taught me to shoot, and now I have to practice.
Heh!
Except it's super-hard because I have to shoot two people at once, and I'll never be able to do it!
BOO HOO HOO!
There, there. Don't cry, Robert.
C'mon buddy...

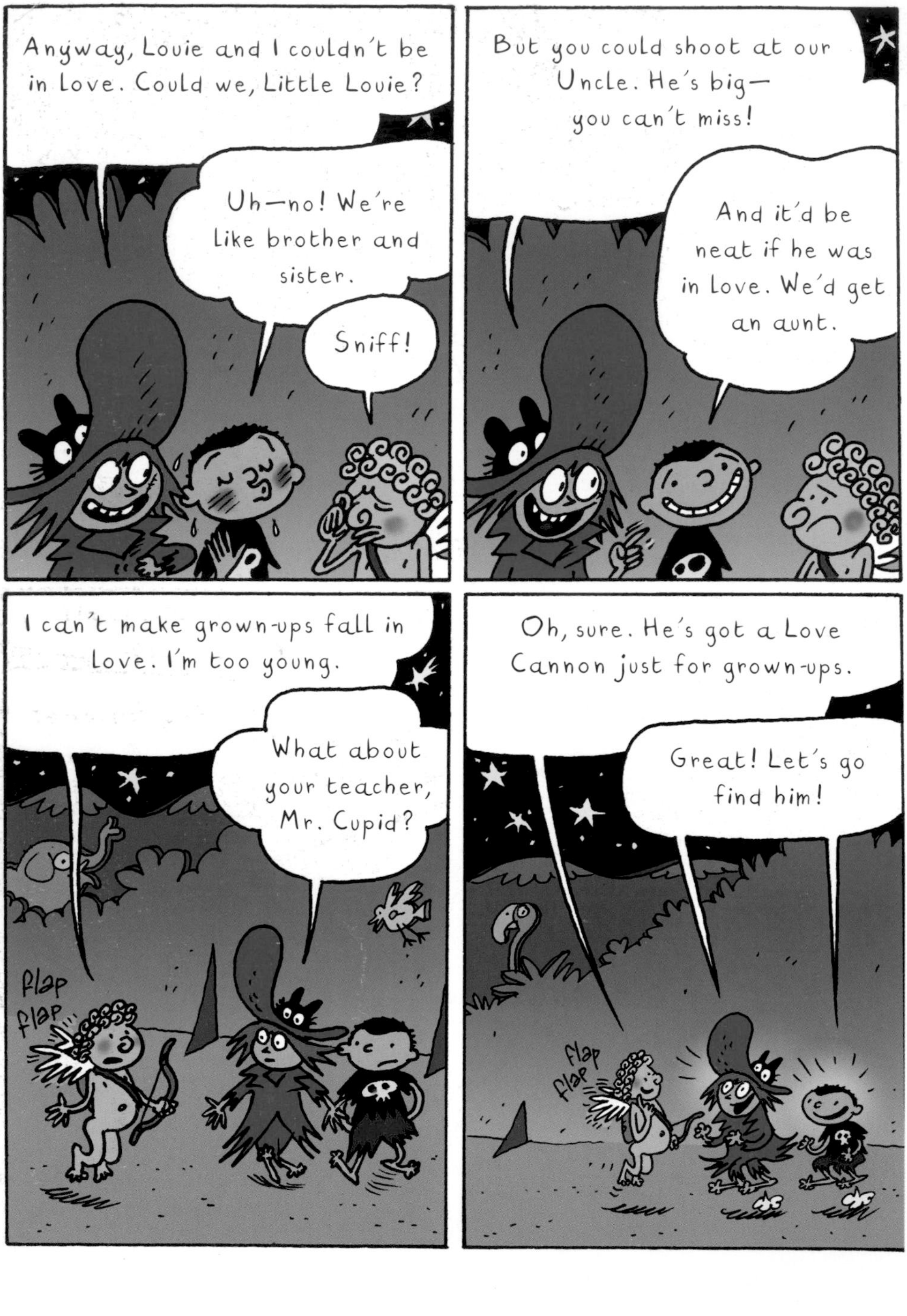
Anyway, Louie and I couldn't be in love. Could we, Little Louie?
Uh—no! We're like brother and sister.
Sniff!
But you could shoot at our Uncle. He's big— you can't miss!
And it'd be neat if he was in love. We'd get an aunt.
I can't make grown-ups fall in love. I'm too young.
What about your teacher, Mr. Cupid?
flap flap
Oh, sure. He's got a Love Cannon just for grown-ups.
Great! Let's go find him!
flap flap

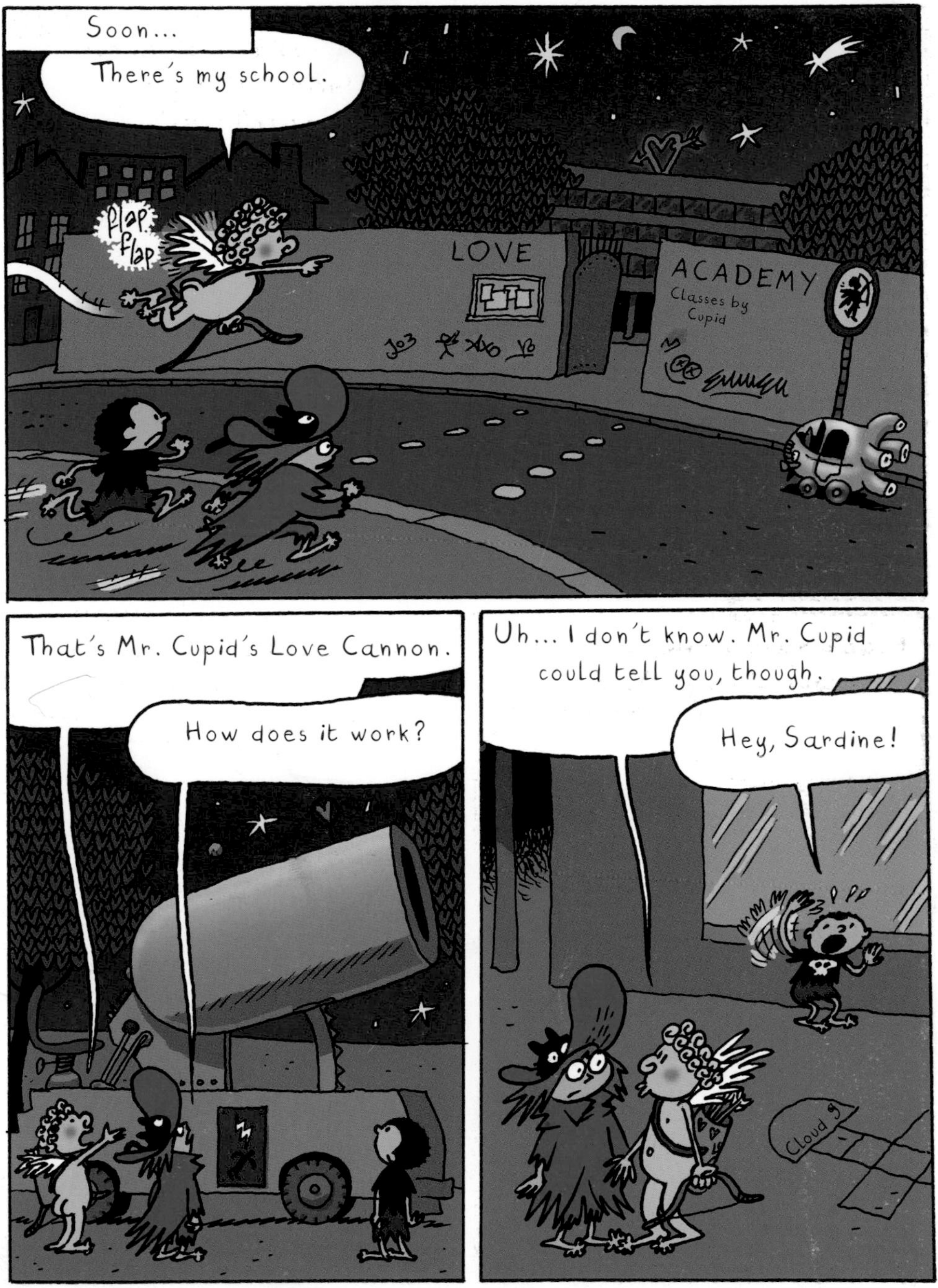
Soon...
There's my school.
flap flap
LOVE
ACADEMY
Classes by Cupid
That's Mr. Cupid's Love Cannon.
How does it work?
Uh... I don't know. Mr. Cupid could tell you, though.
Hey, Sardine!
Cloud 9

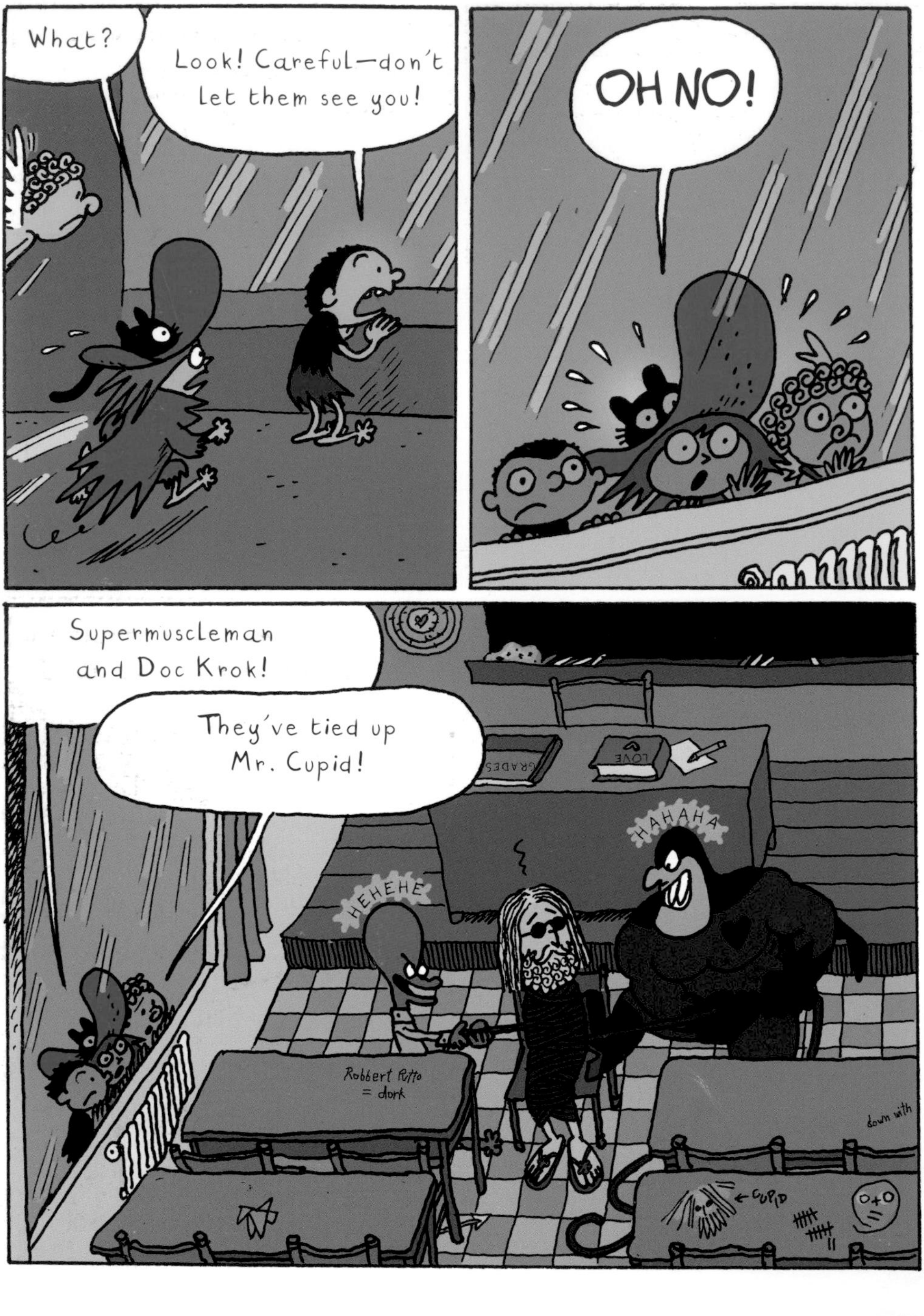
What?
Look! Careful—don't let them see you!
OH NO!
Supermuscleman and Doc Krok!
They've tied up Mr. Cupid!
GRADES
LOVE
HAHAHA
HEHEHE
Robbert Putto = dork
down with
← CUPID

You like kids, Cupid?

I love 'em.

Well, we hate them!

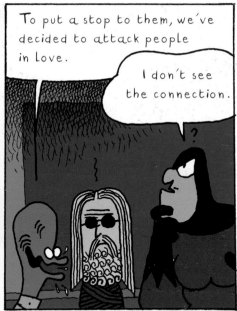

To put a stop to them, we've decided to attack people in love.

I don't see the connection.

Come now, Supermuscleman, you know very well that people in love make children.

Uh, no, I didn't know that.

My mother and father made me, and they weren't in love at all.

And who makes people fall in love, hmmm?

Ow!

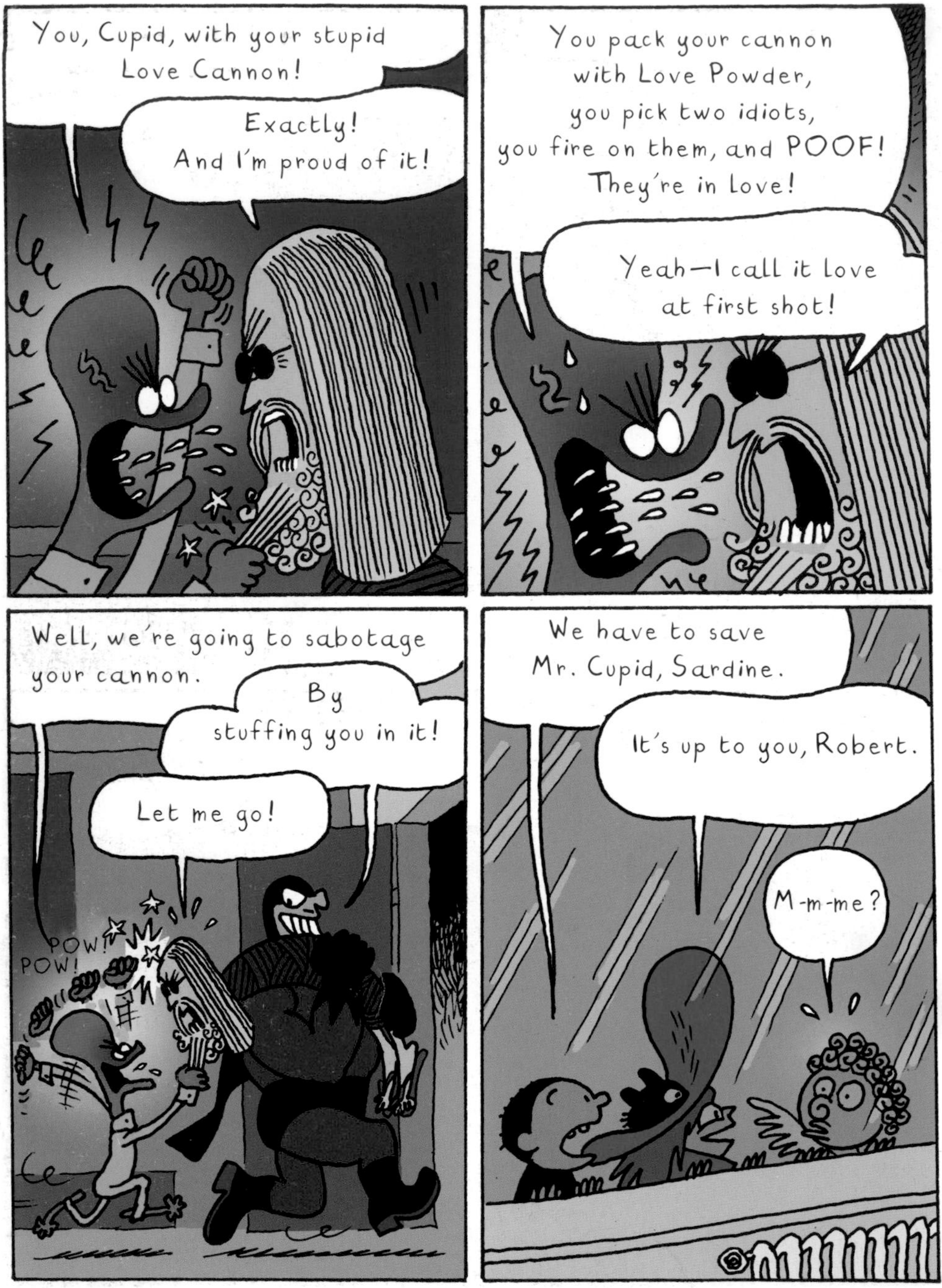
You, Cupid, with your stupid Love Cannon!
Exactly! And I'm proud of it!
You pack your cannon with Love Powder, you pick two idiots, you fire on them, and POOF! They're in love!
Yeah—I call it love at first shot!
Well, we're going to sabotage your cannon.
By stuffing you in it!
Let me go!
POW! POW!
We have to save Mr. Cupid, Sardine.
It's up to you, Robert.
M-m-me?

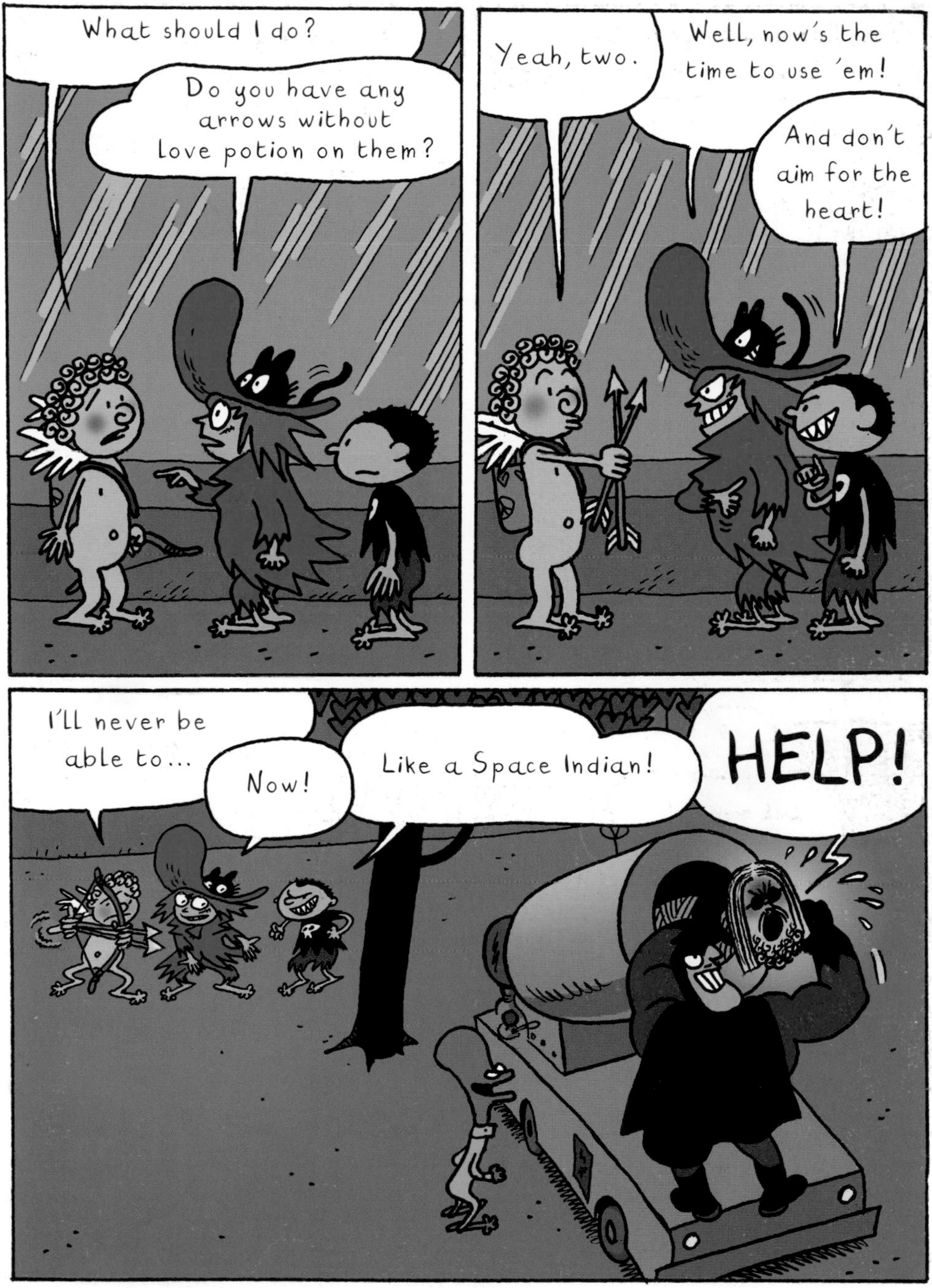
What should I do?
Do you have any arrows without love potion on them?
Yeah, two.
Well, now's the time to use 'em!
And don't aim for the heart!
I'll never be able to...
Now!
Like a Space Indian!
HELP!

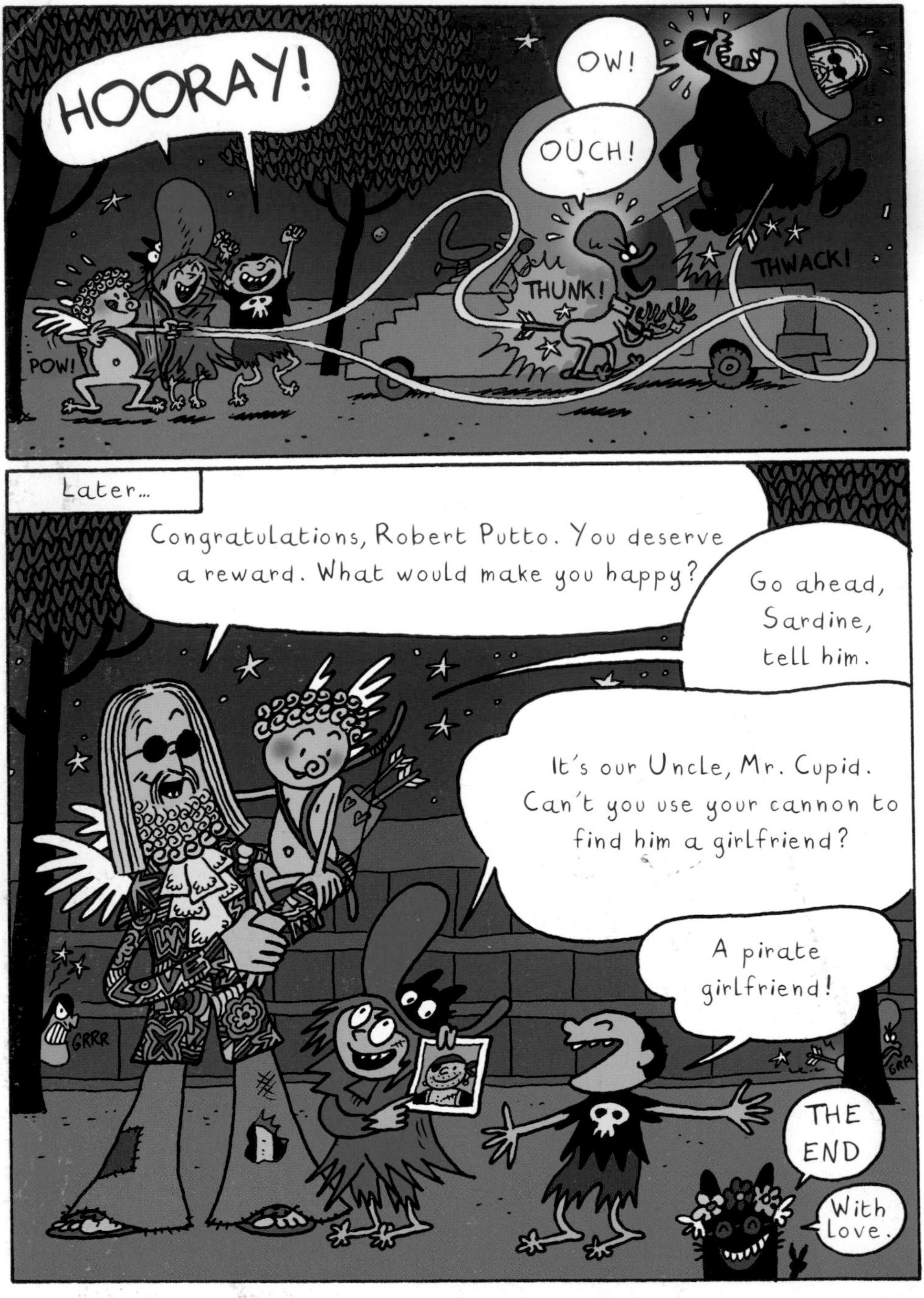
HOORAY!
OW!
OUCH!
POW!
THUNK!
THWACK!
Later...
Congratulations, Robert Putto. You deserve a reward. What would make you happy?
Go ahead, Sardine, tell him.
It's our Uncle, Mr. Cupid. Can't you use your cannon to find him a girlfriend?
A pirate girlfriend!
GRRR
GRR
THE END
With love.

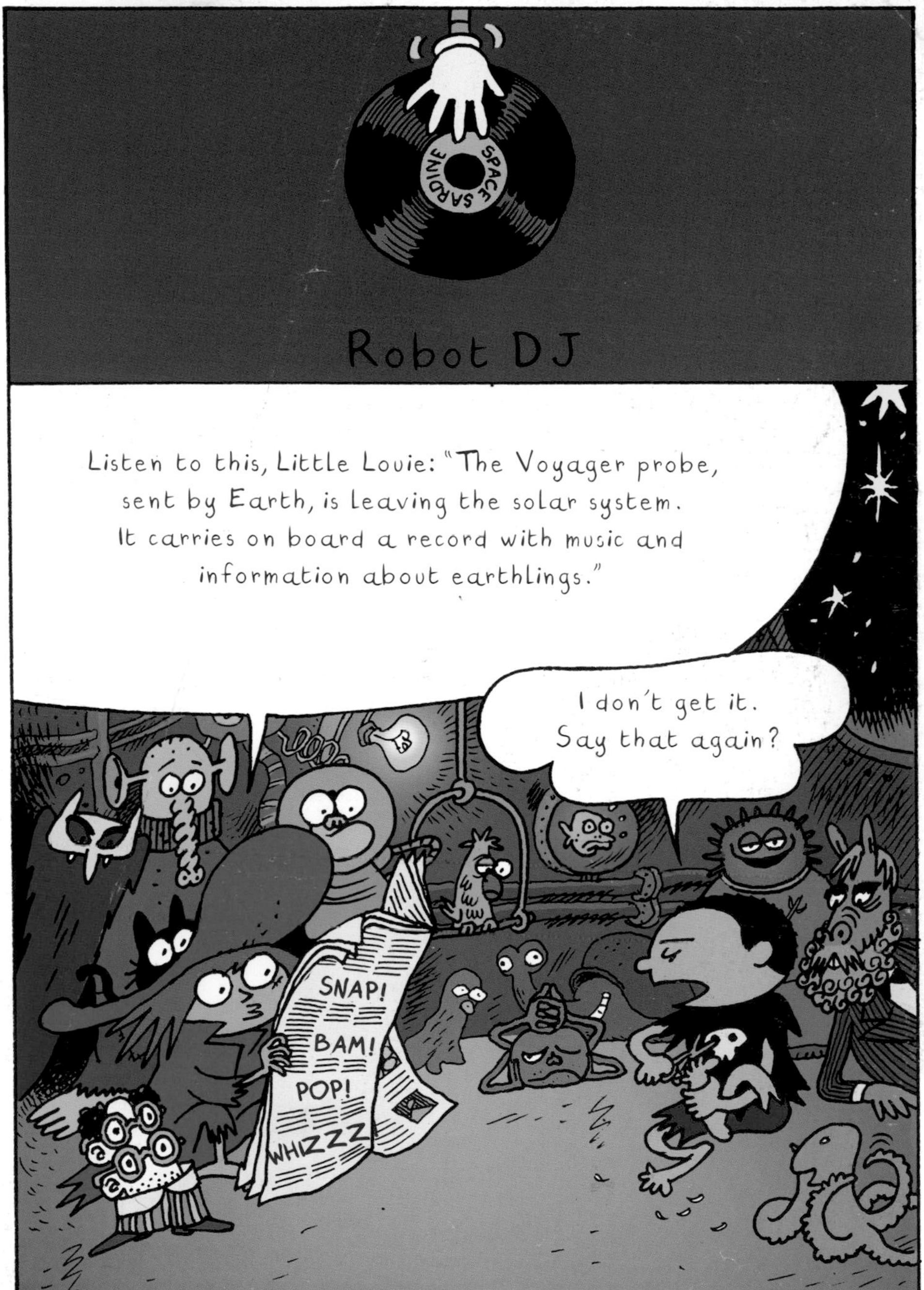
SPACE SARDINE
Robot DJ
Listen to this, Little Louie: "The Voyager probe, sent by Earth, is leaving the solar system. It carries on board a record with music and information about earthlings."
I don't get it. Say that again?
SNAP!
BAM!
POP!
WHIZZZ

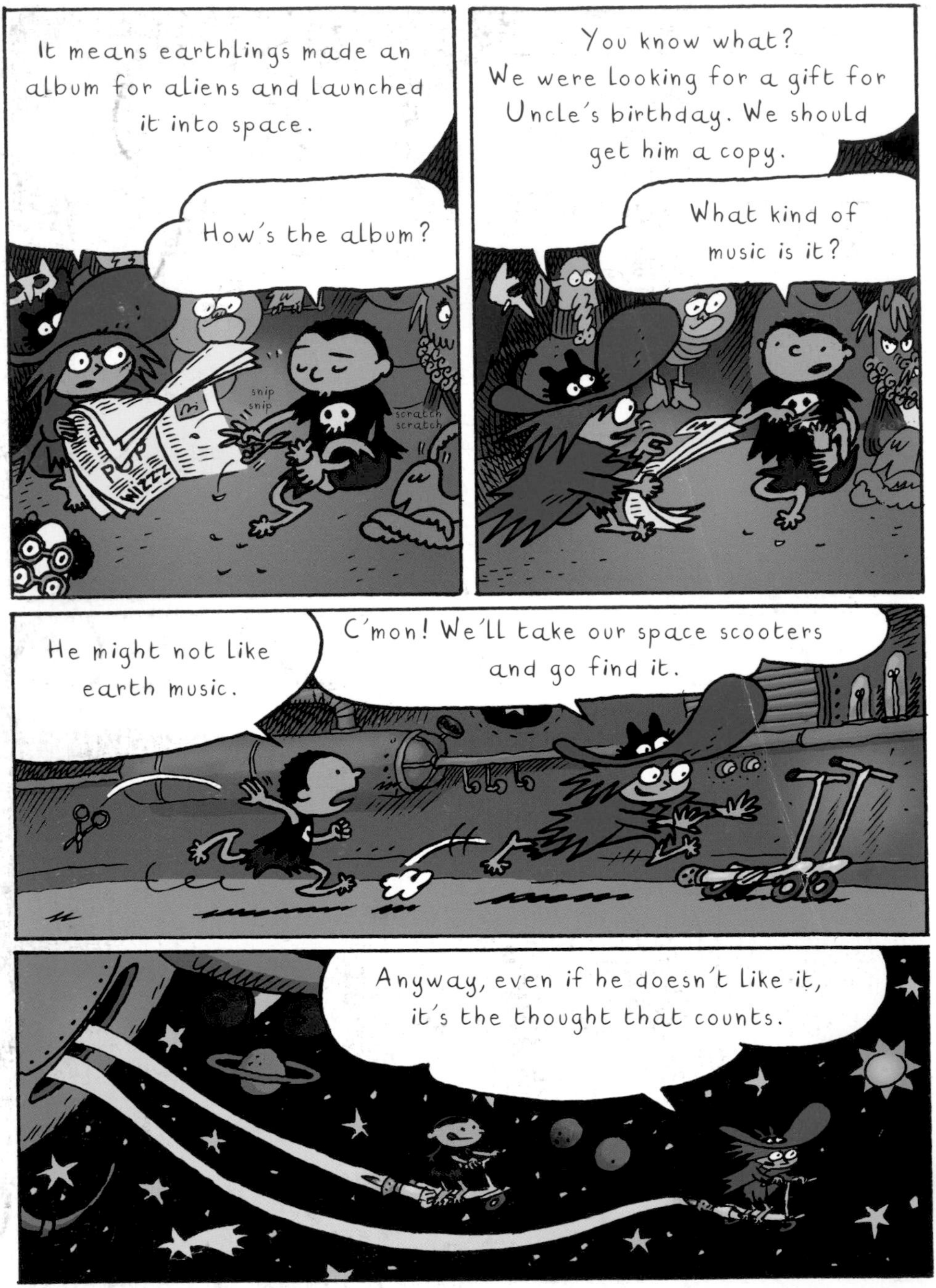
It means earthlings made an album for aliens and launched it into space.
How's the album?
snip snip
scratch scratch
You know what? We were looking for a gift for Uncle's birthday. We should get him a copy.
What kind of music is it?
He might not like earth music.
C'mon! We'll take our space scooters and go find it.
Anyway, even if he doesn't like it, it's the thought that counts.

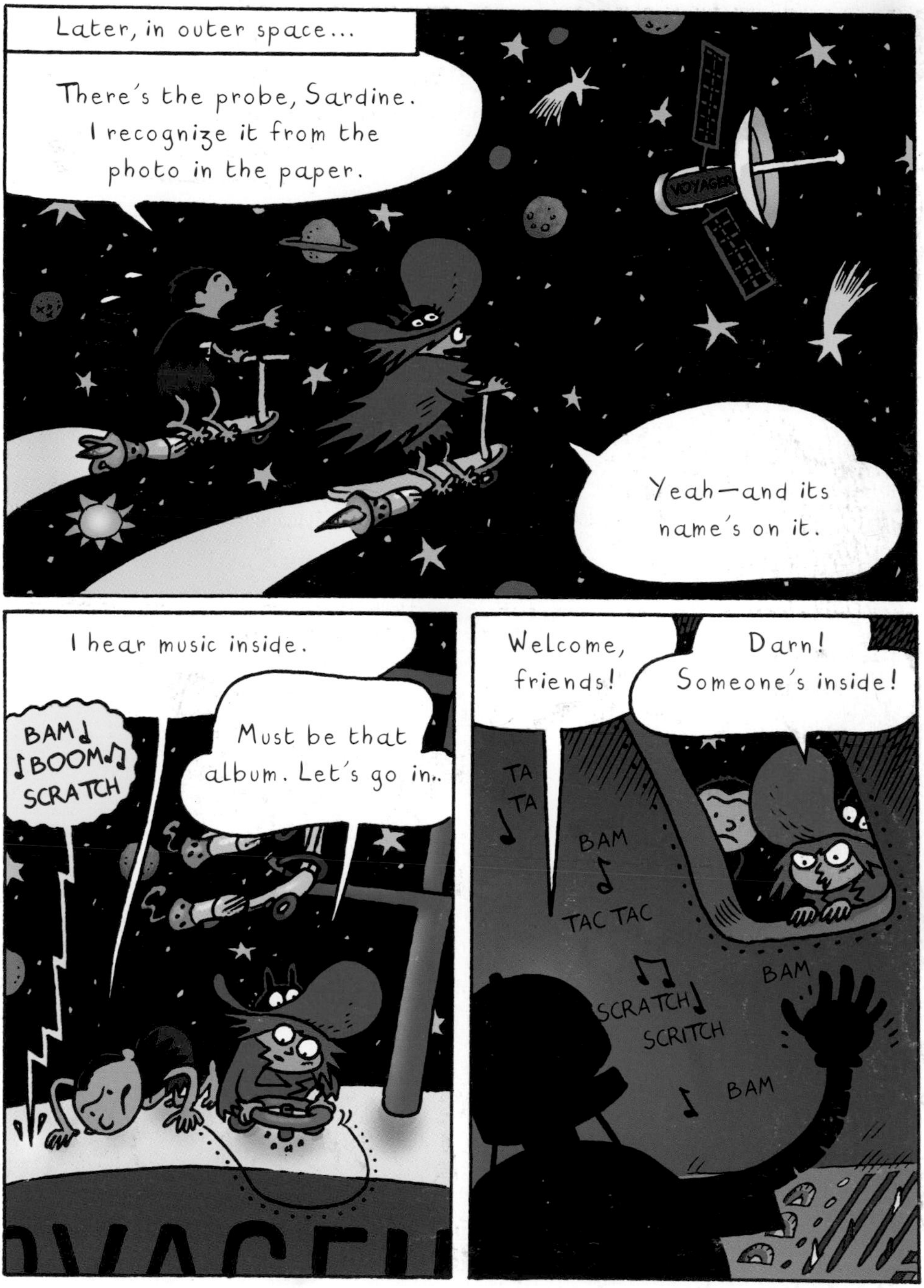
Later, in outer space...
There's the probe, Sardine. I recognize it from the photo in the paper.
VOYAGER
Yeah—and its name's on it.
I hear music inside.
BAM BOOM SCRATCH
Must be that album. Let's go in..
Welcome, friends!
Darn! Someone's inside!
TA TA
BAM
TAC TAC
SCRATCH
SCRITCH
BAM
BAM

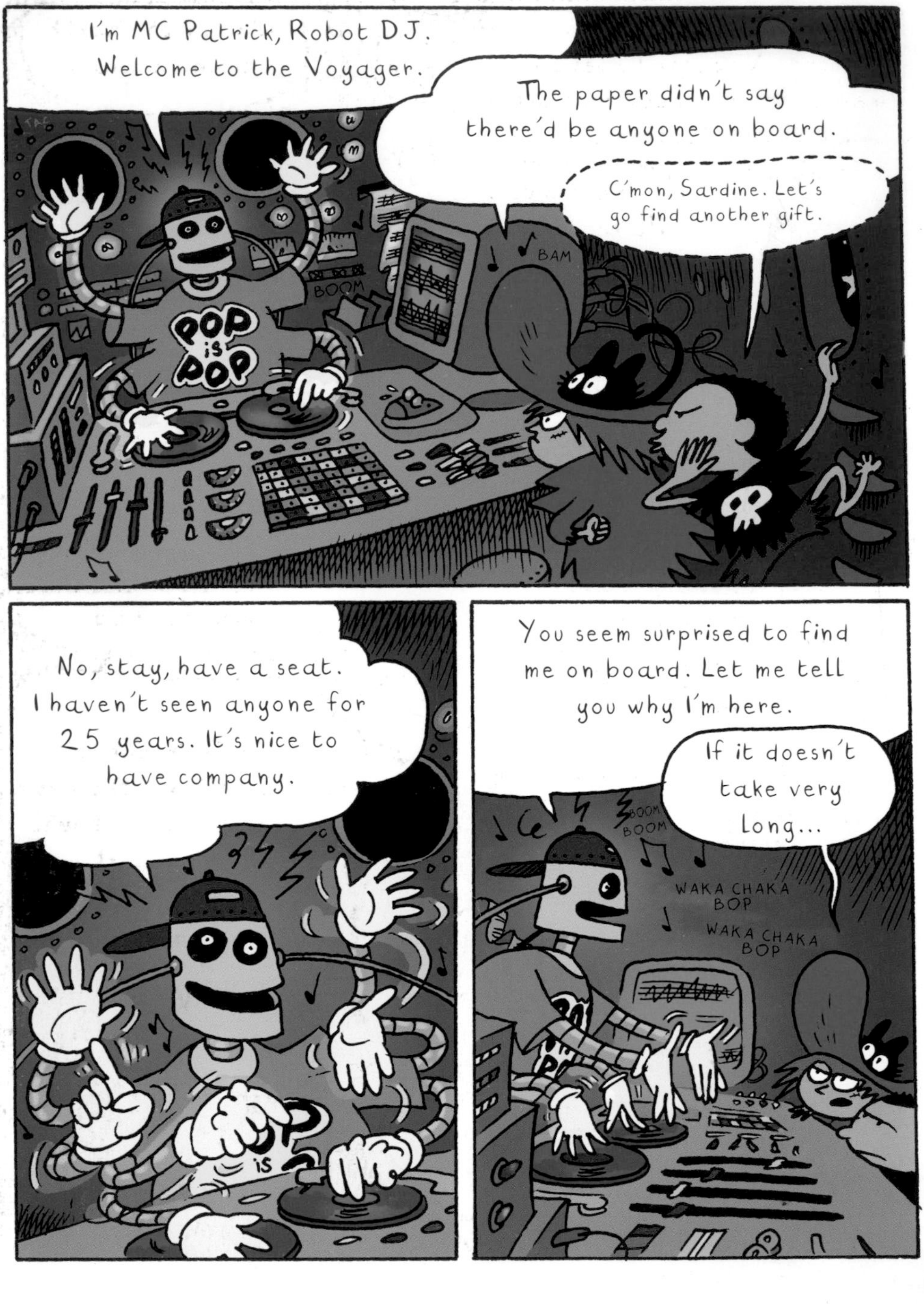
I'm MC Patrick, Robot DJ. Welcome to the Voyager.
The paper didn't say there'd be anyone on board.
C'mon, Sardine. Let's go find another gift.
BAM
BOOM
POP is POP
No, stay, have a seat. I haven't seen anyone for 25 years. It's nice to have company.
You seem surprised to find me on board. Let me tell you why I'm here.
If it doesn't take very long...
BOOM BOOM
WAKA CHAKA BOP
WAKA CHAKA BOP

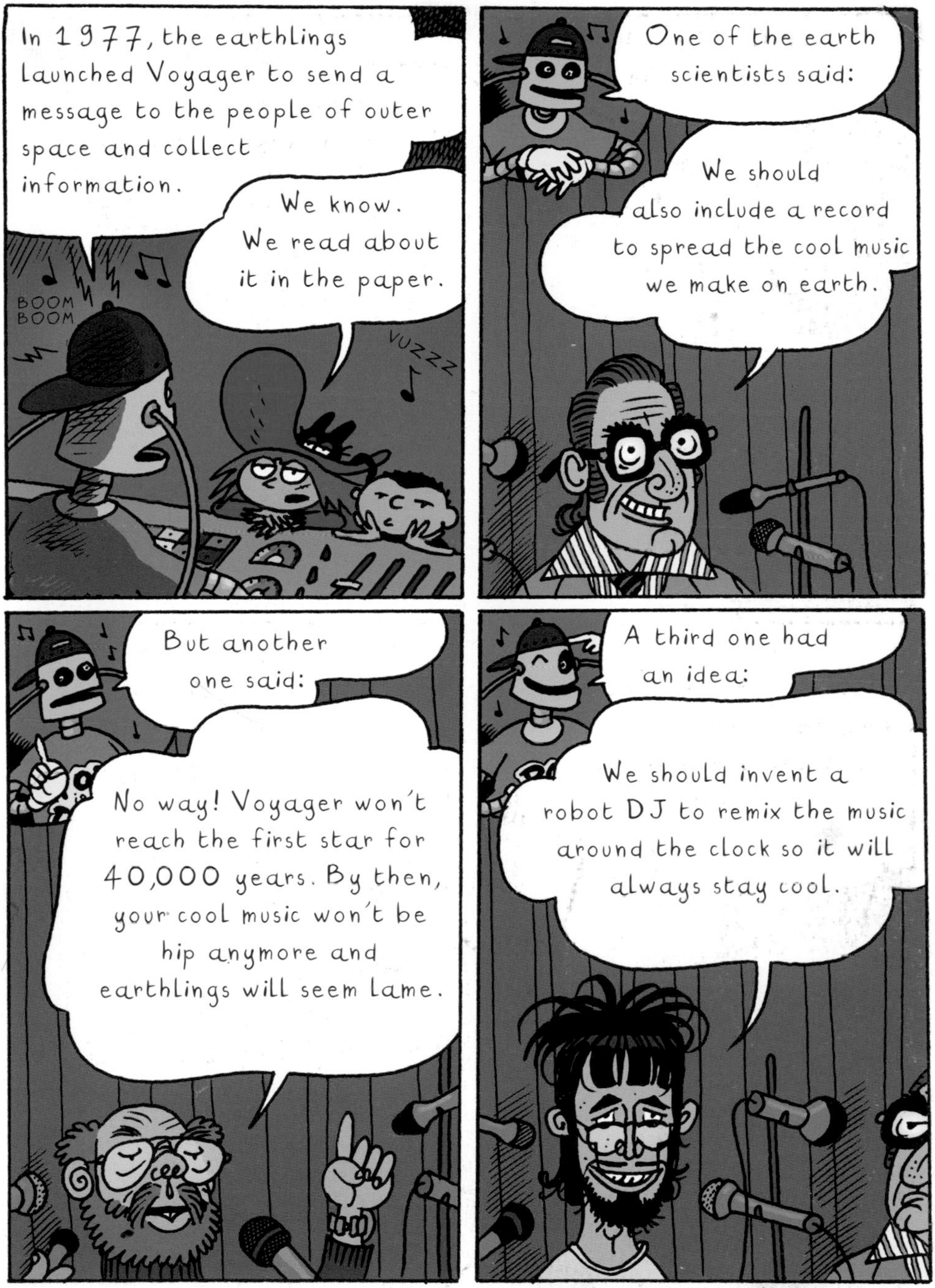
In 1977, the earthlings launched Voyager to send a message to the people of outer space and collect information.
We know. We read about it in the paper.
BOOM BOOM
VUZZZ
One of the earth scientists said:
We should also include a record to spread the cool music we make on earth.
But another one said:
No way! Voyager won't reach the first star for 40,000 years. By then, your cool music won't be hip anymore and earthlings will seem lame.
A third one had an idea:
We should invent a robot DJ to remix the music around the clock so it will always stay cool.

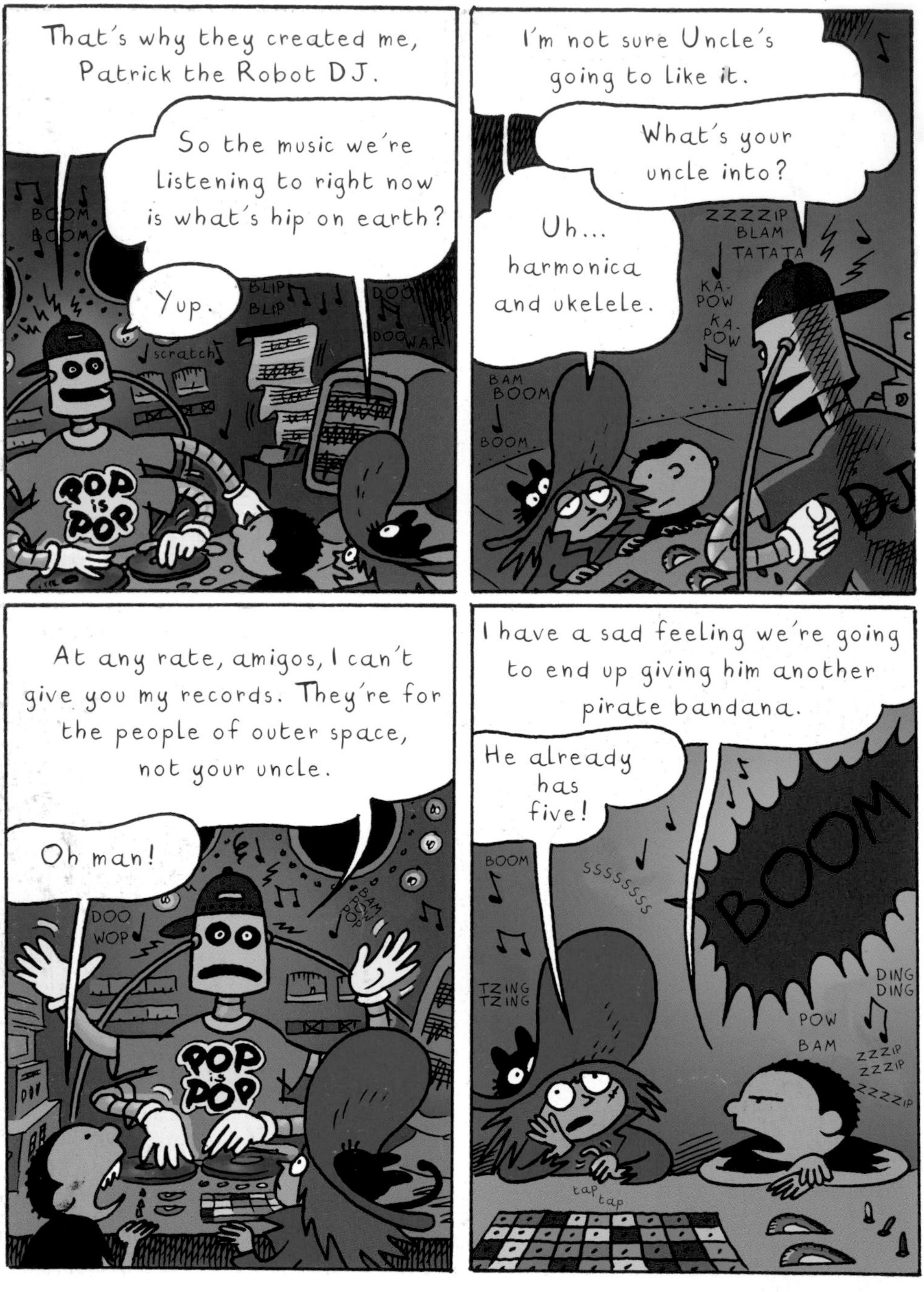
That's why they created me, Patrick the Robot DJ.
So the music we're listening to right now is what's hip on earth?
Yup.
BOOM BOOM
BLIP BLIP
DOO DOO WAP
scratch
POP is POP
I'm not sure Uncle's going to like it.
What's your uncle into?
Uh... harmonica and ukelele.
ZZZZIP BLAM TATATA
KA-POW KA-POW
BAM BOOM
BOOM
DJ
At any rate, amigos, I can't give you my records. They're for the people of outer space, not your uncle.
Oh man!
DOO WOP
BAM POW POP
POP is POP
I have a sad feeling we're going to end up giving him another pirate bandana.
He already has five!
BOOM
SSSSSSSS
BOOM
TZING TZING
DING DING
POW
BAM
ZZZIP ZZZIP ZZZZIP
tap tap

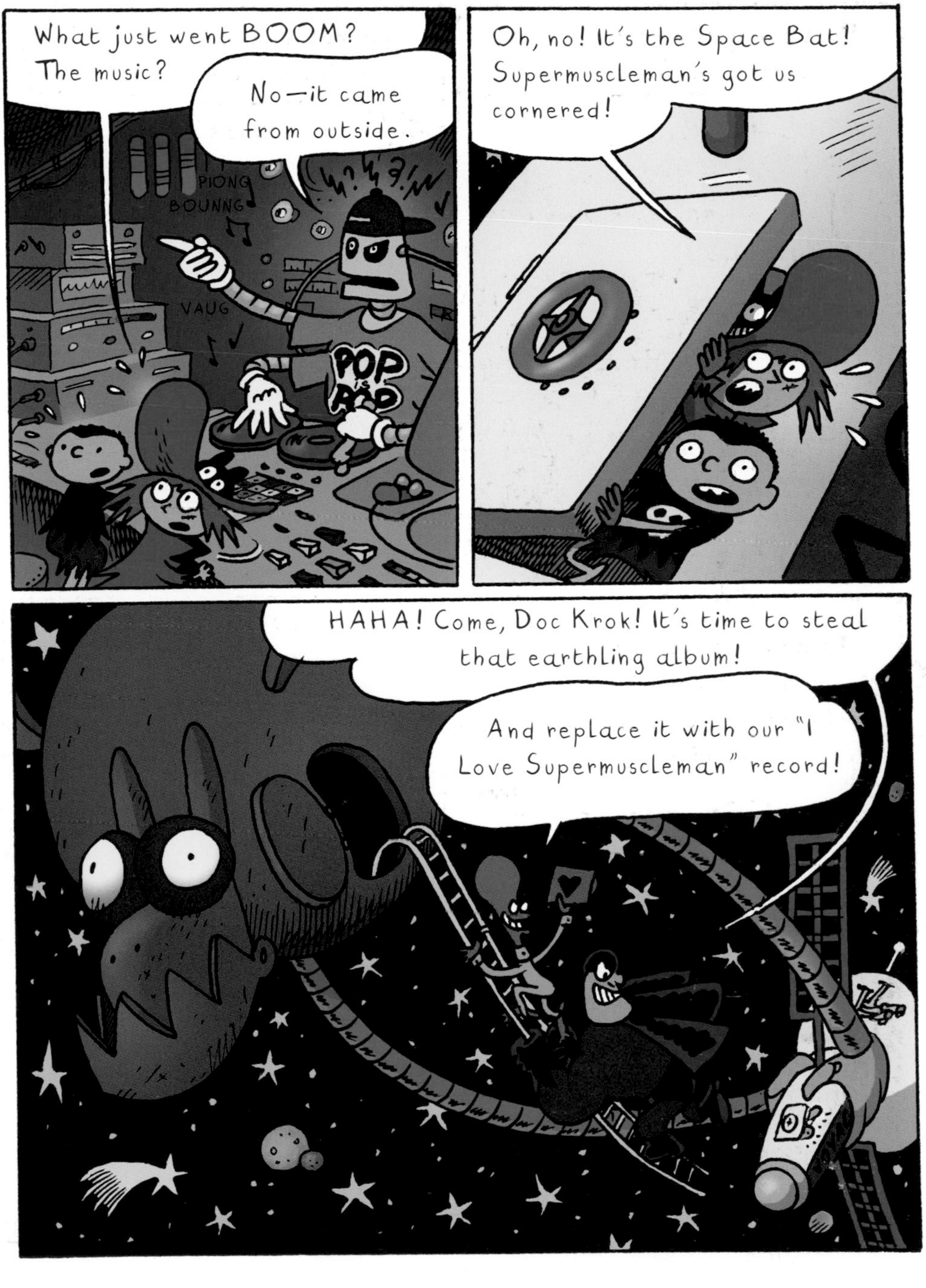
What just went BOOM? The music?
No—it came from outside.
PIONG
BOUNNG
VAUG
POP IS ROP
Oh, no! It's the Space Bat! Supermuscleman's got us cornered!
HAHA! Come, Doc Krok! It's time to steal that earthling album!
And replace it with our "I Love Supermuscleman" record!

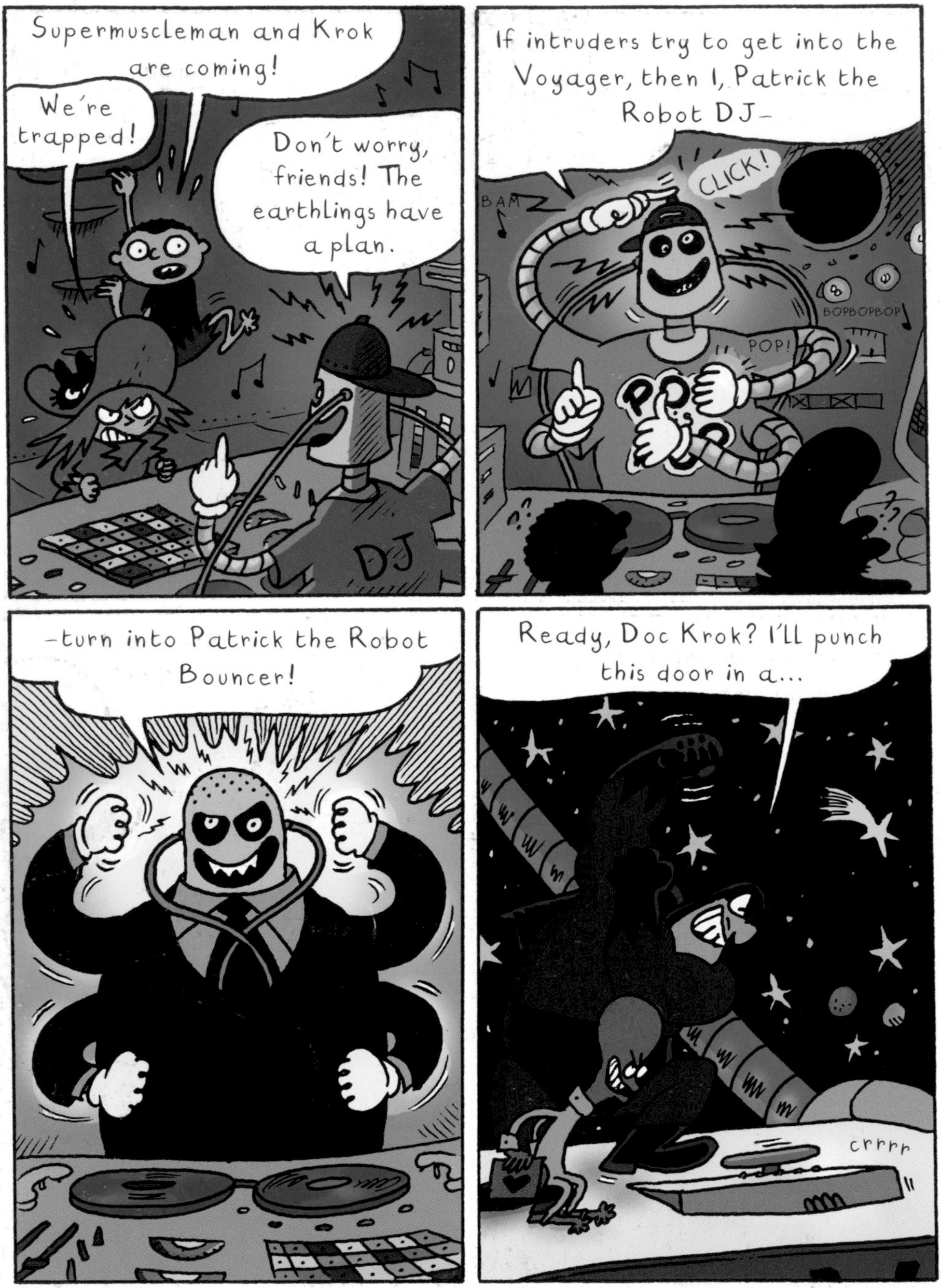
Supermuscleman and Krok are coming!
We're trapped!
Don't worry, friends! The earthlings have a plan.
If intruders try to get into the Voyager, then I, Patrick the Robot DJ-
BAM
CLICK!
BOPBOPBOP
POP!
-turn into Patrick the Robot Bouncer!
Ready, Doc Krok? I'll punch this door in a...
crrrr

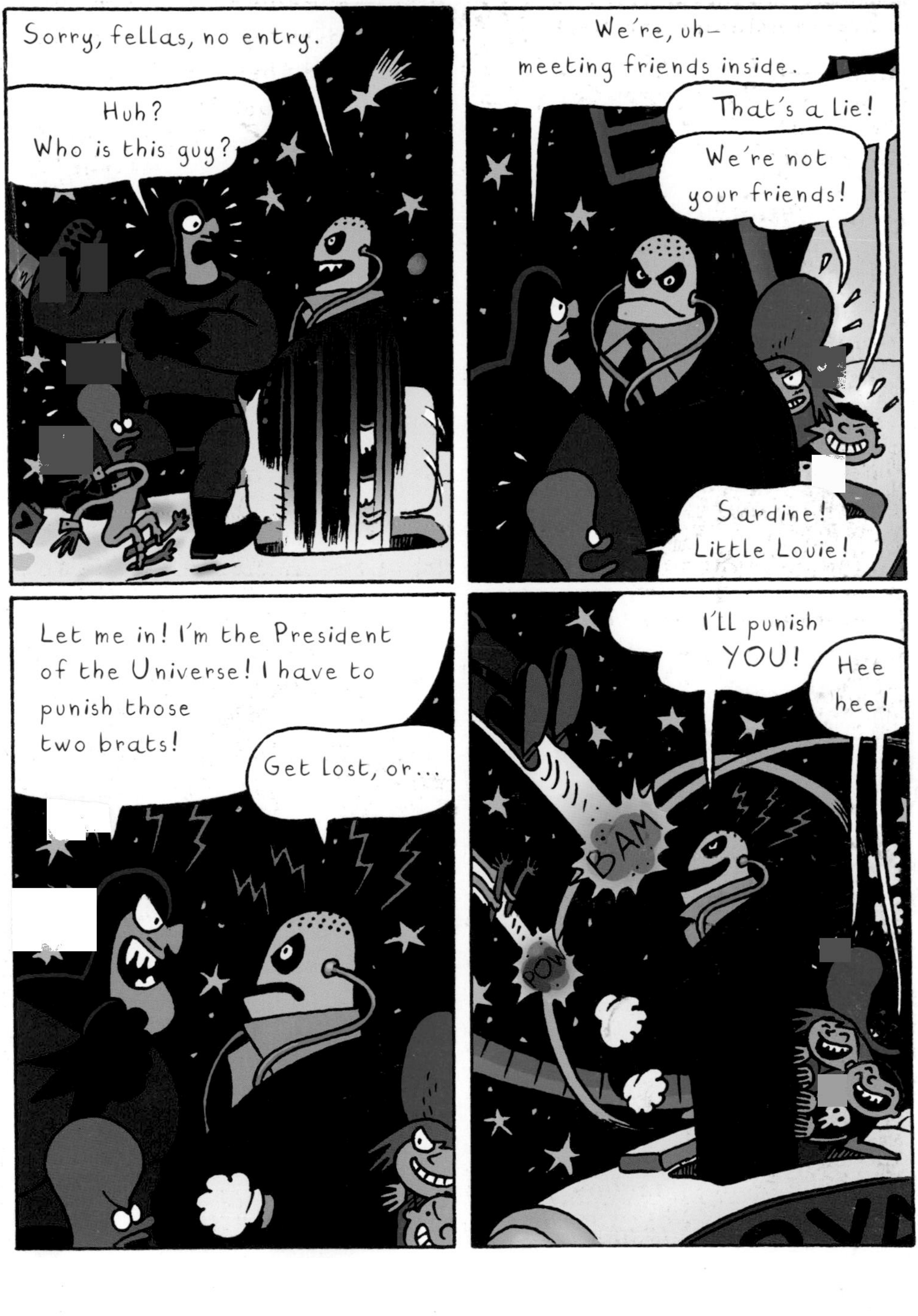
Sorry, fellas, no entry.
Huh? Who is this guy?
We're, uh— meeting friends inside.
That's a lie!
We're not your friends!
Sardine! Little Louie!
Let me in! I'm the President of the Universe! I have to punish those two brats!
Get lost, or...
I'LL punish YOU!
Hee hee!
BAM
POW

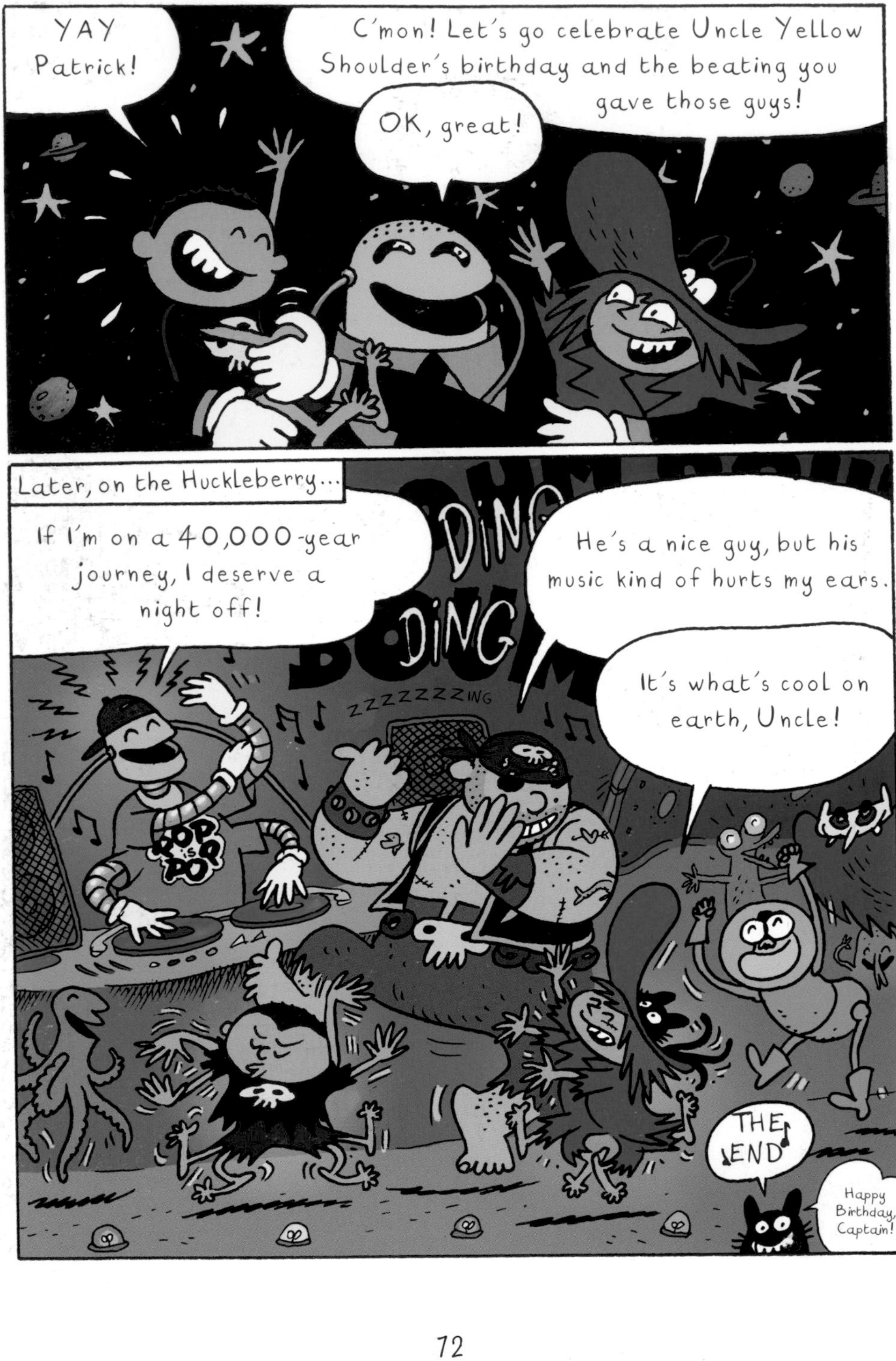
YAY Patrick!
C'mon! Let's go celebrate Uncle Yellow Shoulder's birthday and the beating you gave those guys!
OK, great!
Later, on the Huckleberry...
If I'm on a 40,000-year journey, I deserve a night off!
DING
DING
He's a nice guy, but his music kind of hurts my ears.
It's what's cool on earth, Uncle!
ZZZZZZZING
POP IS POP POP
THE END
Happy Birthday, Captain!

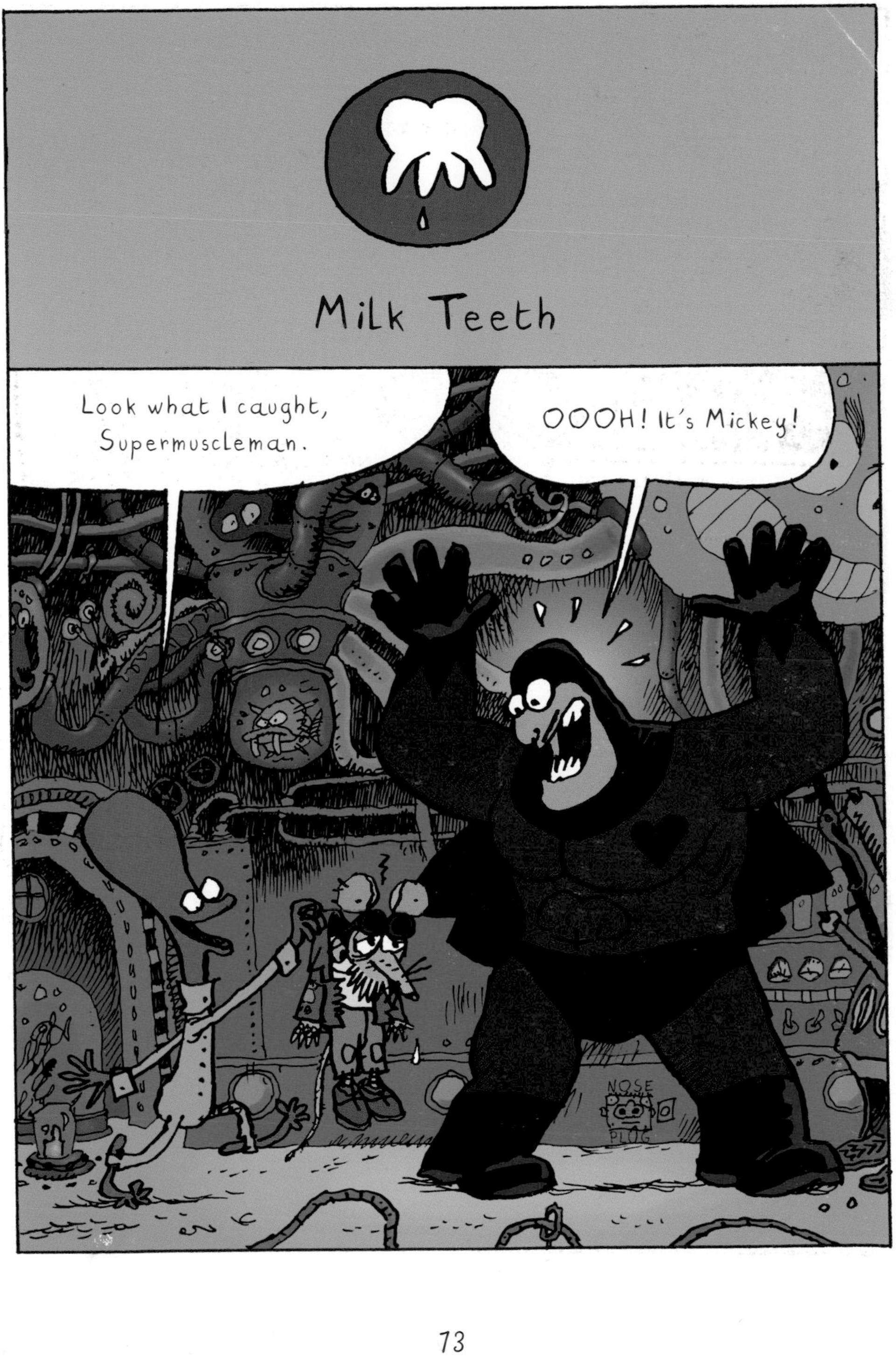
Milk Teeth
Look what I caught, Supermuscleman.
OOOH! It's Mickey!
NOSE PLUG

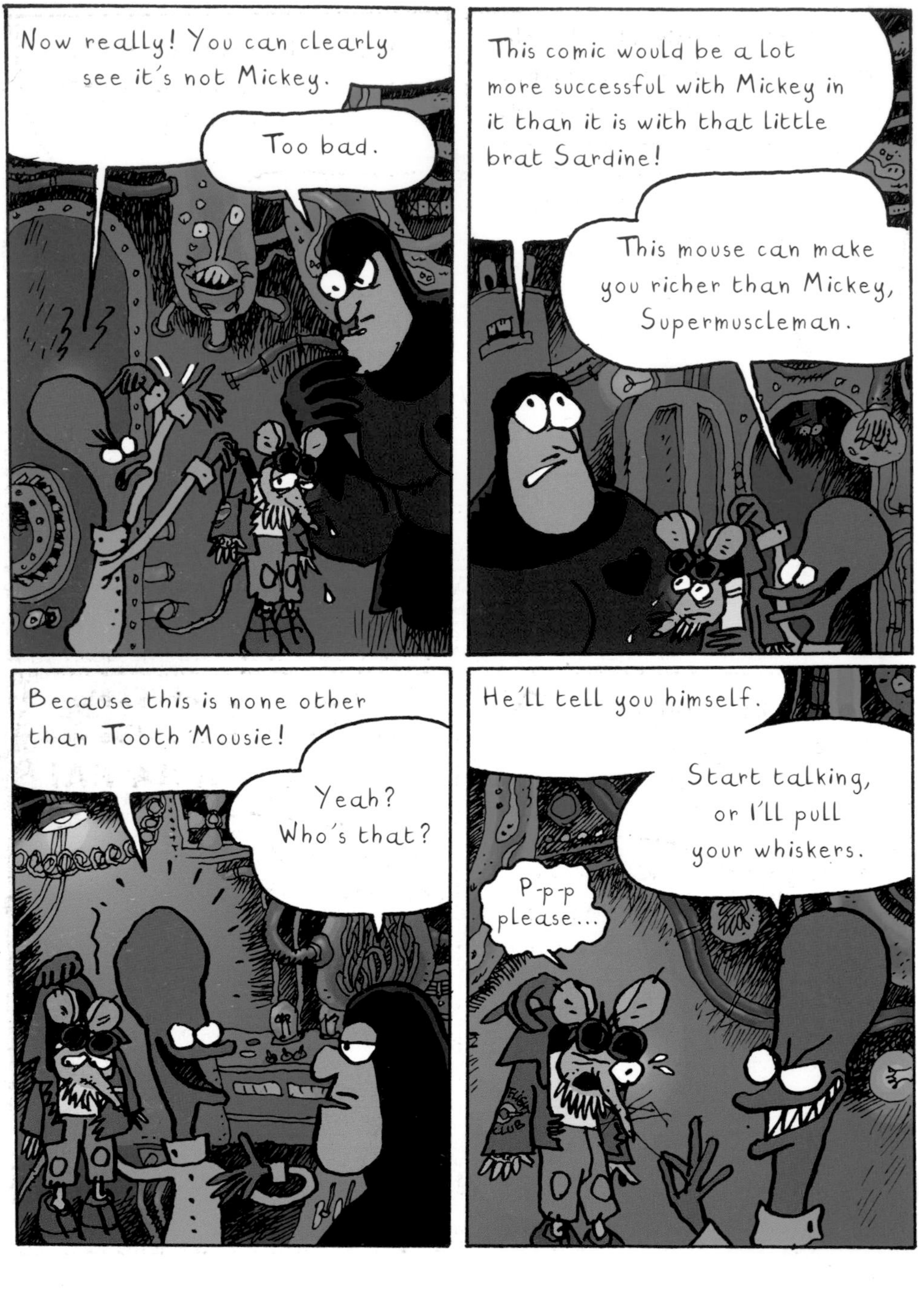
Now really! You can clearly see it's not Mickey.
Too bad.
This comic would be a lot more successful with Mickey in it than it is with that little brat Sardine!
This mouse can make you richer than Mickey, Supermuscleman.
Because this is none other than Tooth Mousie!
Yeah? Who's that?
He'll tell you himself.
Start talking, or I'll pull your whiskers.
P-p-p please...

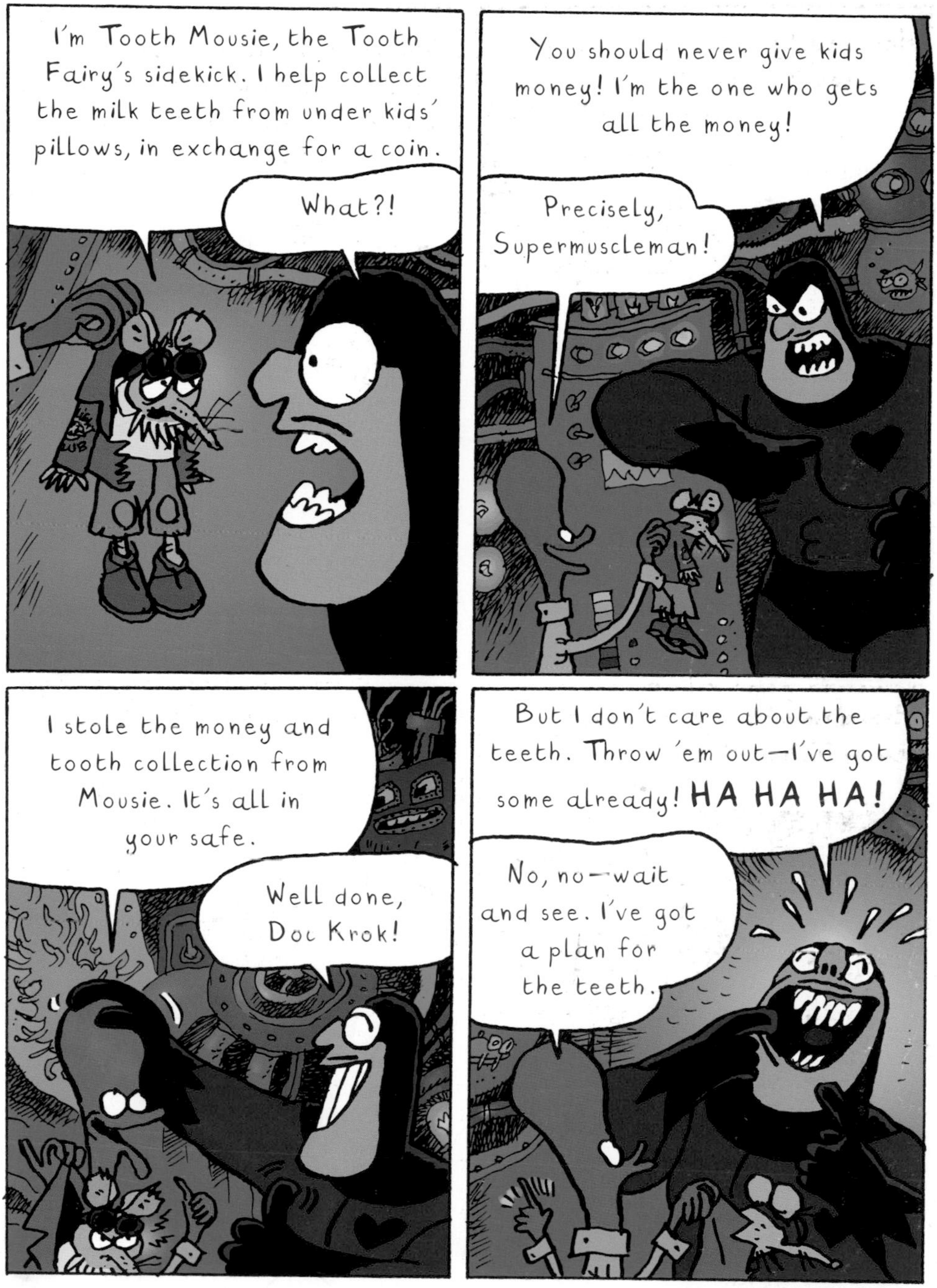
I'm Tooth Mousie, the Tooth Fairy's sidekick. I help collect the milk teeth from under kids' pillows, in exchange for a coin.
What?!
You should never give kids money! I'm the one who gets all the money!
Precisely, Supermuscleman!
I stole the money and tooth collection from Mousie. It's all in your safe.
Well done, Doc Krok!
But I don't care about the teeth. Throw 'em out—I've got some already! HA HA HA!
No, no—wait and see. I've got a plan for the teeth.

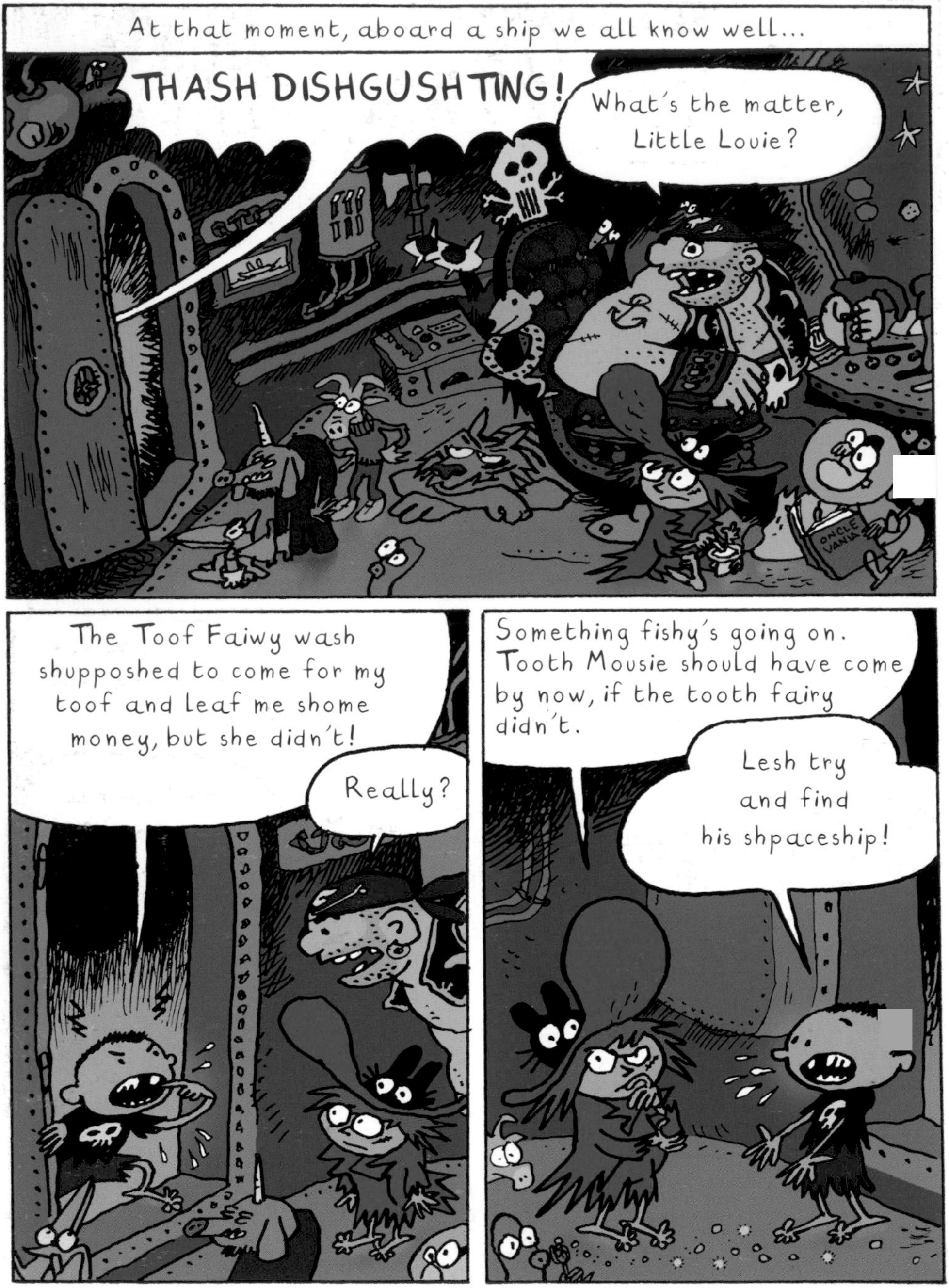
At that moment, aboard a ship we all know well...
THASH DISHGUSHTING!
What's the matter, Little Louie?
ONCLE VANIA
The Toof Faiwy wash shupposhed to come for my toof and leaf me shome money, but she didn't!
Really?
Something fishy's going on. Tooth Mousie should have come by now, if the tooth fairy didn't.
Lesh try and find his shpaceship!

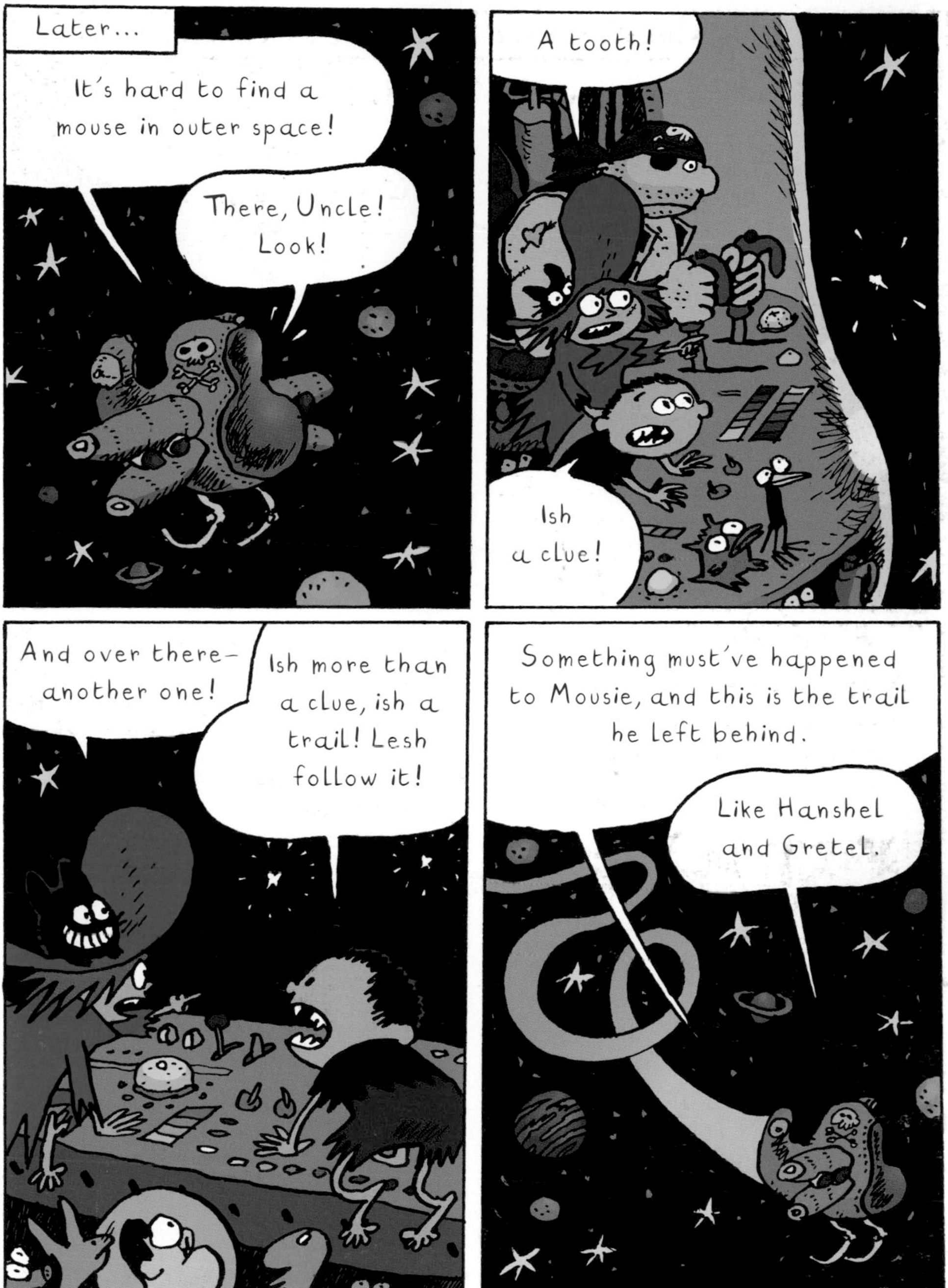
Later...
It's hard to find a mouse in outer space!
There, Uncle! Look!
A tooth!
Ish a clue!
And over there- another one!
Ish more than a clue, ish a trail! Lesh follow it!
Something must've happened to Mousie, and this is the trail he left behind.
Like Hanshel and Gretel.

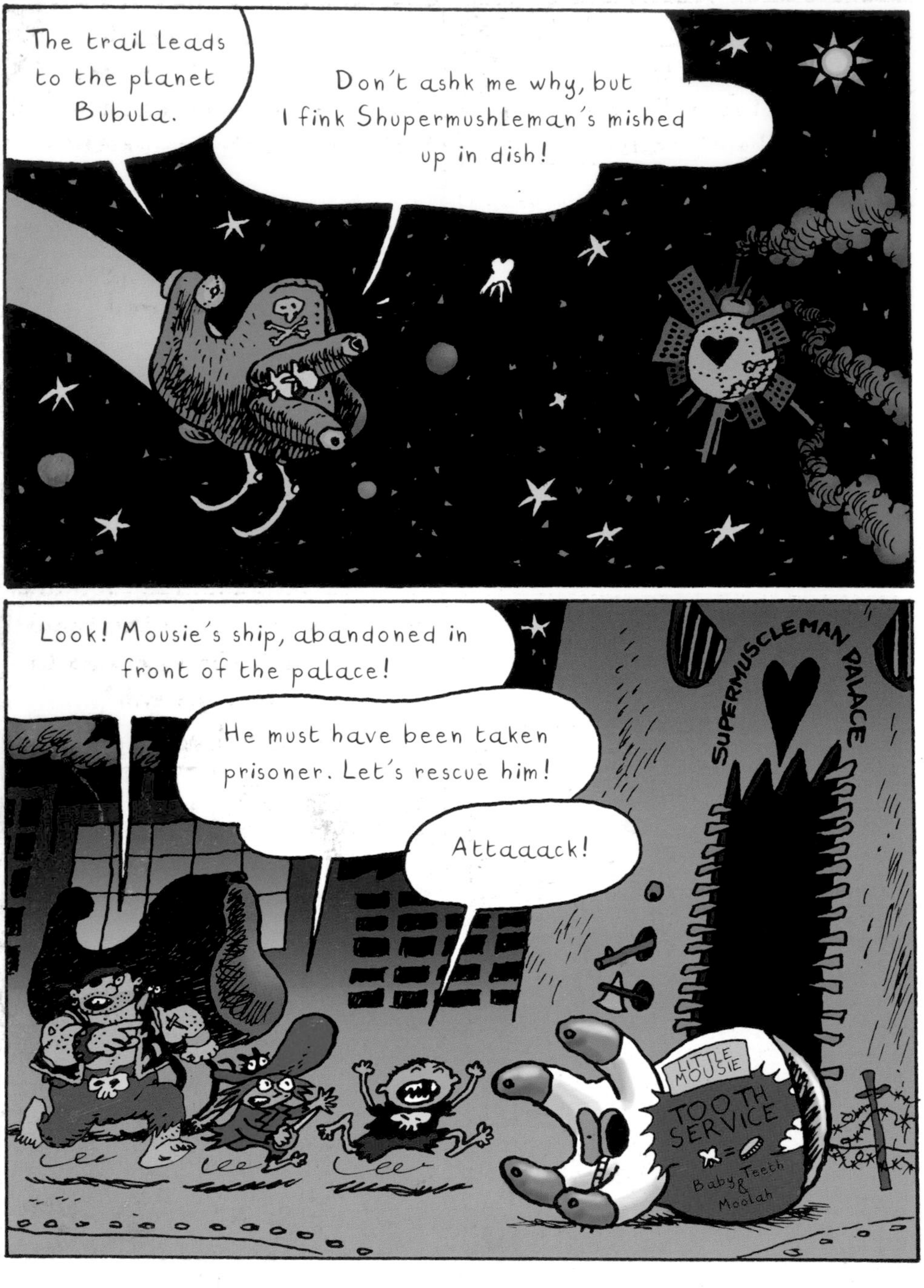
The trail leads to the planet Bubula.
Don't ashk me why, but I fink Shupermushleman's mished up in dish!
Look! Mousie's ship, abandoned in front of the palace!
He must have been taken prisoner. Let's rescue him!
Attaaack!
SUPERMUSCLEMAN PALACE
LITTLE MOUSIE
TOOTH SERVICE
Baby Teeth & Moolah

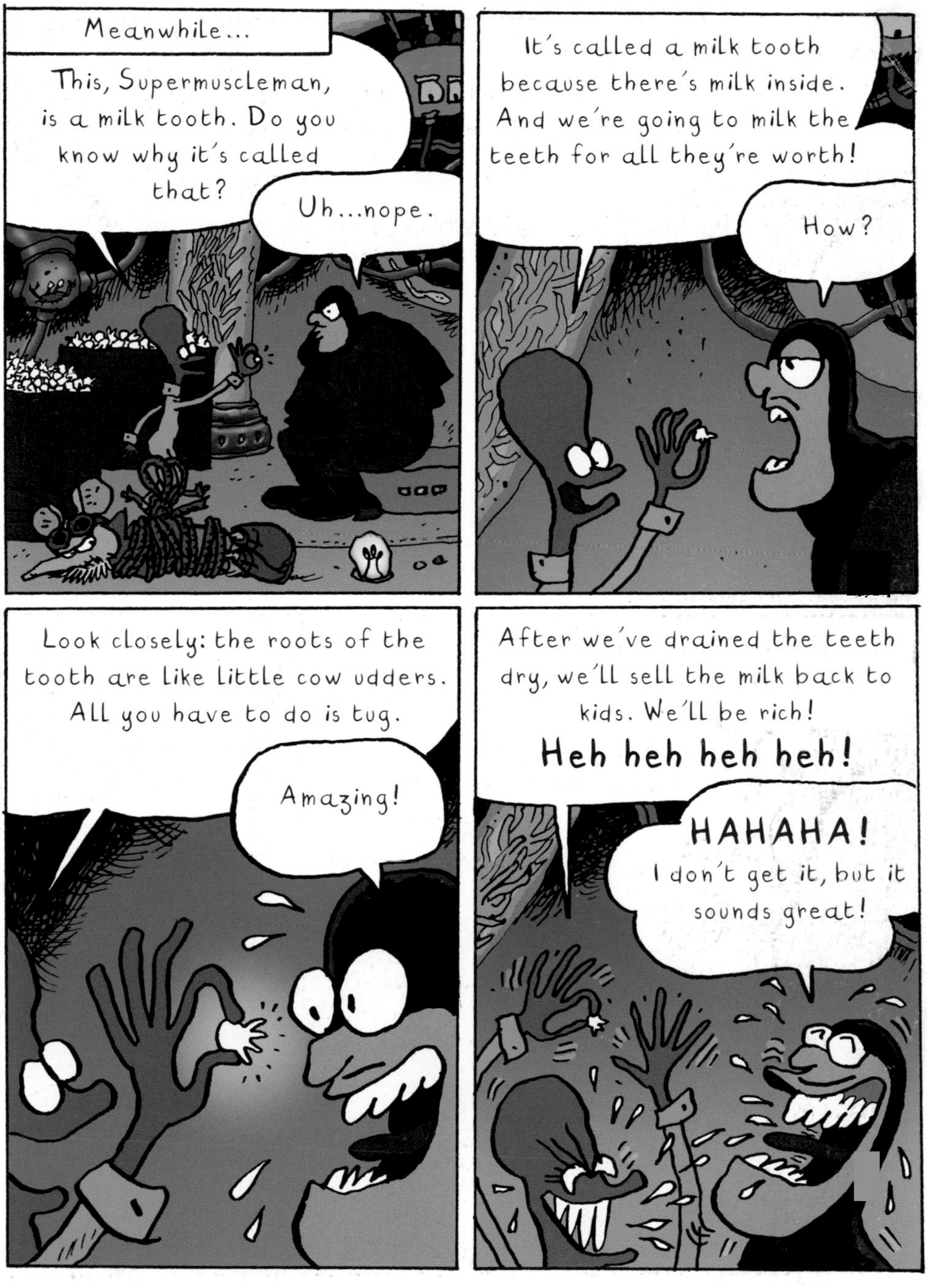
Meanwhile...
This, Supermuscleman, is a milk tooth. Do you know why it's called that?
Uh...nope.
It's called a milk tooth because there's milk inside. And we're going to milk the teeth for all they're worth!
How?
Look closely: the roots of the tooth are like little cow udders. All you have to do is tug.
Amazing!
After we've drained the teeth dry, we'll sell the milk back to kids. We'll be rich!
Heh heh heh heh!
HAHAHA!
I don't get it, but it sounds great!

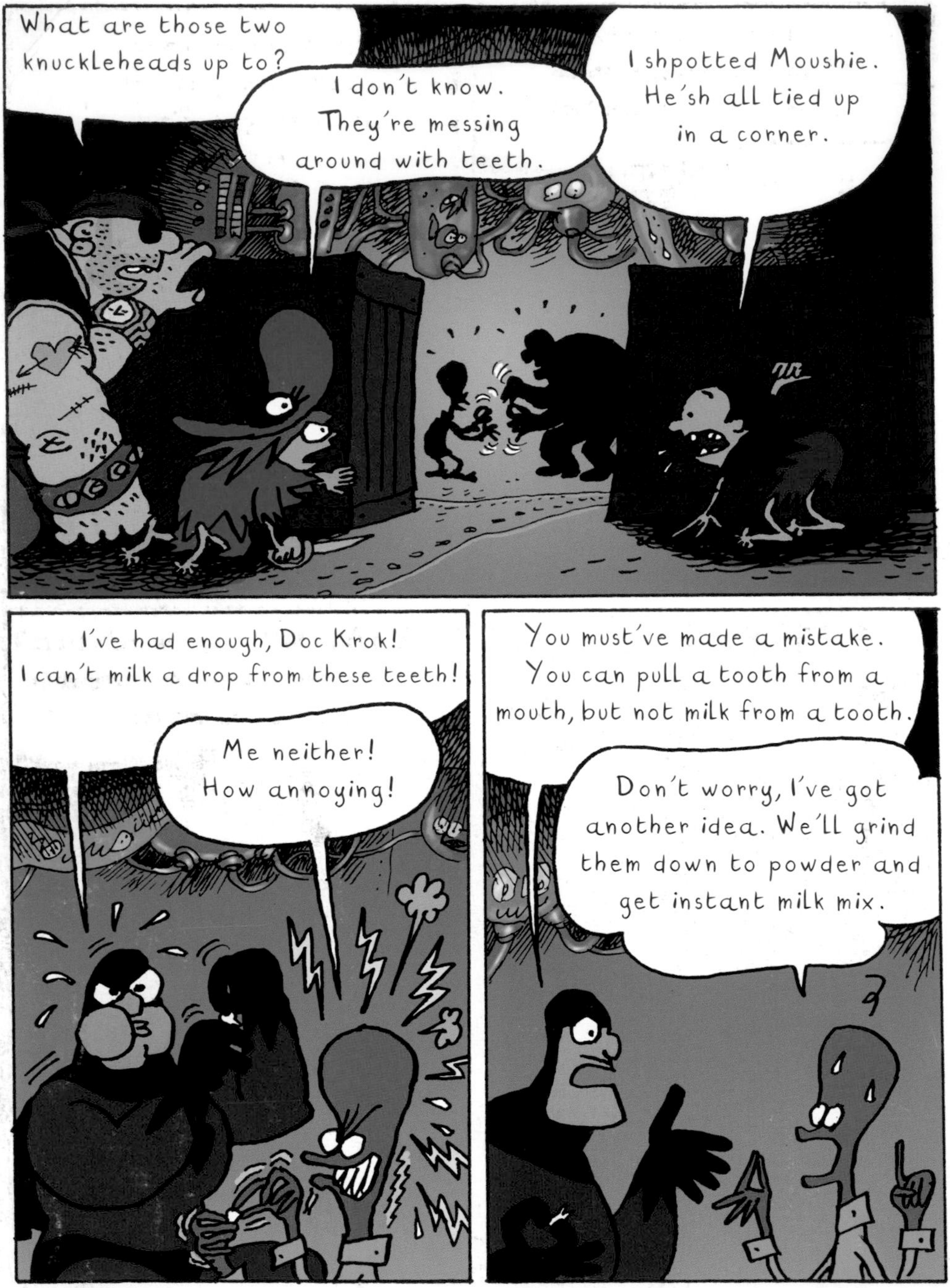
What are those two knuckleheads up to?
I don't know. They're messing around with teeth.
I shpotted Moushie. He'sh all tied up in a corner.
I've had enough, Doc Krok! I can't milk a drop from these teeth!
Me neither! How annoying!
You must've made a mistake. You can pull a tooth from a mouth, but not milk from a tooth.
Don't worry, I've got another idea. We'll grind them down to powder and get instant milk mix.

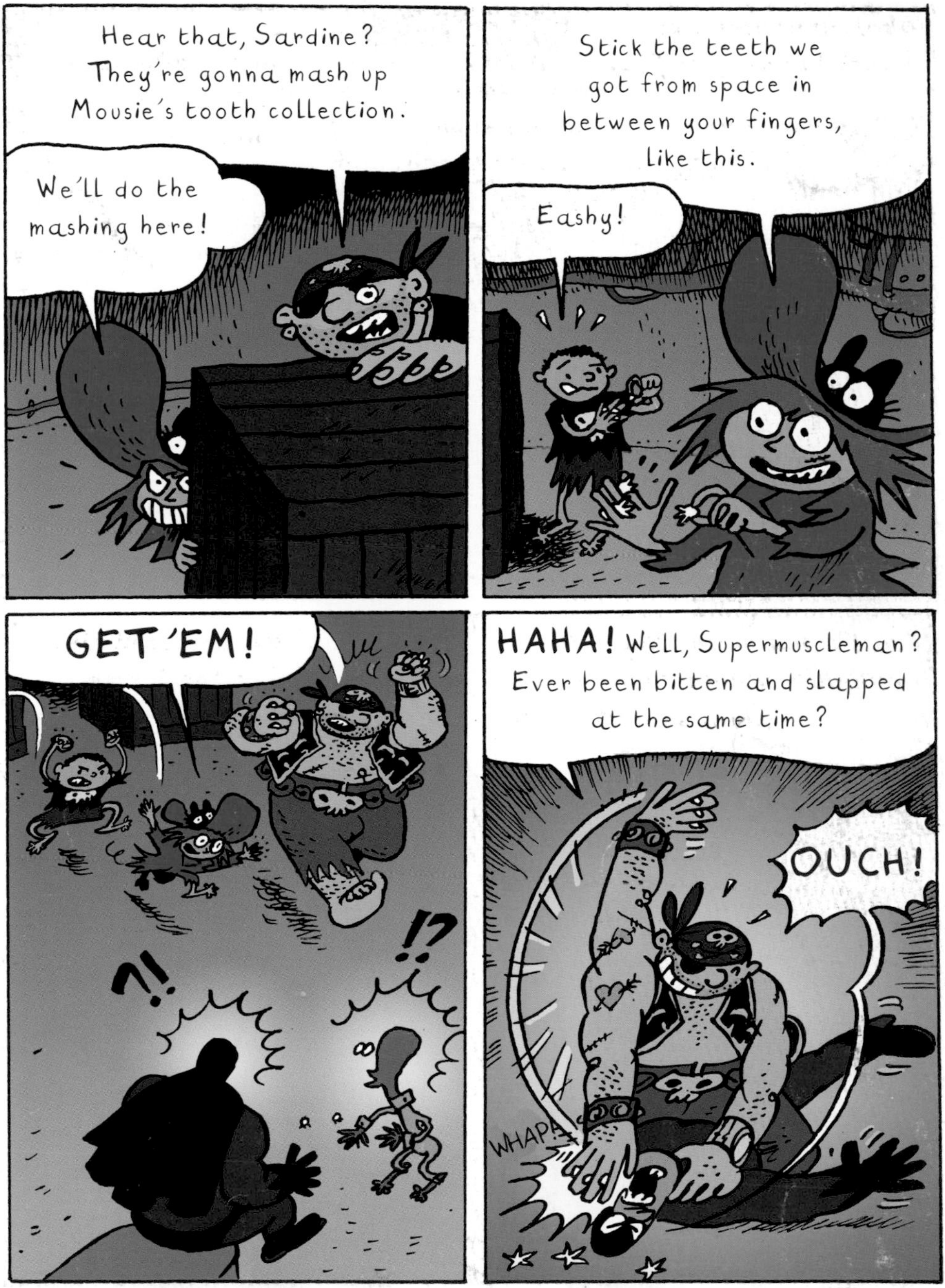
Hear that, Sardine? They're gonna mash up Mousie's tooth collection.
We'll do the mashing here!
Stick the teeth we got from space in between your fingers, like this.
Eashy!
GET 'EM!
?!
!?
HAHA! Well, Supermuscleman? Ever been bitten and slapped at the same time?
OUCH!
WHAP!

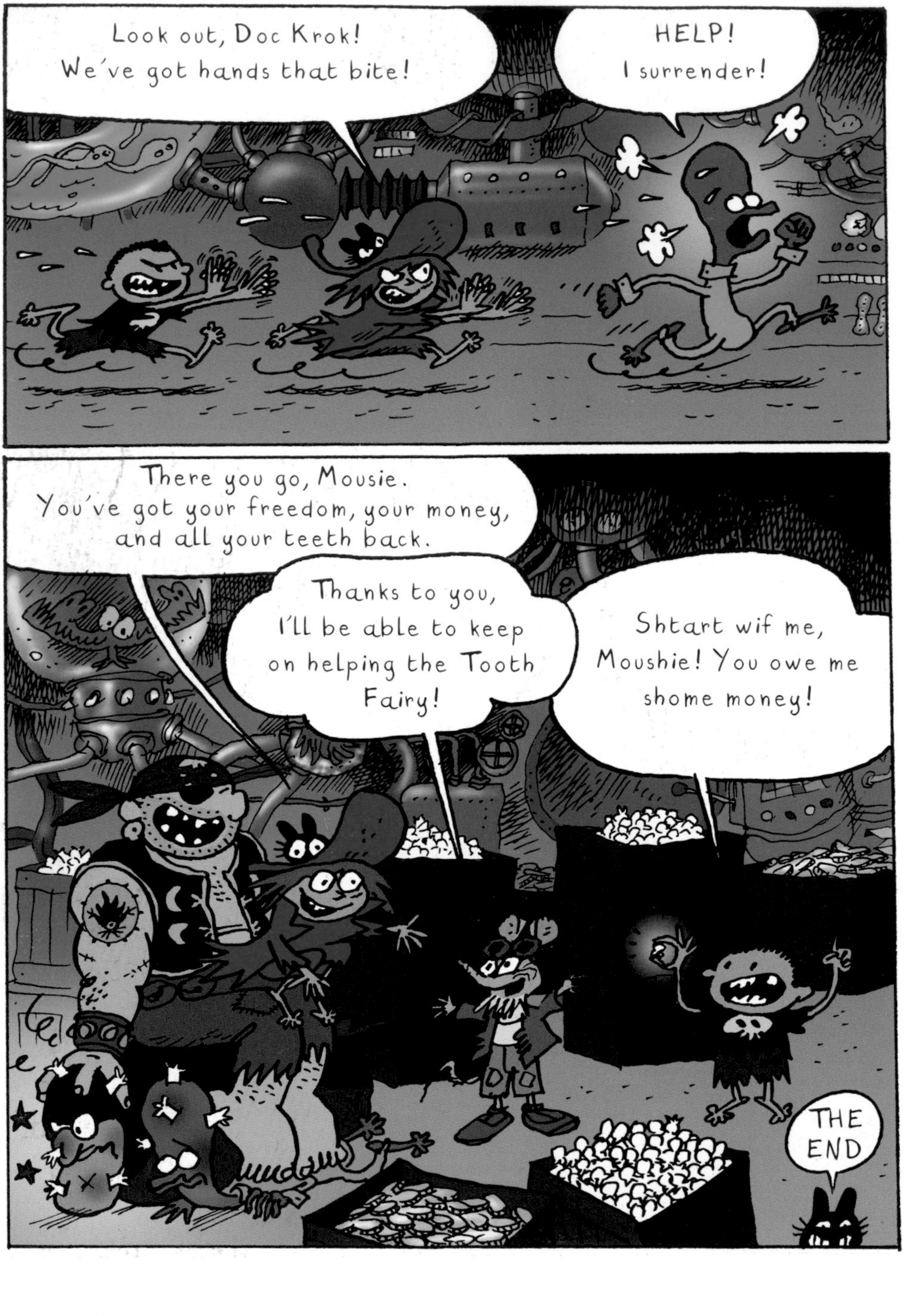
Look out, Doc Krok!
We've got hands that bite!
HELP!
I surrender!
There you go, Mousie.
You've got your freedom, your money,
and all your teeth back.
Thanks to you,
I'll be able to keep
on helping the Tooth
Fairy!
Shtart wif me,
Moushie! You owe me
shome money!
THE
END

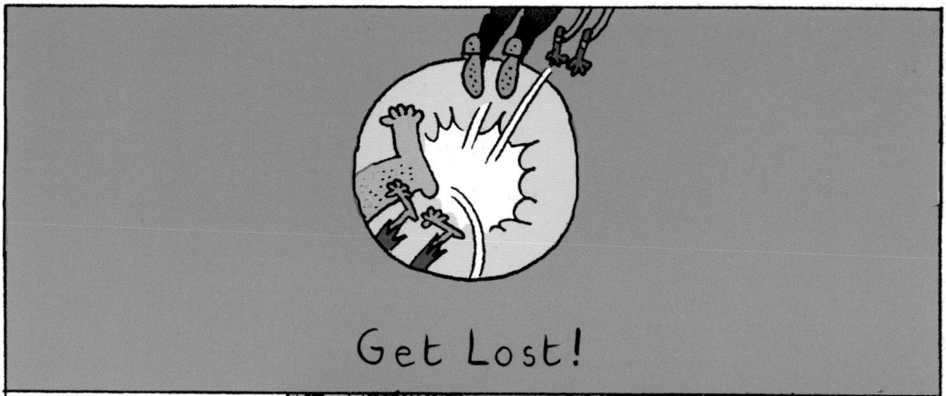
Get Lost!

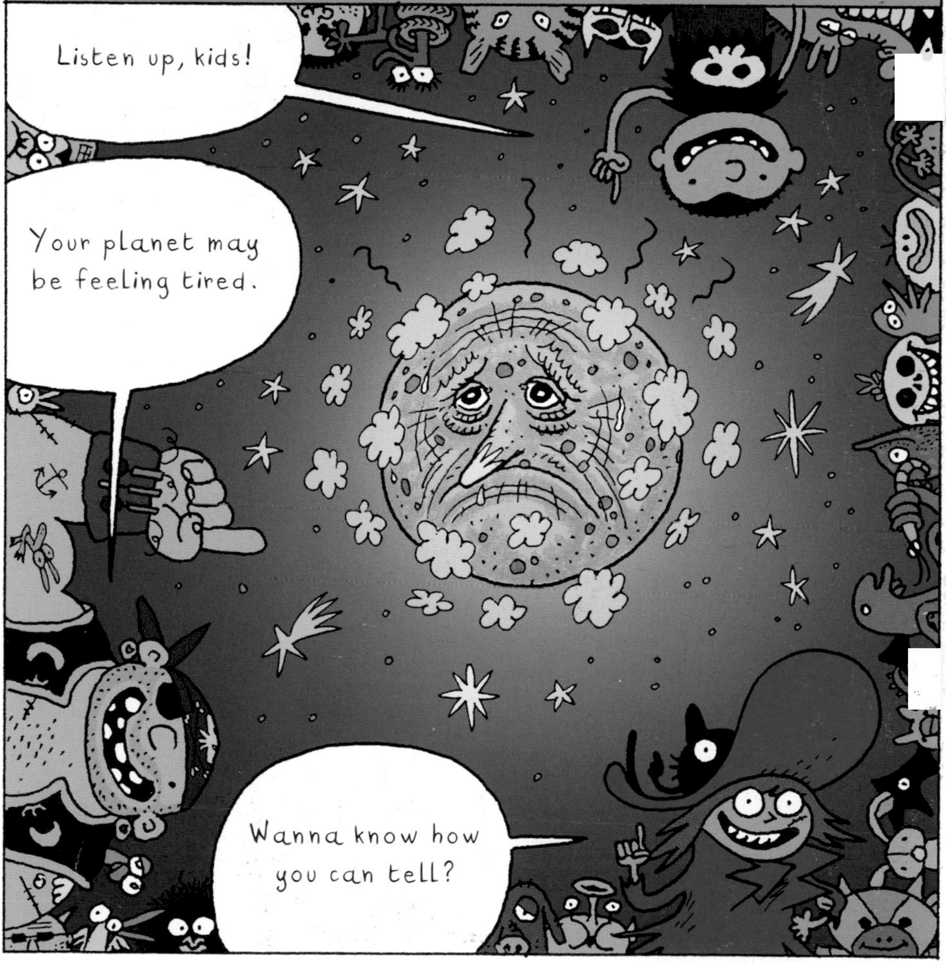
Listen up, kids!
Your planet may be feeling tired.
Wanna know how you can tell?

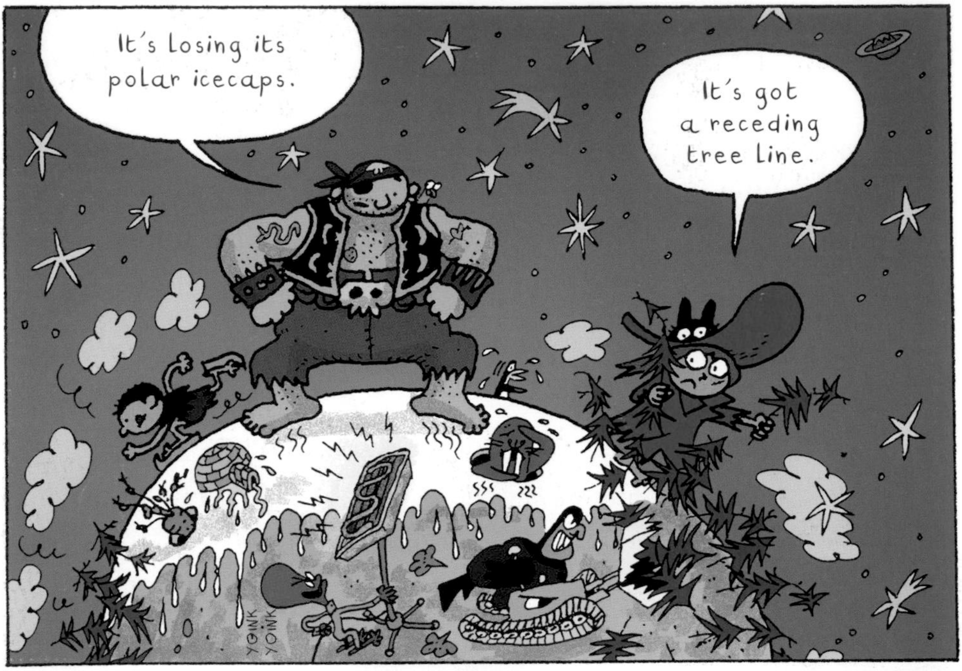
It's losing its polar icecaps.
It's got a receding tree line.
YOINK YOINK

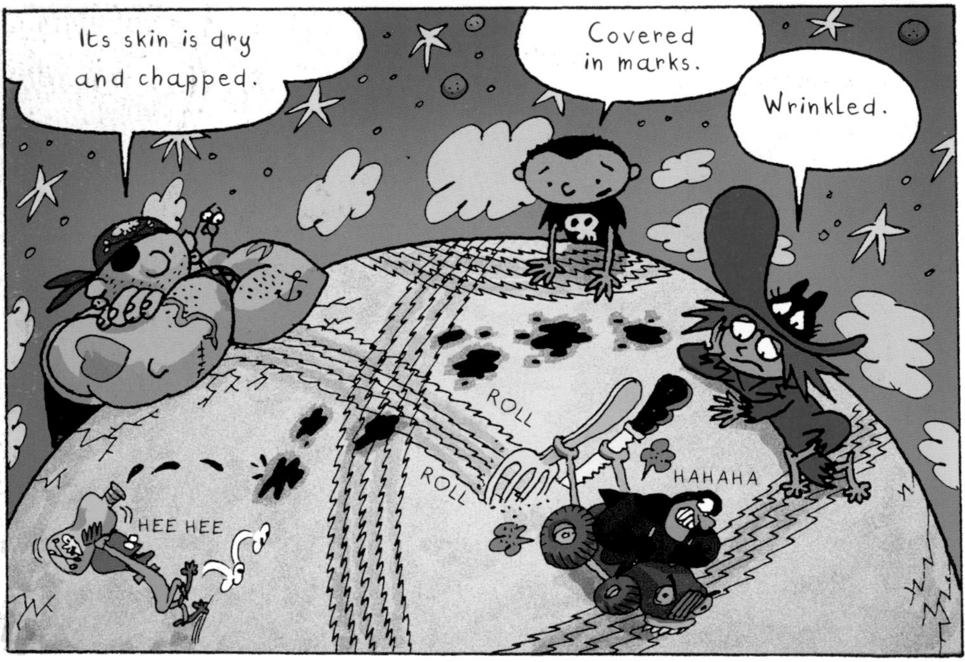
Its skin is dry and chapped.
Covered in marks.
Wrinkled.
ROLL
ROLL
HAHAHA
HEE HEE

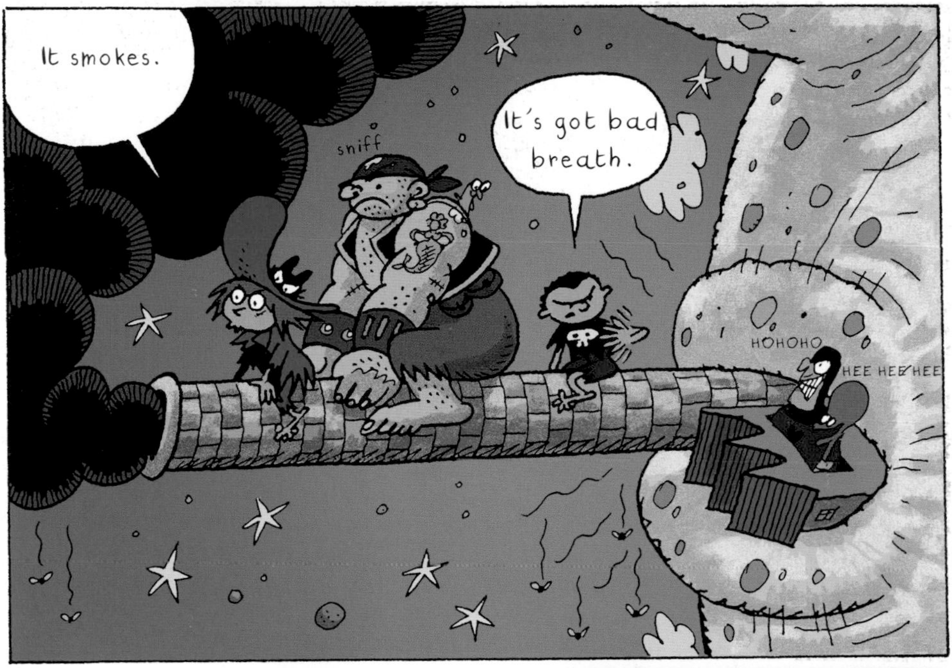
It smokes.
sniff
It's got bad breath.
HOHOHO
HEE HEE HEE

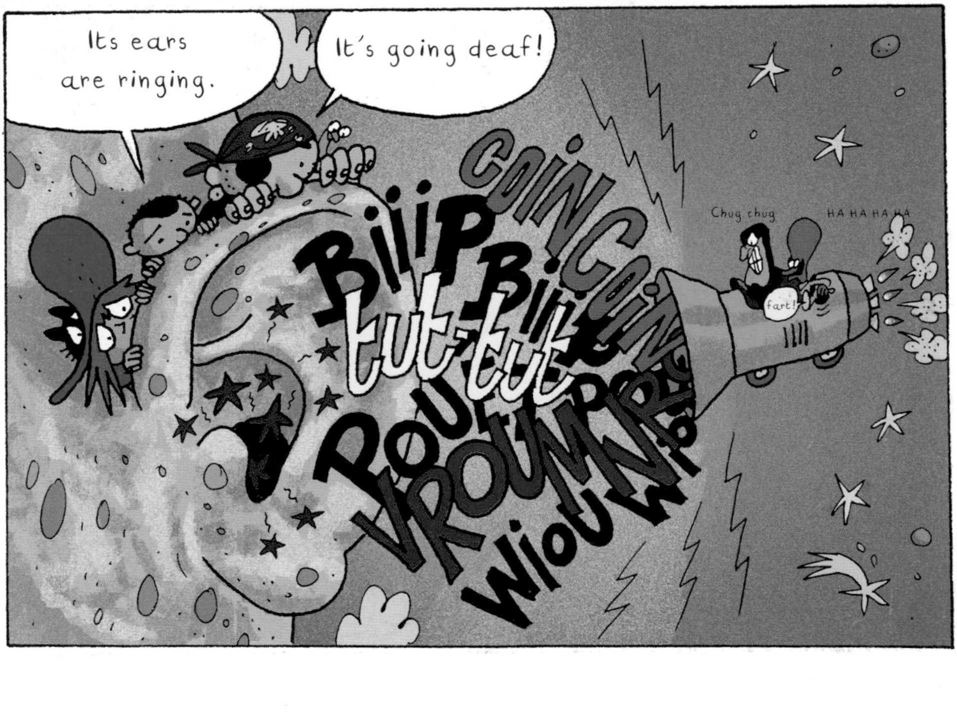
Its ears are ringing.
It's going deaf!
Chug chug
HA HA HA HA
fart!
COIN COIN
Biiip Biiip
tut-tut
POU POU
VROUM VROUM
WIOU WIOU

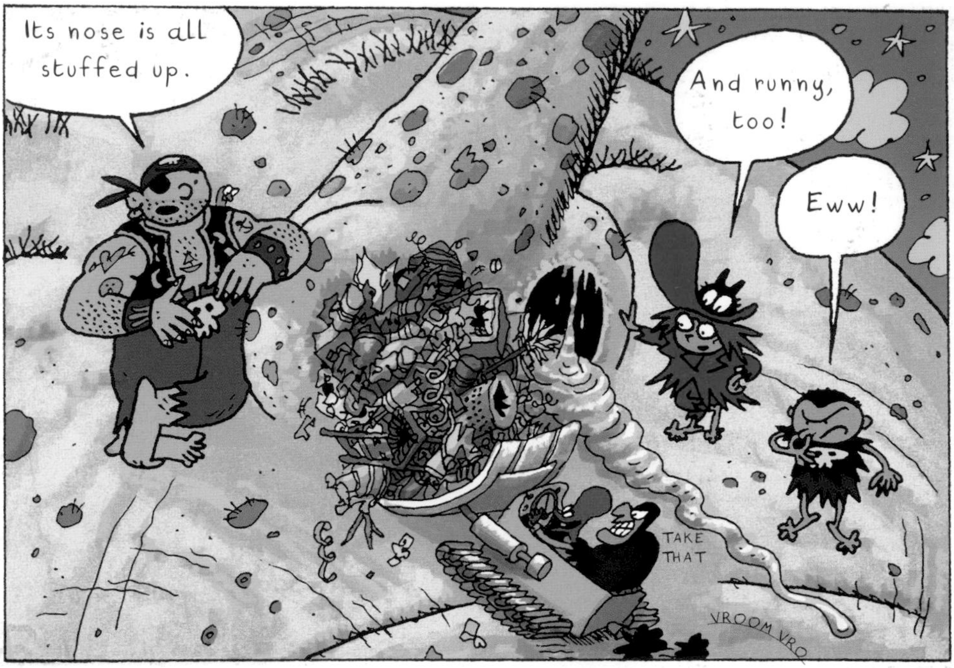
Its nose is all stuffed up.
And runny, too!
Eww!
TAKE THAT
VROOM VRO

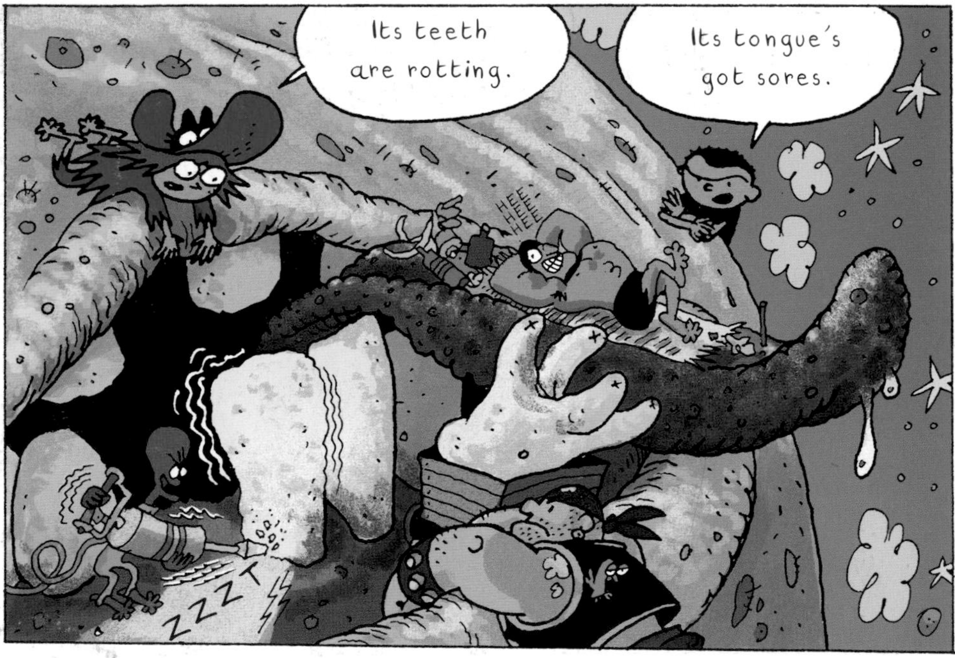
Its teeth are rotting.
Its tongue's got sores.
ZZZT

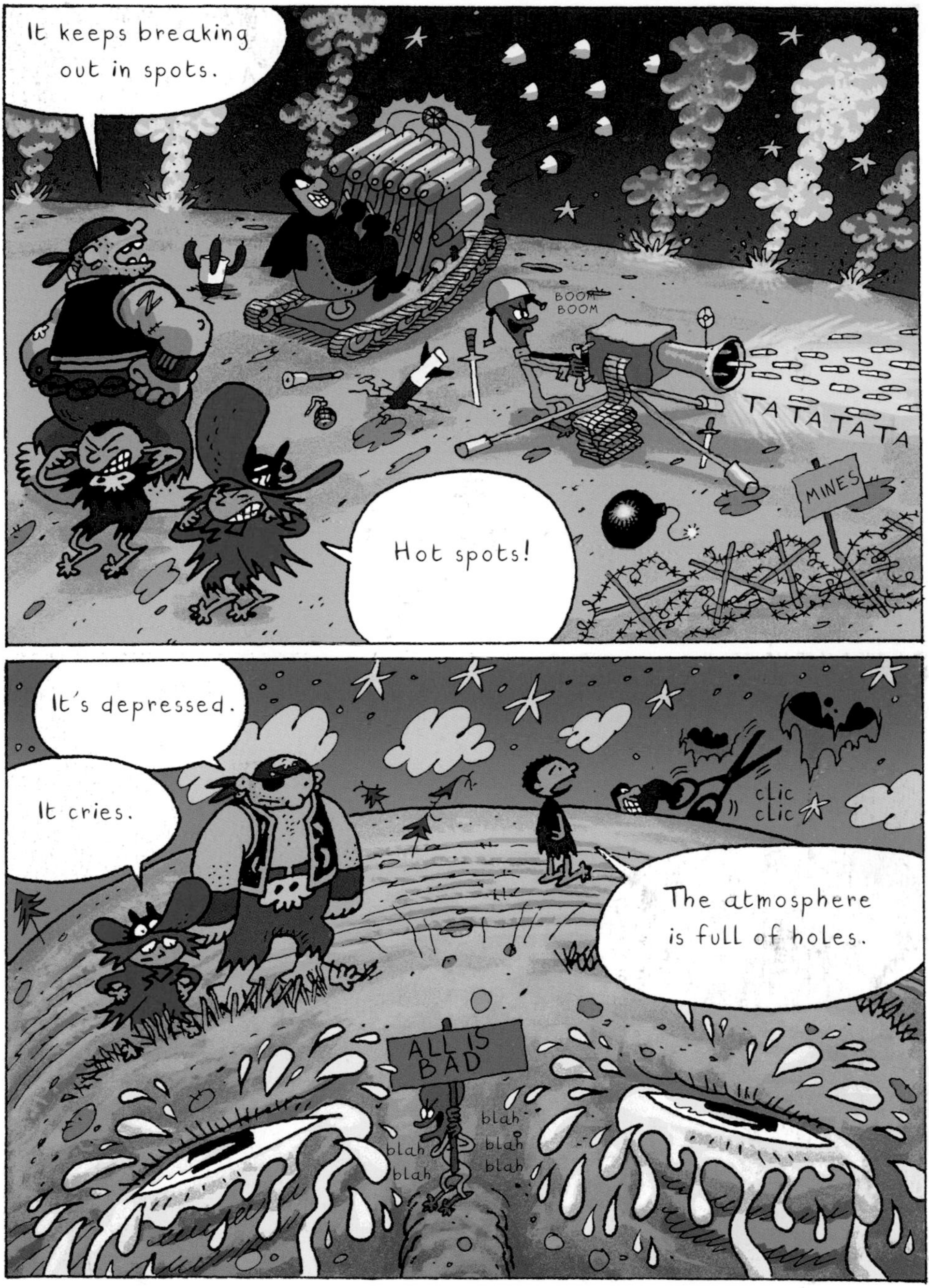
It keeps breaking out in spots.
BOOM BOOM
TATATATA
MINES
Hot spots!
It's depressed.
It cries.
CLIC CLIC
The atmosphere is full of holes.
ALL IS BAD
blah blah
blah blah blah

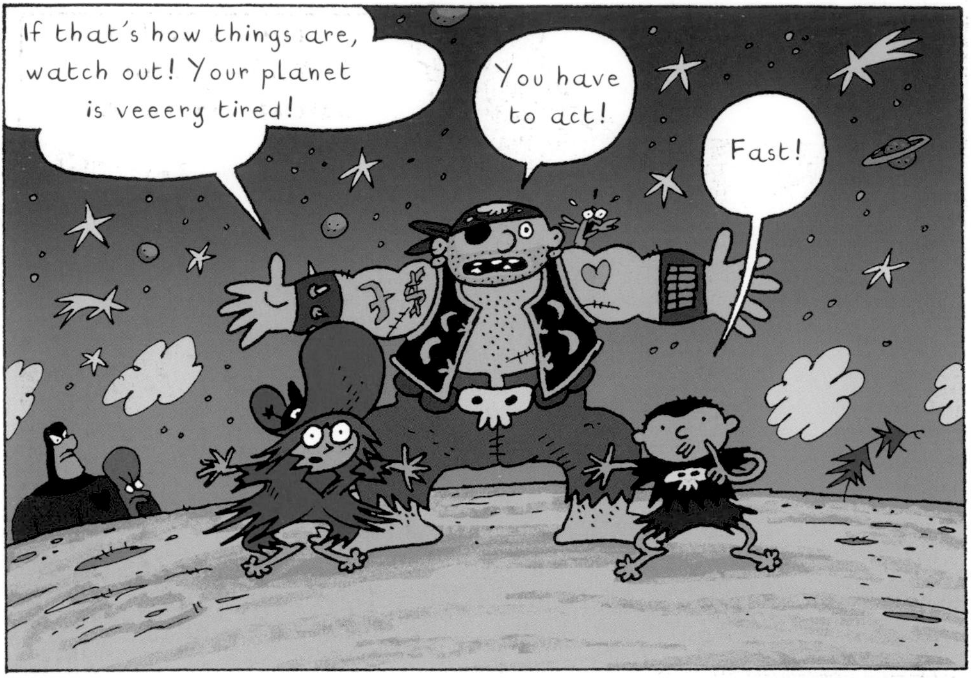
If that's how things are, watch out! Your planet is veeery tired!
You have to act!
Fast!

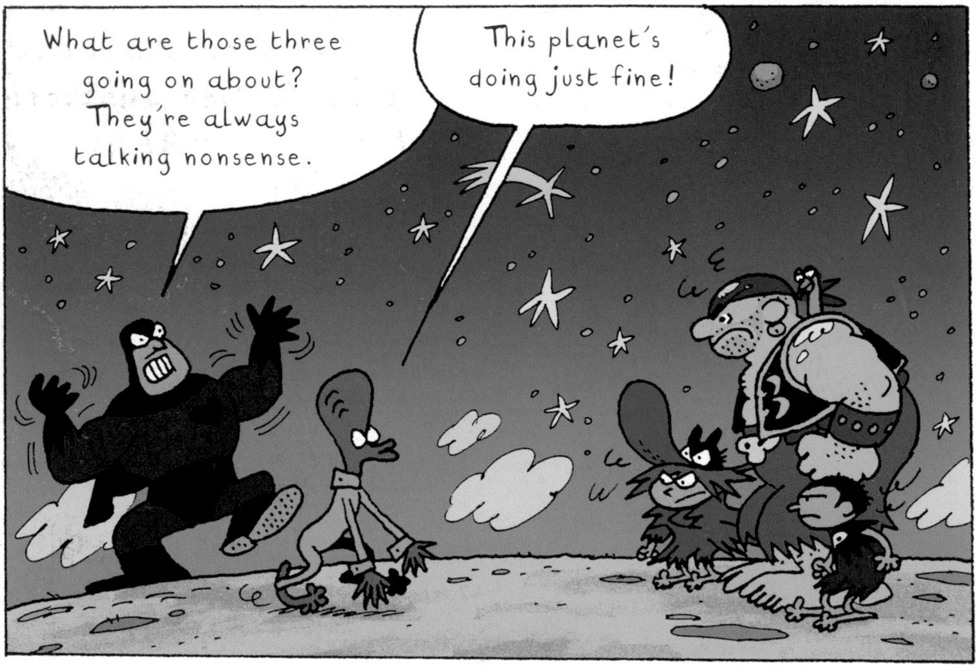
What are those three going on about? They're always talking nonsense.
This planet's doing just fine!

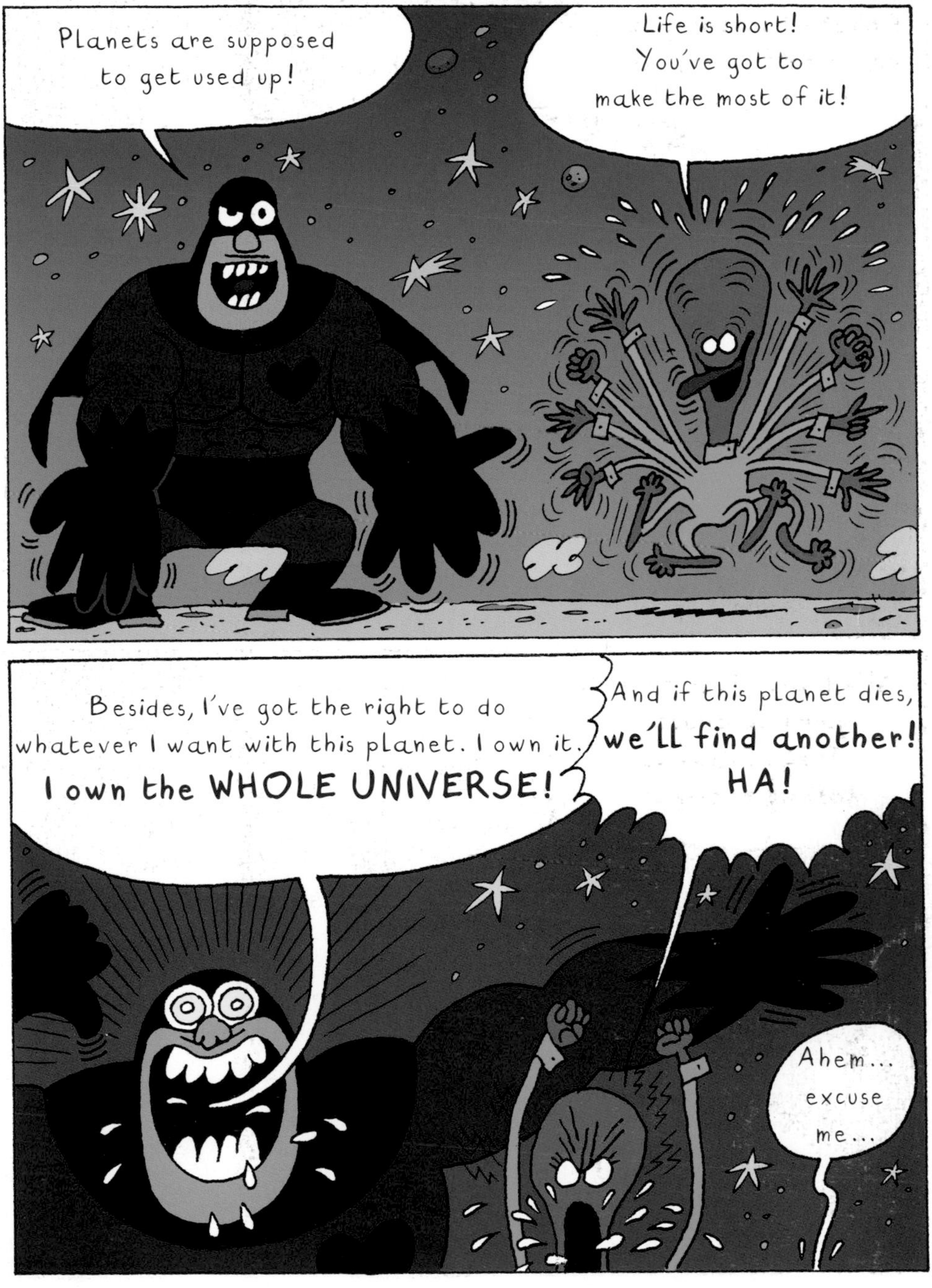
Planets are supposed to get used up!
Life is short! You've got to make the most of it!
Besides, I've got the right to do whatever I want with this planet. I own it. I own the WHOLE UNIVERSE!
And if this planet dies, we'll find another! HA!
Ahem... excuse me...

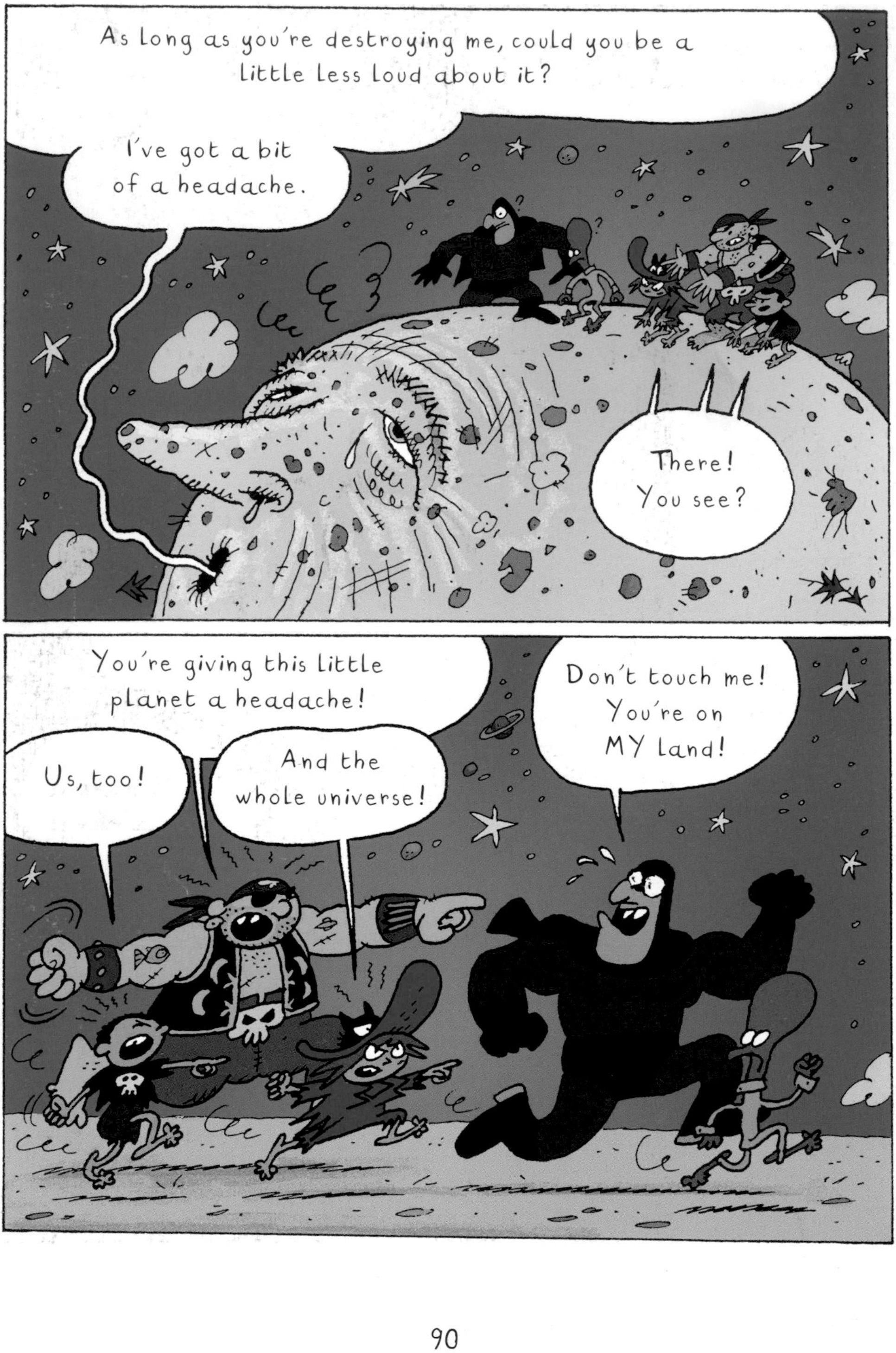
As long as you're destroying me, could you be a little less loud about it?
I've got a bit of a headache.
There! You see?
You're giving this little planet a headache!
Us, too!
And the whole universe!
Don't touch me! You're on MY land!

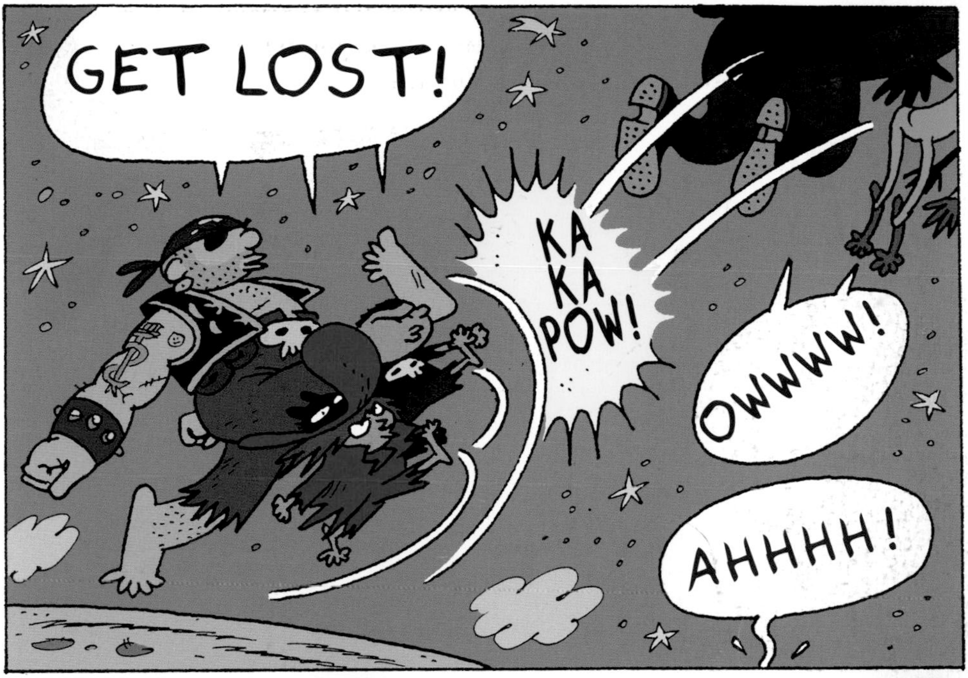
GET LOST!
KA KA POW!
OWWWW!
AHHHH!

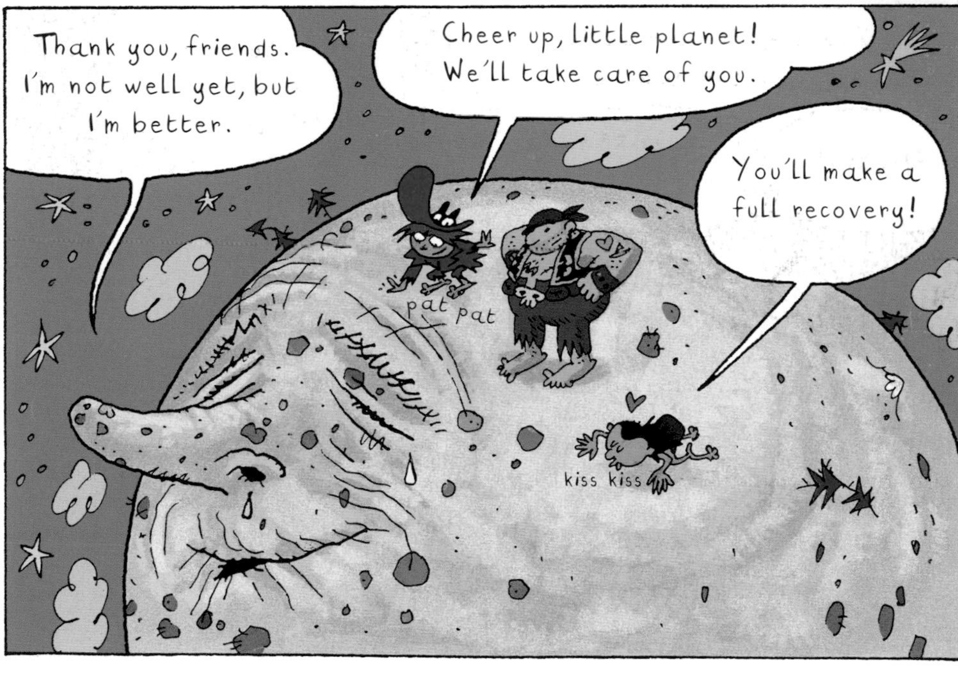
Thank you, friends. I'm not well yet, but I'm better.
Cheer up, little planet! We'll take care of you.
You'll make a full recovery!
pat pat
kiss kiss

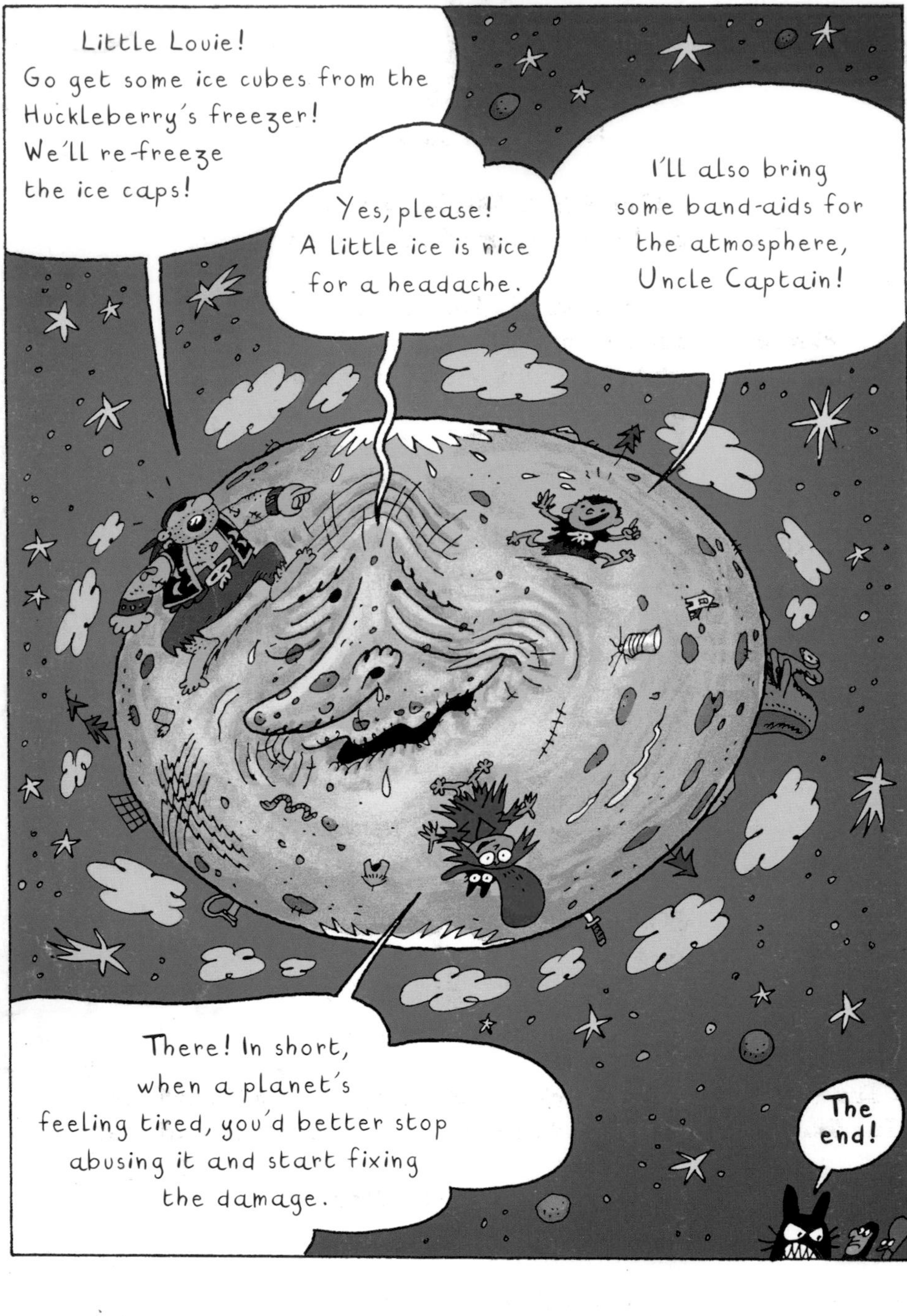
Little Louie! Go get some ice cubes from the Huckleberry's freezer! We'll re-freeze the ice caps!
Yes, please! A little ice is nice for a headache.
I'll also bring some band-aids for the atmosphere, Uncle Captain!
There! In short, when a planet's feeling tired, you'd better stop abusing it and start fixing the damage.
The end!